'I don't need your help.'

Her tongue slid over the fullness of her bottom lip, sweeping through him as her crisp verbena perfume swept over his senses.

'Oh, I think you do.' He held steady as he leaned in, matching her enticing look with one of his own, refusing to let the student best the master, no matter how tight his dark breeches grew. 'Why else would you invent such a dramatic reason to call on me?'

'You flatter yourself.' Her fingers swept her chest, the little half-moons of her fingernails matching the high curve of her breasts.

'And you can't recover the register without me.' He shifted closer, the wood beneath him creaking and almost covering the slight hitch in her breathing. He laid one hand on top of her knee, the curve of it filling his palm. 'You need me.'

AUTHOR NOTE

I read a lot of historical non-fiction—for fun and for inspiration. My inspiration for THE COURTESAN'S BOOK OF SECRETS came from a biography of Nell Gwyn, mistress of King Charles II of England. In the biography, the author mentioned a book kept by a servant of Charles II that listed all the women who had slept with the King at Whitehall Palace. The book was destroyed, and with it a number of secrets.

Reading about this book, I began to wonder what might happen if a book of secrets everyone had thought was lost suddenly reappeared, and the secrets in it had the power to destroy titled families. My wondering eventually became Rafe and Cornelia's story. To craft their tale I had to dip into the darker underworld of Regency England. It was a treat to see a slightly seedier side of London, and to help my characters rise above the temptation of cards and blackmail to overcome the threat of the book and find love and success.

I hope you enjoy THE COURTESAN'S BOOK OF SECRETS. It is my fourth Regency story with Mills & Boon® including ENGAGEMENT OF CONVENIENCE, RESCUED FROM RUIN and HERO'S REDEMPTION from Carina Press.

Please check out my website www.georgie-lee.com for more information about me and my novels. I love to hear from readers and you can e-mail me at georgie.lee@yahoo.com. You can also find me on Twitter @georgieleebooks and Facebook www.facebook.com/georgieleebooks

THE COURTESAN'S BOOK OF SECRETS

Georgie Lee

A dedicated history and film buff, **Georgie Lee** loves combining her passion for Hollywood, history and storytelling through romantic fiction. She began writing professionally at a small TV station in San Diego, before moving to Hollywood to work in the interesting but strange world of the entertainment industry. During her years in La-La Land she never lost her love for romance novels and decided to try writing one herself. To her surprise, a new career was born. When not crafting tales of love and happily-ever-after, Georgie enjoys reading non-fiction history and watching any movie with a costume and an accent.

Please visit www.georgie-lee.com to learn more about Georgie and her books. She also loves to hear from readers, and you can e-mail her at georgie.lee@yahoo.com

Previous novels by the same author:

ENGAGEMENT OF CONVENIENCE
RESCUED FROM RUIN

DEDICATION

Thanks to Tami and Melissa
for giving the cougar her bite and
helping me get this story to the end.

Chapter One

Lord Twickenham's address to the House of Lords on the Bill of Attainder for the Treasonous Acts of Lords Seduced by the French during the American Rebellion, July 8, 1783:

Mrs Ross convinced weak men of title and station to provide the French with secrets of his Majesty's Government during the American Rebellion. My own brother perished because of their treachery. How many other fine men died because it?

She might be gone, along with the evidence of her conspirators' crimes, but those deceitful men are still among us. My lords, I crave the day when proof of their villainy finally emerges and the full power of this Bill of Attainder is

*brought against them. If they think time can
erase their guilt, then they are mistaken.*

*Through this Bill of Attainder, if evidence
ever comes to light of their guilt, even if God
has struck them from this earth, they will be
convicted of High Treason as though they still
walked among us. All their titles and lands will
be forfeit to the Crown and their heirs will bear
the burden of their fathers' disgrace.*

London, July 1803

Rafe Densmore, Fifth Baron of Densmore,
marched up the stone staircase of Mrs Ross's un-
imposing town house off Gracechurch Street. He
rapped his knuckles against the door and the black
ribbon hanging from the brass knocker fluttered in
the breeze. He eyed it with a frown, wondering if
the ancient courtesan's sudden demise would be to
his benefit or his detriment. She'd been perfectly
alive and well when she'd penned the letter in his
pocket, summoning him to her sad doorstep.

The old shrew.

He shifted back and forth on his feet. Deep in
his boot, his toe caught the beginning of a hole in
one stocking.

Damned cheap wool. If he employed a valet,

the man would do something about it. Perhaps he might charm Mrs Linton, his landlady, into mending it for him. Though if her needlework proved anything like what she did to the meagre meals she deigned to deliver to his room, he might as well mend it himself. He wondered if her meals were the true extent of her culinary skills or revenge for his grossly outstanding rent.

The hackney horse waiting at the kerb whinnied, failing to disturb the thin driver leaning against the vehicle, smoking a long pipe. The smoke swirled around his head before the wind carried it over the back of his stocky grey animal.

Rafe eyed them both. Whoever had hired the poor beast and his horse must still be inside and it was time for them to draw their business to a close. He hadn't fought so hard to reach Mrs Ross, or to raise the blunt needed to meet her demands, only to be stalled on the doorstep by a dawdling caller.

He raised his fist to knock again when the bolt scraped and the door creaked open to reveal the drooping eyes of a withered old butler. Rafe brushed past him and into the small entrance hall, his throat tightening from the thick dust covering every surface. A spider scurried behind a dark painting. Compared to this house, his current lodgings seemed breathtakingly opulent.

'Lord Densmore to see Mr Nettles,' Rafe announced. 'He's expecting me.'

'Yes, of course. This way, my lord.' The butler shuffled across the hall.

Rafe followed before something along the edge of his vision brought him to a halt at the morning-room door.

A tall, voluptuous woman draped in gauzy black silk stood by the cold fireplace. She didn't move or greet him, but remained silent beneath the dark veil covering her face. A slow smile spread across Rafe's lips, his fever in obtaining the register momentarily dampened. Despite her silence, something about her called to him and he moved closer to the doorway. The slight tensing of her shoulders made him stop, but not turn away. Her dress, dark and wispy like smoke, swirled around her curves. She clutched a book to her chest. The leather tome obscured the full roundness of her breasts, except for the creamy tops which were just visible beneath her black-net chemisette.

'Good morning.' He swept off his hat and dropped into a low bow, noting the few white petals scattered on the faded carpet at her feet, probably the remains of Mrs Ross's funeral. By her own account, Mrs Ross was a recluse, but apparently she wasn't completely devoid of friends to mourn her.

And what a delightful friend this is. Rafe straightened, admiring the woman's generous measure of height. Heat flooded through him as he imagined tucking the statuesque creature into the curve of his body and brushing his lips along the bit of exposed neck caressed by her short veil. He tapped his fingers against his thigh, sensing her height would match his perfectly, the way Cornelia's once did.

His hand tightened into a fist, the sharp edge of betrayal cooling his ardour. He relaxed his fingers and struggled to keep smiling. Why the deuce was he thinking of Cornelia? He'd left that business in France where, with any luck, it would stay.

He focused on the woman's face, trying to catch a glimpse of her features beneath the thick veil. Nothing was visible except the flush of skin and the faint red of full lips. Hopefully, her features were as appealing as the hint of body beneath the close-cut French style of her dress. If the solicitor proved problematic with the register, this woman might be more obliging.

'If you please, my lord,' the butler urged.

Rafe stroked the tall woman with one last glance, reluctantly offering a parting nod before following the butler to a room near the back of the house.

They reached the end of the hallway and the butler pushed open the door to an old study, the bare, sagging shelves held up by dust. A round man with spectacles sat at a desk, reviewing stacks of yellowed papers. He stood as Rafe entered, a wide smile drawing back the jowls framing his mouth.

'Mr Nettles, Lord Densmore to see you,' the butler rasped.

'Lord Densmore, what a pleasure.' A few loose threads from his cuff waved as the man motioned Rafe to the wood chair in front of the desk. 'Sit, please.'

'I'm sorry I didn't arrive when my letter said I would, but business in France delayed me.' *It damn near killed me.* If he hadn't enjoyed a small winning streak at the tables, he'd still be stuck in the stinking place. 'My condolences on Mrs Ross's passing.'

'Yes, poor woman. Takes her first trip outside in over twenty years and some runaway carriage strikes her. Terrible business.' The solicitor tutted as he lowered himself into his chair, the wood creaking beneath his weight. 'I suppose she was right to stay hidden away for so many years.'

'If would seem so.' *If only the carriage had finished off the wretched blackmailer before she'd mailed the blasted letter.* Then who knew whose hands the register might have fallen into. At least now there existed the chance of buying the entire rotten thing, not just the page with his late father's name on it, and the proof of his treason. 'Mrs Ross wrote to me while I was in Paris, offering to sell me a certain book of hers.'

'Yes, I know of it. Not a very interesting read. Nothing but lists of nobility and numbers next to their names. Probably accounts from the men who paid for her company in her youth. According to the butler, she was quite a beauty back then.' The man chuckled, his round belly bouncing up and down beneath his wrinkled waistcoat. Then his jowls dropped, giving him the look of an innocent bloodhound waiting for its master's command. 'Why do you want such a thing?'

'I have my reasons.' Rafe didn't elaborate, unwilling to enlighten the man on the true nature of the register.

'Yes, I suppose you do.' The mask of innocence slipped just a bit, reminding Rafe of an exceptional card player he'd once bested in France whose ability to bluff almost matched his. Then the solicitor rubbed his chins, the look gone. 'It's a pity you didn't arrive a hair sooner.'

Fear snaked up his spine, all thoughts of gambling or what the puffy man might know about the register gone. Obtaining it was almost the only thing he'd thought about since landing in Dover. He'd torn through Wealthstone Manor in search of anything left of value to sell to obtain it. The delightful set of silver spoons he'd discovered in the attic, wedged in their wooden box between two trunks and somehow missed by his father, had just been sold this morning.

Rafe shifted forward in the chair, his hand tight on the arm. 'What do you mean?'

'It seems you weren't the only one Mrs Ross wrote to about the register. Judging from her papers, she'd been in straitened circumstances for some time and was forced to part with a number of possessions. There are still outstanding debts and I'll have a hard time settling them with what valuables are left.' He grabbed a crinkled paper with each hand, flapping them in the air. 'Though it would be a might easier to sort through it all if she hadn't called herself Mrs Ross at one time, Mrs

Taylor in later years and now Mrs Ross again. I wish she'd made up her mind about who she was.'

'And the book?' Rafe tensed, eager for him to get on with it.

'A young woman arrived just before you did, a French Comtesse, though she didn't sound French. I sold it to her.'

'Hell.' Rafe jumped up and ran to the door. He flung it open and raced down the hall, sending balls of dust whirling out of his way. At the morning room he stopped. Only the wilted white flowers greeted him. 'Blast.'

'Lord Densmore.' The solicitor came down the hall behind him as Rafe rushed to the front door and pulled it open. Outside, everything was the same as before, except for the hackney. It rolled down the street, a familiar face watching him through the back window before the vehicle turned the corner and disappeared in the traffic on Gracechurch Street.

Cornelia, Comtesse de Vane.

What's she doing here? Rafe slammed his fist against the doorjamb and a small splinter slid beneath his skin. She shouldn't be here. She should be in France, rotting away with her crooked old husband at Château de Vane, counting the silver or ordering the servants about, not stealing the register out from under him.

'Lord Densmore, I'm truly sorry for your inconvenience.' The solicitor puffed from behind him. 'Had I known the book was so important to you—'

Rafe held up one hand to silence the man, in no mood to be polite. 'Thank you, Mr Nettles, but I'm no longer in need of your services.'

Rafe stormed off down the street, the slam of Mrs Ross's front door echoing off the buildings.

He moved into the bustle of Gracechurch Street, his toe sliding through the now-widened hole in his stocking. If it weren't for the crush of people, he'd pull off the boot and toss the offending garment in the gutter. Instead, all he could do was keep walking, the wool grating with each step like the memory of Cornelia watching him from the back of the hackney.

He passed a wagon loaded with apples and plucked one from the pile without the seller noticing, turning the smooth fruit over and over in his fingers. *What's she doing here?*

She couldn't have convinced her husband to abandon his native shore. The Comte wasn't likely to leave after everything he'd done to regain his ancestral home. It meant the old man had either given up the ghost in a fit of ecstasy over his nubile young bride, or Cornelia had spent her time at the château plotting to run out on him just as she'd so cleverly plotted to run out on Rafe.

His hand tightened on the apple, the hard skin pressing against the splinter and making it sting. If it hadn't taken him so long to raise the money to purchase the register page, he might have beaten her to it today.

Now she had it and the ability to destroy him.

He took a bite of the apple and cursed, spitting out the mushy piece and flinging the whole rotten thing under the wheels of a passing carriage.

Damn his luck. Nothing was working out as he'd planned.

Cornelia leaned back against the squabs and let out a long breath, relief flooding through her as if she'd faced a man at dawn and prevailed.

Her fingers tightened on the register, the leather cracking a little under the pressure. If she'd dallied a few minutes longer this morning or walked instead of hiring the hack, she might have lost the register to Rafe. Then all her plans to protect Andrew, her half-brother, would have come to nothing.

She eased her grip on the book and closed her eyes, struggling to see Andrew's dark hair tousled over his small head, to remember the warmth of his little hand in hers as they'd explored the river behind Hatton Place, their father's slurred and roaring voice blocked out by the rush of water over the rocks. However, one image remained stubbornly fixed in her mind.

Rafe.

His deep tones had rolled into the town house ahead of him, drawing her back two years ago to their first nights together in the tiny room in Covent Garden. The image of him standing over her as she'd lain in the narrow bed, his shirt open at the neck, his dark breeches tight against his hips, made her heart race as fast as it had when he'd smiled at her from across Mrs Ross's entrance hall.

Except today it wasn't desire quickening her pulse, but fear. If he'd recognised her through the veil or noticed the register clutched against her like a shield, who knew how he'd have reacted. Thankfully, more carnal thoughts had distracted him from seeing what was plainly in front of him.

She opened her eyes and shifted against the worn leather, irritated at the way her traitorous body warmed with the memory of Rafe's dark eyes caressing her like a fine shift. She swept her fingers across her neck, the light gauze covering her breasts suddenly as heavy as wool. After the Comte's waxy hands, even Rafe's gentle touch would be a welcome relief.

Emptiness slipped in beneath the desire. She rubbed her cheek, still able to feel the scratch of Rafe's shirt against it as he'd held her in their Paris apartment two months ago. She'd been so terrified that night, clinging to him as she'd repeated the rumours of British men being arrested once war was declared. She'd feared for him and their future. As a woman, she would have been free to go, but he faced the threat of being caught and left to linger in some disease-ridden prison.

If only he'd received such a deserving fate.

She clenched her hands, the black gloves pulling taught over her knuckles. Like a fool, she'd trusted him, sending him off to the card room with the last of their money, believing his promise to return with enough to buy their passage home. Instead he'd fled like a coward, saving himself and leaving her to her fate.

She banged her fists against the worn-out squabs. After all he'd done for her before, how could he have been so cruel?

The hackney made a sharp turn and she gripped the strap above the door. In the rattle of the wheels, she could almost hear Fanny, her stepmother, laughing at her change in fortune. Thankfully, her father would never learn of it. When the letter from Fanny had finally reached her, she hadn't cried. She couldn't bring herself to mourn the man who'd felt nothing for her his entire life.

Out of the window, the arch of St Paul's dome stood over the tops of short buildings and marked the end of long streets. The familiar sight eased some of her anger and pain. There were too many days during her thankfully brief time at Château de Vane when she'd thought she'd never see this beautiful sight again. During the endless hours she'd spent wandering the dark hallways, she'd tried to convince herself marrying the Comte had been a great victory. Who knew the Comte was a bigger charlatan than any she'd ever encountered in a card room?

The hackney hit a bump and she clutched the register to keep it from sliding off her lap. When the vehicle settled back into a rocking gate, she opened the worn leather cover, the papers beneath it yellow with age. The past no longer mattered. In her lap lay a better, more secure future for her and

Andrew. With the money she'd raise from the register, she could keep paying for Andrew's school and prevent Fanny from making good on her threat to send him to her brother in the disease-ridden West Indies.

She closed the book, knowing it wasn't only Andrew's future she held.

The fate of Rafe's entire legacy now rested on her thighs.

The tart taste of revenge filled her mouth, followed by a pang of guilt. She ran her finger down the first list of names, wondering on which page Rafe's father's name appeared.

He'll come after it.

She snapped the book closed, wrinkling her nose against the dust escaping from the paper. Let him come, let him try to charm the book out from under her with all his wit and games. She'd listen, all the while dangling it before him like a sweetmeat in front of a dog's nose. Then she'd pull it back and watch him writhe in frustration.

It's exactly what he deserved.

Rafe stepped through the crumbling brick arch into the narrow alley filled with the deafening chorus of men's cheers. The noise called to him, drawing him through the sharp turns like a sweet smell draws a child to the kitchen. He stepped around the last corner and into an open courtyard. A large crowd circled two men, yelling and jeering as the hulks in the centre pummelled one another. They fought bare from the waist up, their broad backs covered in open cuts and dark bruises, each blow sending sweat and blood splattering into the dirt.

A smile eased Rafe's jaw as the crowd's excitement vibrated through him, shifting the lingering tension from this morning's escapade in Gracechurch Street. He'd spent the better part of the past hour walking the streets and considering his options, of which there were few. Cornelia possessed the register and there was no way to raise enough blunt to tempt it away from her. He owed more than he cared to remember to several moneylenders, including the garlic-loving Mr Smith. It was a wonder the cockroach hadn't scurried out of the shadows to demand repayment since the debt was almost a year outstanding. Rafe wouldn't even have dealt with the rat if he hadn't needed money to keep his mother from starving while he was in Paris and to buy his and Cornelia's passage to France and their way into the most lucrative card rooms. He'd hoped to repay the moneylender with their winnings, but like too many other plans, it hadn't proceeded as he'd expected.

Now, the outstanding loan was just another of the heavy debts hanging around his neck. With any luck, one of Mr Smith's less-than-genteel clients would find a more creative way to eliminate his debt and save Rafe from the money man's foul breath. Rafe doubted he'd get so lucky. Luck had avoided him like the pest house these past few months.

He tapped his pocket, making Mrs Ross's letter and the pound notes from the sale of the spoons crinkle. It was a shame he couldn't use the letter to settle the old bet in the book at White's and prove it was the maid and not the old trollop who'd died in the fire twenty-two years ago. His smile widened at the idea of entering the club and watching a few faces go pale as he held up the missive and collected his money. He could also imagine the stampede to Cornelia's door. No doubt she'd get rich selling the damning evidence to all those heirs and then where would he be? Certainly not sharing in the wealth.

If I'd have known this was how she planned to repay me, I'd have left her at Lord Perry's where I found her. He tugged the bottom of his waistcoat straight, not believing his own words. Her father might have been hard hearted enough to consign his own daughter to the pawing hands of Lord Waltenham, but Rafe hadn't been cruel enough to condemn a young woman to such a fate.

'Densmore,' a voice hailed. Lord Hartley, a short fellow made higher by his tall hat, pushed his way out of the crowd, pausing to let a young urchin scurry in front of him before he trotted up to Rafe. 'I see Napoleon threw you out. Afraid you'd steal Josephine's jewels?'

'I wouldn't be the first to touch her baubles.' Rafe took the Viscount's extended hand as the other clapped him on the back. Another cheer went up from the crowd and they turned to watch the smaller of the two fighters stagger back. He quickly regained his footing and landed a sharp hook on his opponent's jaw. 'No, I couldn't stay in France, not with such cultural delights beckoning.'

'Then you'll want to bet on the next fight, on Joe James.' Hartley stepped closer, holding one hand to his mouth and dropping his voice as much as he could in such a racket and still be heard. 'I spoke to a man who knows his trainer and assures me he can't lose.'

'Sounds like a most reliable source,' Rafe chided.

Hartley shrugged. 'More reliable than most. Come, what do you say?'

He knew too much about bribed pugilists to risk his money on a fight. 'No, thank you. I prefer the certainty of cards, where if a man slips a deuce from his boots, justice against him is swift.'

'Yes, you've always been eccentric that way. Come with me anyway. Keep me company while I take my chances.'

Rafe swung his arm towards the two men in the dirty tricorns sitting behind the betting table. 'Lead the way.'

He followed Hartley around the circle of men, catching glimpses of the fighters over the heads of the ever-shifting mass of bodies. The larger man pounded the smaller one to the delight of the spectators whose bloodthirsty cheers grew louder, eager for the larger man to deliver the *coup de grâce* and put his poor contender out of his misery.

'Whatever happened to the delightful little widow I used to see you with in Paris?' Hartley asked.

The larger boxer slammed his fist into the smaller man's face, sending him spinning to the ground in a puff of blood and dust. 'She married the Comte de Vane.'

Hartley's eyebrows shot up before scrunching down in disbelief. 'The relic from the Ancien Regime who used to haunt Madame Boucher's card parties?'

'The very one.' The old codger used to enjoy playing Cornelia at the tables, his rheumy eyes raking her body as he tried to capture her interest. Rafe once admired the artful way she'd kept him at bay, flirting with him just enough to encourage more wagers. Never in all the games had Rafe guessed she was scheming to win more than the Comte's counters.

'Well, I suppose it's a more practical way for a woman to earn her wealth.' Hartley shrugged, more amused than disgusted by the pairing. Unlike Rafe.

'Apparently.'

Rafe picked at a small chip on a waistcoat button, recalling her saucy smile their first night at Madame Boucher's when she'd laid down her cards to win a tidy sum and the notice of all Paris society. He'd proudly watched her from across the room as she'd risen from the table and tucked the bills into the small pocket sewn into the front of her stays. She'd been so beautiful, the cunning fox. Her yellow dress hugging her full breasts and emphasising her willowy height had made her a rare daisy among roses. As she'd crossed the gilded and mirrored ballroom, she'd collected every man's gaze. Then, when her vivid blue eyes and radiant smile had fixed on him, he'd almost forgotten the terms of their arrangement and dropped to his knees to propose.

Almost.

If he had, he certainly wouldn't be in his current predicament. Though she wouldn't have accepted him, not with men like the Comte sniffing about her skirts, but he hadn't known that back then.

His big toe rubbed at the ragged edge of the hole in his stocking. If the soft weight of her cheek on his chest and the delicate tears moistening her lashes during their last night together in Paris hadn't muddled his thoughts, he might have caught her ruse. Instead he'd strode out to the card rooms like some besotted fool, thinking himself the hero for finding the money to get them home before the impending blockade could trap them in France.

It'd been a nasty awakening when he'd returned to see her driving away in the Comte's carriage. She hadn't even possessed the decency to write him a note. Instead, she'd left the empty wardrobe and missing portmanteaus to explain everything, the finishing stanza of her message delivered when he'd overheard Lord Rollingham in a card room discussing her marriage to the Comte.

Never once in all their time together had he thought her so manipulative, so hard hearted and cunning. How wrong he'd been.

The sneaky wench.

The crowd shoved past Rafe, knocking against his shoulders as it surged forward to congratulate the winner. The boxer raised his hands in triumph, flashing a near-toothless smile through a cut lip and one swelling eye.

Rafe ground his jaw at having been so easily duped, but as much as he cursed the Comte for winning Cornelia, he should've thanked the decrepit crook for forcing their separation. Marriage was never meant to be part of their partnership. He hadn't saved her from one disgrace only to pull her into a poverty he couldn't even describe as genteel, living with his mother in the few habitable rooms of Wealthstone Manor or huddled in his draughty lodgings in Drury Lane.

Two men dragged the unconscious boxer from the ring and into one of the brick buildings flanking the yard. The crowd moved away from the centre, breaking into small groups to commiserate over their losses and plan their next wager.

'Last chance to bet, Densmore.' Hartley moved forward in line, eager to part himself from his blunt.

'No, thank you.' Rafe stepped to one side to make room for others.

Movement in a small window overlooking the square caught Rafe's attention. He looked up at the sagging building to meet the hard eyes of a dark-haired woman watching the gathering. The image of Cornelia in the hackney rushed back to him and he swallowed down the foul taste in his mouth.

He could imagine a number of reasons why she might want the register, none of them good. It certainly wasn't to protect her father's name. The soused country Baronet couldn't have known anything of value to sell to the French. There was something more nefarious behind her acquisition. If there wasn't, she wouldn't have skulked past him this morning like some sharper creeping off to plan her next swindle.

Worry crept over him like the small hand sliding into his pocket.

Rafe snatched the arm of the ragamuffin standing next to him. 'Nothing for you there.'

'I didn't do nuffin',' the boy squealed, trying to twist free, but Rafe held him tight. 'I'm only running an errand for me ma.'

The panicked boy shot a look up at the building and Rafe followed it to see the dark-haired woman gripping the window pane. Her narrow chin and the mole above her lip reminded him of the daughter of a squire, a Miss Allen, he'd met some years ago at a country garden party. It was the last one he and his mother had attended before his father's mounting debts had forced them to shun invitations. If it was the same young lady, then she'd fallen a long way since he'd last seen her in Sussex.

Rafe studied the thin boy, his face streaked with dirt, his hair covered with a threadbare cap. He was hardly worth the hangman's rope. He dug a coin out of his pocket and pressed it into the boy's grimy palm. 'Take this to your mother and don't come back in this crowd again.'

He let go and the boy staggered back, clutching the coin to his chest as he darted through the door of the tumbledown rookery. Rafe tipped his hat to the woman in the window.

She mouthed 'thank you', then receded back into the shadows.

If only all cheats were so easily dealt with. The

sense this round was lost to Cornelia still rubbed, the frustration of Rafe's current situation more annoying than the ever-widening hole in his stocking. Without the register, any effort to protect and build back the Densmore fortune and name, to spare his mother from further poverty and degradation, would come to nothing. If Cornelia showed anyone in the House of Lords the evidence of his father's crime, he and his mother were finished. The Bill of Attainder was still in place and the greying Lord Twickenham still intent on enforcing it. Wealthstone would be seized and Rafe's title forfeit.

It was enough to ruin a good boxing match.

Hartley appeared at Rafe's side, holding his ticket and practically fluttering with excitement. 'Come on, I want to get a good place.'

They walked around the edge of the circle of men. Rafe's height gave him the advantage in the crowd, but they moved three times before Hartley was content with his view. A cheer went up as the fighters appeared in the doorway of one building. The crowd parted, allowing the two boxers to pass into the circle of spectators. They stood across from each other, looking less like a pair of Hercules and more like two blocks of stone some sculptor had hacked at to give them arms, legs and something of a face.

'Which one is your man?' Rafe asked.

'The ox with the scar on his arm.' Hartley rubbed his hands together in anticipation. 'This should be good.'

Rafe studied the scarred fighter, agreeing with Hartley's description of his bovine features. The man walked in a tight circle, his steps heavy, his arms swinging about his body like two logs. 'A fiver says your man goes down in the first round.'

Hartley adjusted his hat. 'That's no way to wish a man luck.'

'You're confident in your tip?'

'It's the best one I've had in weeks.'

'Then ten pounds says he falls like a chopped oak.'

Hartley levelled a finger at Rafe. 'I'll take the bet and you'll wish you hadn't made it.'

The fight began and the two boxers moved to the centre of the ring, circling and jabbing at each other. The unblemished man moved faster than his opponent and landed one good punch to the ox's gut before catching him with a right hook. The crowd went silent as the ox tipped on his heels and landed flat on his back in the dirt.

The smaller man lifted his arms in triumph.

Somewhere in the distance a dog barked.

Grumbles rippled through the crowd as men exchanged money.

Hartley groaned, peeled a ten-pound note off his roll of money and handed it to Rafe. 'I should have known better.'

'And next time you will.' Rafe tucked the note into his pocket.

He thought of Cornelia and his determination swelled with the crowd's excitement as the next pair of fighters took to the ring. Rafe might be short his entrance fee, but he'd be damned if he'd let Cornelia knock him out of the game. Gaining access to the register wouldn't be as easy as walking into Mrs Ross's house and purchasing it, but he'd find a way to slip between Cornelia's covers, so to speak, make her see how much she owed him for everything he'd done for her and overcome whatever grudge she'd developed against him in France.

As a newly minted Comtesse, she was sure to be at the Dowager Countess of Daltmouth's salon tonight, worming her way into society. Rafe would be there, too, to remind her of her debt to him.

Whatever her plans for the register, she owed him at least the safety of removing his father's name from the book and it was time to call in her vowel.

Chapter Two

Rafe strolled into the Dowager Countess of Dalt-mouth's salon, taking in the number of ladies in white, high-waisted gowns scattered between the furniture. Their presence on every sofa and chair gave the long room the look of a conservatory filled with pregnant Greek marbles. The women huddled in groups around the thin intellectuals, twittering like birds at the men's flashes of brilliance. The husbands took up more sober positions near the tables of wine and food, fortifying themselves against any taint of intellectual or poetic leanings.

Rafe moved down the centre of the long room, passing a group of dandies in blue silk coats, their waistcoats cinched so tightly, he could count the pence in their pockets. As if on cue, they lifted their lorgnettes and scrutinised Rafe's plain black

coat and tan breeches, sneering down their powdered noses at his understated dress. He ignored
them as his gaze skipped over a few nymphs surrounding a consumptive-looking youth extolling
his latest drivel.

'Lord Densmore, what a pleasure it is to have
you here tonight.' The Dowager Countess of Daltmouth glided up to him in a cloud of rosewater
perfume. 'I didn't think you'd come.'

Rafe took her extended hand, nearly folding himself in half to offer a greeting of substance. She'd
aged gracefully, her blonde hair arranged to favour
her regal nose and high cheekbones. The deep-
purple dress flowed over her still enviable curves,
revealing a touch of the bosom which had once
been the envy of all the ladies. If the lights were
lower, Rafe might have mistaken her for a much
younger woman. 'There's nowhere else in London
I'd rather be.'

'Liar,' she chided, her thumb brushing the underside of his palm before she let go.

Rafe straightened, cautious of the mature coquette. 'You've assembled an impressive gathering tonight.'

'Not as impressive as the pillar of the Densmore
family.' Her eyes stroked the length of him, paus-

ing at the buttons of his breeches before rising to meet his eyes. 'I believe you've surpassed even your father in height.'

'And wit and charm.' As well, it seemed, as respectability and love for his country.

'Yes, I greatly admire your *charm*.'

'Careful, Lady Daltmouth, or I might mistake your flattery for flirting.'

She laughed like a newly married girl impressing her unmarried friends with her recently acquired experience. 'I assure you, Lord Densmore, nothing could be closer to the truth.'

'I'm flattered,' he lied, more amused than aroused. The woman wasn't without appeal and if he were eighteen, he might be tempted, but not at eight and twenty. 'I must warn you, I'm a rogue and not worth trifling with.'

'I like rogues, they're so much more interesting than ordinary gentlemen.' She adjusted the creamy strand of pearls looped around her neck, making the beads rattle together as she settled them against her voluptuous bosom. 'I hope to see more of you at my card party next week. Perhaps we can knock hands and you'll find me above you.'

'I look forward to the challenge.' He bowed again, but not quite so low. It wasn't the first time a woman long in the tooth and even longer in the purse had tossed him an offer. He wasn't about to become a kept man, but he wasn't about to make an enemy of the Dowager Countess either. Whatever her hungers and family reputation, she possessed connections and he valued them as much as the sovereigns in his pocket.

Her offer delivered, she whirled with the grace of an empress and made for a group of sombrely dressed matrons surrounding a thick-waisted poet. The Dowager Countess tossed Rafe one last suggestive glance before taking her place at the centre of the semicircle. Rafe struggled not to laugh at her imperiousness and her brazen suggestion before another sight knocked the humour out of him.

Cornelia.

She stood just beyond the old crows, near the open window. The evening breeze rustled the sheer gauze of her embroidered blue overdress and the white under-dress hugging the lines of her round hips. Her dark hair was drawn up in a mass of loose curls wound with a black-satin ribbon, leaving the arching line of her neck exposed to tease him. He opened and closed his hand, eager to slide his fingers up the warm skin, dislodge the hairpins and send the tangle of ebony ringlets cascading over her shoulders. There was nothing more beautiful than her dark curls hanging just above the tips of her pointed nipples, the pink buds eager for his touch, her rich, blue eyes wide with anticipation.

He tightened his fingers into a fist before releasing them one by one. Tonight wasn't about some dalliance from his past. It was about protecting his future and he couldn't allow the tightness in his breeches to distract him from his goal.

He strolled around the outside of the gathering, watching Cornelia's gaze slide from one guest to another, sizing up her prey like a wolf waiting to pick off the weakest lamb.

At last her eyes met his, dipping down the length of his body before she flashed him a dazzling smile. Rafe stopped as if he'd hit a wall. He knew this smile. It was a warning, not a welcome.

She settled herself on a nearby sofa as he approached, arranging her skirts over her legs before laying her hands in her lap to greet him like a queen. His ego chafed at her arrogance. How dare she take airs with him? He knew her history, both the real one and the one they'd invented the night she ran away with him from Sussex. Pride demanded he cut her, but he forced himself forward.

'My dear Cornelia, what a pleasure it is to see

you back in London.' He swept into a low bow, noticing a small stain on one of his stockings before he straightened, careful to keep his smile wide and gracious.

'I'm the Comtesse de Vane now, or have you forgotten?' She held out her hand, a large diamond glittering on her middle finger.

'How could I forget?' He slid his fingers beneath hers, squeezing them as his lips brushed the knuckles, catching more of the large stone than her skin. The clear gem danced with small rainbows and jealousy cut through him. Even before Paris, he didn't possess the means to offer such tokens. No wonder she'd abandoned him for the Comte. 'Especially after the trouble you took to secure it.'

'It was hardly any trouble at all.' Cornelia slid her hand out of his grasp, tilting it to view the stone, as if checking to make sure it was still in its setting. 'The Comte didn't possess the necessary vigour to fulfil his conjugal duties.'

The ever-so-subtle tightening of her full lips didn't escape Rafe's notice. So, the marriage hadn't been all bliss. He should have taken delight in the subtle revelation, but he couldn't, nor could he believe she'd sold herself to the old man for a few thousand francs and a title. The idea of the Comte's gnarled hands pawing at Cornelia made his meagre dinner roil in his gut, but he hid it as he would a disappointing hand in a tight game.

She'd chosen the hunched old man as her bedmate. No one had forced her into it.

'And now you've returned, the happy, wealthy widow.' He sat down next to her, the cushion beneath him sinking and making her lean closer.

Her full lips eased into a gloating smile as bright as the diamonds dangling from her ears. 'I couldn't have imagined a more delightful way to come home.'

He motioned to an exceptionally tall footman carrying a tray of champagne and selected one of the offered flutes. He took a sip, allowing the tart liquid to cool the acid remarks dancing on his tongue. 'And you've also stumbled upon an inventive way to increase your widow's portion. Tell me, who do you intend to threaten for money?'

He'd never thought her cruel enough for blackmail, but after the clever way she'd duped him with the Comte, he wouldn't put anything shady past her now.

She tilted her head to one side, placing a small amount of distance between them. Pulling open her fan one stick at a time, she revealed the painting of Venus lounging nude in Mars's arms. He knew the fan. She always carried it when on the hunt for a lucrative and less talented opponent. 'What makes you think I purchased the register for such a sinister reason?'

'What other reason could you have? It's hardly pleasurable reading.'

'Oh, you'd be surprised at how much fun it is to peruse.' She fanned herself with three quick flicks, making the candles on the pillar behind them waver. 'The full list of every titled man Mrs Ross ever paid to betray our country during the colonial revolt. Some of the names are quite shocking.'

'For instance?'

She cast him a sideways glance, her eyes skimming the length of him, focusing on his foot before rising to meet his face. For a moment he didn't think she'd tell him, then he saw the sense of satisfaction widen her eyes. He inwardly cringed. She wasn't just going to tell him about the register, she was going to torture him with it.

'For instance, the Dowager Countess of Daltmouth.' She lowered her arms, levelling her fan at the imperious woman. 'It appears her late husband accepted quite a generous amount from the French to turn coward at the Battle of Saratoga.'

Rafe let out a low whistle. 'Which means all the old rumours are true.'

She sat back, adjusting her diamond bracelet. 'Given her massive efforts to reform the Daltmouth name, she can hardly afford to have any evidence of his treason come to light.'

'Which she'll avoid by paying for your silence.'

'It is but one possibility.'

She flicked the top edge of her teeth with her tongue as she always did at the end of a well-played hand. He eyed her mouth, bitter desire twisting his insides. He wanted to brush his lips across the delicate blush of her cheek, take one small ear-lobe in his teeth and remind her of everything he could do to her, to make her want him beyond reason. Then he could leave her the same way she'd abruptly left him.

He straightened and set his champagne glass on the side table. There would be time for more pleasurable business later. 'An interesting plan, but incredibly flawed. She's weathered worse storms than you. Threaten her and she'll crush you.'

Cornelia's eyes flashed with irritation before she took a deep breath and they softened to their usual languid blue. 'Ah, Rafe, ye of little faith. I have no plan to blackmail the Dowager Countess.'

A loud laugh from the far end of the room silenced the gentle murmur of conversation and everyone turned to watch the current Earl of Daltmouth, the dowager's pudgy son, throw back his head so far, he nearly stumbled into the sharp-jawed footman passing behind him. The Earl straightened himself with a great deal of effort and the footman's assistance. 'I'm going to blackmail him.'

Rafe studied the stout fellow. The Earl's eyes were nearly lost in the large cheeks underneath them and his round chin was beginning to disappear into the second one forming just beneath it.

A chill shot through Rafe as Cornelia leaned in close to his ear, her verbena perfume as shocking to his senses as her warm breath on his neck. 'He isn't as astute as his mother and much more inclined to pay.'

Rafe nodded, hating to admit even to himself the logic of her choice. The Earl was known in society for many things. Astounding feats of genius were not one of them. 'You've improved a great deal since Paris.'

'I learned from the best.' She flicked her fan

over her chest and the memory of her in his bed, the white sheets wrapped around her naked body as she curled herself around him, flashed through his mind. His manhood tightened and he shifted on the sofa, determined to maintain a steady course.

'Since I taught you so much, allow me one favour.' He leaned in to her and she looked up at him through her dark lashes. The beautiful blue irises surrounded by clear white fixed on him, sending another jolt of need through his body. Curse the minx for this hold she had over him. 'Give me the page with my father's name on it. I have no money to pay you and you can gain nothing by hurting me. Consider it a thank you for everything I taught you.'

'My dear Rafe.' She laid one gloved hand along the side of his face, her lips moist, parted and so temptingly close. 'I see poverty has not robbed you of your sense of humour.'

She patted his cheek, then rose, the sweet sway of her hips not lost beneath the high-waisted dress as she strolled away. A cold dunk in a pond couldn't have done more to wilt his need and he drummed his fingers on the velvet cushion, the bitterness he'd tasted in Paris filling his mouth again.

* * *

Cornelia struggled to walk a smooth, straight line as she left Rafe, her whole body shaking with excitement and rage. She hadn't been this close to him since their last night together in France. The tart scent of tobacco smoke and wine clinging to his coat from a long night in the hells had nearly been her undoing. It reminded her of too many evenings with him in the card rooms of Paris, and then in their apartment afterwards, his hard chest pressed against her breasts, his skilful touch making her insides ache.

A shadow wavered in the corner near a heavy sideboard, reminding her of the dark hallways of Château de Vane and the cold bite of Rafe's betrayal. She shivered, all desire to rush back across the room to him gone. Instead she continued forward, savouring the memory of Rafe's surprised eyes. She'd struck a blow, even if it had taken every ounce of self-control to remain calm while he sat so close and to not break her fan over his head for abandoning her in Paris.

She eased her grip on the delicate accessory to keep from crushing it. How dare he brazenly approach her after what he'd done and expect her to hand over the register pages. She was no longer the naive daughter of a country Baronet in need of his guidance. She was the Comtesse de Vane, even if the title was worth little more than the tin heraldic shield hanging above her mantel.

Joining the circle of women surrounding Lady Daltmouth and a poet, Cornelia shifted back and forth in her slippers. She tried to focus as the poet extolled the virtues of womanhood, nodding along with the other ladies, but his words were a meaningless jumble. Rafe's mere presence in the room made her jittery. If this continued, she'd be unable to put together a coherent thought by the end of the poet's stanza. Taking a deep breath, she focused as she exhaled, settling herself the way Rafe had once taught her to do before engaging in a high-stakes card game.

Curse him, he seemed to be everywhere in her life.

As she exhaled the second breath, Cornelia focused on the Dowager Countess. She sat like a petite queen on a low gilded chair, scrutinising the people around her, the small lines at the corners of her eyes relaxing or hardening depending on whom she took in. Cornelia followed her gaze around the circle, noting the lesser nobility who flocked to her salon. After the late Earl's cowardly retreat at the Battle of Saratoga, there were few in the *ton* willing to show the Daltmouths favour. This collection of people was the Dowager Countess's answer to their snub, an attempt to create an alternate society of mushrooms and nobles of questionable lineage. Cornelia had counted on this cultivation when she'd left a card at the Dowager's Mayfair town house yesterday morning. Her effort was rewarded when tonight's invitation arrived with the Dowager's gold engraved card.

Lady Daltmouth's haughty, scrutinising look fell on Cornelia, dipping down the length of her sheer blue overdress. One sculpted brow rose a touch, but the lines of the Dowager's face remained smooth. Like many of the other matrons, Cornelia imagined the older woman disapproved of her choice of dress so soon after the Comte's passing. Let the Dowager think what she wanted, Cornelia refused to mourn the old dog.

Her silent judgement given, Lady Daltmouth turned to the poet and cut him off mid-sonnet.

'I think you've extolled the virtues of your work enough for one evening, Mr Keans.' She rose and crossed to Cornelia, sending the flock of ladies surrounding her scurrying out of her way. She stopped in front of the younger woman who offered a deep curtsy before rising.

'Comtesse, I see you have a preference for French fashion,' the Dowager announced.

So, it wasn't the lack of black, but the tighter cut of Cornelia's dress the Dowager disapproved of. *'Oui, madame.'*

The Dowager's eyes narrowed ever so slightly. 'I hope you did not bring back too many other French customs such as papist beliefs.'

Cornelia looked down at the short woman, careful to keep her face free of any emotion. 'No, my lady. I kept my Protestant faith. It wasn't my beliefs which interested my late husband.'

A surprised gasp escaped from someone behind the Dowager, whose mouth twitched up in one corner. 'I'm glad to hear it. Good evening, Comtesse.'

She swept past her and across the room in the direction of her son, who watched her pending approach with dread. His face drooped in relief when his mother passed him to speak to one of the many tall footmen stationed around the room. It was then Cornelia noticed the impressive height of the liveried young men. They were all exceptionally tall, almost as tall as Rafe, and scandalously handsome.

Well, well, well, it seemed Lady Daltmouth wasn't such a strict Protestant after all.

Cornelia opened her fan, her amusement fading. It was time to focus on less appealing sights.

She sauntered into the Earl's line of vision, offering him a coy smile when his eyes met hers. His face rumpled in confusion and he turned to look over first one shoulder and then the other.

She curtsied, tilting forward a touch to give him a better view of her chest and drive home her invitation. His piggy eyes flicked to her breasts with the same greed she remembered lighting up the Comte's watery eyes from across many card tables. Despite the queasy roll of her stomach, she maintained the look of pleasure as he approached, his girth making him waddle more than walk.

'Comtesse, we're honoured to have you grace our little gathering,' he gasped, winded with the exertion of crossing the room.

The hypocrite. He wouldn't have deigned to speak to her if she was still the Honourable Cornelia Trofton.

'It's I who am honoured to be at such an intellectual gathering.' She fluttered the fan over her breasts, drawing attention to them and the sensual painting. 'You're so clever to bring together so many intelligent men.'

'Yes, of course.' His thick fingers ruffled the lace of his cravat. 'I'm quite the cultivator of the intellect and the arts. How I enjoy Mr Langello's poetry.'

'I believe Mr Langello is the composer,' Cornelia corrected, lowering her fan a touch to reveal more of her *décolletage.*

'Yes, of course,' Lord Daltmouth said to her breasts. 'It's Mr Keans who writes poetry in praise of womanhood.' His tongue slid over his large lower lip and she squelched the urge to slap the greedy look from his face.

'I'm not very familiar with Mr Keans's work. Please, tell me more about it.' She lowered the fan another inch, slowly reeling him in.

While he blathered on about the poet, guilt blackened the edges of her triumph. Blackmail wasn't her preferred game, but she had no choice. Another letter from Fanny had arrived today, demanding the tuition for Andrew's school fees at once or she'd write to her brother in Barbados about sending Andrew there in the autumn. There wasn't time to trust Andrew's safety to the fickle chance of cards. If all went as planned, she'd soon have enough to keep him at school and away from the West Indies for good. She knew she shouldn't take advantage of the Earl, but he was one of the few people with a relative in the register who could pay her demand without jeopardising his estate or his legacy. Besides, she would do anything to save Andrew. He was the only person who mattered to her now.

Rafe tapped the table and Lord Brixton laid another card on top of the first. After the disaster of the Dowager's salon, he'd hoped to find more success in this hell.

So far, both events had proved disappointing.

'Twenty-three. Tough luck Densmore.' Lord Brixton scraped up Rafe's cards, then moved on to deal an equally poor card to Lord Sewell.

Rafe narrowed his eyes at the young buck, noting the large diamond glittering in his cravat pin. The thought of losing at *ving-et-un* in front of this fop made his mouth burn more than the cheap wine the proprietress served.

A woman moving along the periphery of his vision caught his eye and he turned, thinking for a moment it was Cornelia. Expectation filled him before he realised it was only a molly searching for a new client among the players. She seemed young, though every soiled dove in this gaming den did, and with her blonde hair and small chest, she looked nothing like Cornelia. Only the way she stopped along the edge of the tables, observing everything and revealing nothing, reminded him of his former partner. He shifted in his chair, the weight of Cornelia's absence from his side heavier than he wanted it to be.

Lord Brixton dealt himself another card. 'Twenty-one. Looks like I win again.'

He collected the stacks of money from in front of each player, adding them to the large pile of notes and coins already piled in front of him.

Rafe took another swig of the hell's sour wine, blanching at the swill. The only game he'd won in the past three months was the game of life when he'd escaped from a Parisian moneylender who'd threatened to kill him over a sizeable debt and sell his corpse to an anatomist. The rogues were not as civilised in Paris as they were in London. He smiled wryly as he remembered giving the greasy Frenchman the slip in Madame DuMonde's. He'd even managed to collect his paltry winnings before sliding out through the ground-floor window of an obliging *putain*. His brief spate of luck ended when he'd returned to their lodgings to see Cornelia driving away in the Comte de Vane's carriage.

He downed the rest of the bitter wine, then tossed the empty goblet to a passing server.

'What do you say, Densmore? Up for another round?' Brixton asked with a smile Rafe wanted to punch from his round face.

'Come on, Brixton, give poor Densmore a break,' Lord Sewell chided, removing notes from his waistcoat pocket. 'I'll play again.'

Rafe fingered the few remaining notes from the sale of the silver spoons and his lips curled up in a wicked smile. It wasn't for nothing he'd followed his father through the card rooms of London, learning how to play. It was the only education his father had seen fit to provide him.

'Deal,' Rafe demanded, laying the notes on the table.

The two men exchanged stunned glances before Brixton took up the deck, shuffled twice, then dealt the first round of cards.

He laid a five of clubs in front of Lord Sewell.

The young man frowned. 'Not a good way to open.'

Brixton turned the next card over and laid it in front of Rafe.

The king of hearts.

Rafe didn't say anything as Brixton laid a ten of diamonds in front of himself.

A loud cheer went up from the table across from theirs. Rafe looked over as Lord Edgemont collected a pile of bills from the centre of the green baize, a smug grin on his chiselled face. He folded two notes and held them out to the harlots flanking his chair, his dark eyes raking their ample assets like a dog eyeing a bone. Across from Edgemont sat Monsieur Fournier, a refugee who'd once served as a geologist under Louis XVI and enjoyed the king's generosity. Rafe had hired the man three years ago to search Wealthstone for the lead vein his grandfather went to his grave believing existed. As they'd wandered the fields, the aged Frenchman had told Rafe stories of women and parties from before the Revolution, each marvellous enough to make a man long for Louis XVI's court. He'd also told Rafe of horrors to chill a man, but neither Robespierre nor Bonaparte had succeeded in knocking the life from Monsieur Fournier.

The laughing old man was gone now, his face long, his eyes sunken. He rose, broken defeat weighing down his steps as he left, unnoticed by the others.

Cold passed over the back of Rafe's neck as if the spectre of his own future had just slid by.

He rubbed away the chill and focused on his game.

Lord Brixton laid a card face up on top of Rafe's. The queen of hearts.

Rafe kept his face impassive, eyeing Lord Sewell and Lord Brixton's cards, none of which were face cards. Rafe could stand and hope neither of them reached twenty-one, or he could separate his cards and double his wager.

Brixton dealt two more cards to Sewell, pushing him over twenty-one.

'Rats, out again,' Lord Sewell complained, propping his elbows on the table.

'What about you, Densmore? Another card or are you happy with what you've got?'

'Split.' He moved the queen next to her king.

'Haven't lost enough tonight, eh, Densmore?' Brixton taunted.

'Then let's make this even more fun.' Rafe narrowed his eyes at the fop. 'Two twenty-ones say I take the entire pile of winnings sitting in front of you.'

'You're mad,' Brixton scoffed.

'No, just man enough to take a risk. Are you?'

'He has you now,' Lord Sewell heckled, goading his friend.

Rafe knew it would force Brixton into the wager. He was counting on it.

A faint flicker of fear rolled through Brixton's eyes before he regained his courage. 'All right. I'll take your wager, but you're going to lose what's left of your blunt.'

Rafe didn't answer. He didn't smile, flinch or move. 'Deal.'

Brixton's bravado dimmed as he dealt the first card.

'Oh, ohh!' Lord Sewell clapping. 'The ace of diamonds. He has you now, Brixton.'

'Shut up,' Brixton spat.

'Deal,' Rafe demanded.

Brixton's lips screwed tight in frustration as he slid the top card off the deck and laid it over the queen.

The ace of clubs.

'Well played, Densmore.' Lord Sewell applauded.

Brixton collapsed back in his chair, one hand over his eyes.

'Good evening, gentlemen.' Rafe rose and scraped up Brixton's substantial pile of notes and coins. 'It was a pleasure playing you.'

He tucked the money in his waistcoat pocket and stepped outside.

Two sad lamps flanked the front door, their dancing flames casting a faint glow across the pavement, but doing little to pierce the darkness of the street. Rafe stood in the flickering light and inhaled. Mould and rot hung heavy in the damp air, burning his nose more than the stink of stale wine and old cologne from inside.

Perhaps my luck is changing for the better.

'Did ya 'ave a good night in there, Lord Densmore?' A familiar voice slid out from the shadows across the street.

Or perhaps not.

Mr Smith, the moneylender, took shape in the twin circles of the lamps. Two henchmen perched on either side of him, one burly with wide shoulders, the other lean and lanky like his employer.

'My luck was tolerable.' Rafe shifted his foot to feel the weight of the knife hidden in his boot.

Mr Smith stopped a few feet from Rafe and flipped opened a slim toothpick case. 'I was beginning to think ya didn't want to see me.'

Rafe dropped his hands to his side, ready to reach for the knife. 'How could a gentleman not want to see a man of your esteem?'

Mr Smith pointed his toothpick at Rafe and the two thugs rushed forward. Rafe snatched the knife from his boot, held it up and the two men jerked to a halt.

'Rough handling isn't necessary. Wouldn't you agree, gentlemen?' Rafe waved the men back with the knife and they dutifully moved closer to Mr Smith.

He ran his thumb down the length of the ivory handle, painfully aware of the thin bit of metal standing between him and real trouble.

'Please excuse our lack of manners.' The hammer clicked back before Rafe noticed the gun in Mr Smith's hand. 'But I want to impress upon ya the importance of repaying the money ya owe me.'

Damn.

Mr Smith stepped closer, the stench of his garlic breath rising above the manure in the street. The moneylender slipped the toothpick between his teeth, letting it dangle on his chapped bottom lip as he reached into Rafe's pocket and pulled out the folded notes. Rafe didn't lower the knife, but kept it raised between them, the blade shining orange in the lamplight. If Mr Smith pulled the trigger, the bullet might tear through Rafe, but not before he got a swipe at the cockroach. He might have lost the advantage, but he wasn't about to roll over and die in the dirty street like his father had done.

Mr Smith's dull eyes flicked to the blade. Even with his limited intelligence, he seemed to grasp the threat. He danced back out of Rafe's reach before his dirty thumb flipped through the notes, calculating their worth. 'It won't pay your debt, but it's a start. Ya can keep the coins.'

'You, my good man, have an astounding lack of respect for your betters,' Rafe spat, hoping the man hadn't left any greasy fingerprints on his waistcoat. He couldn't afford to replace it.

Mr Smith stuffed the bills into the pocket of his dark trousers, careful to keep the pistol pointed at Rafe. 'I don't care who ya father was or what hoity-toity title you have. Ya owe me and I know your estate ain't worth a brass farthing. All of London knows it, so ya'd better hope Lady Luck slips into your bed because I want me money by next week. If I don't get it, I'll sell your hide to the anatomists.'

Rafe took one large step forward, pressing his chest into the hard end of the barrel and staring down at the slack-jawed rat. The metal quivered with Mr Smith's surprise. One slip and the moneylender would send a ball tearing through him.

'You may remind me of my debts,' Rafe hissed

in a voice as hard as chipped flint. He wasn't about to back down or be cowed by the rodent, no matter how much money he owed the man. 'But you will do so in full remembrance of your station and mine.'

The toothpick dropped from Mr Smith's open mouth before he clamped it shut. He staggered back, his eyes wide as he stuffed the pistol in his belt and, without a word, scurried off. His thugs hurried after him, the clomp of their footsteps fading into the misty darkness.

Rafe slid the knife back into his boot, ignoring the slight tremble in his hand. Brandishing the weapon might have startled the rat tonight, but it wouldn't stop him from scurrying out of the dark again and making good on his threat.

It seemed fashions weren't the only Paris trends to have crossed the Channel.

He looked down at the faint black circle on his waistcoat. 'Hell.'

He shouldn't have let his pride goad him into taking such a risk with Mr Smith. He brushed at the spot, relieved to see it fade. He'd already lost his winnings, he didn't need to lose his life like his father had done and leave his mother to starve.

'You were very brave, *mon ami.*' The weathered

voice with a thick French accent drifted out from the shadows behind him.

Rafe whirled to see Monsieur Fournier pulling himself up off the front step of the house next door. 'Or foolish.'

Monsieur Fournier raised his arms with a wide shrug, his limbs as thin as wrought iron. 'It appears we're both down on our luck.'

'Yes, Lady Luck is proving a most inconsistent mistress.'

'They're all inconsistent, *les belles femmes*.' He smiled, the glint of his spirit evident beneath the heavy weight of his lot.

'Then let's hope we both meet a more willing vixen tonight.' Rafe took the Frenchman's hand and pressed the remaining coins from his waistcoat into the palm, feeling the man's bones through the flesh. 'Good luck, *mon ami*.'

The older man's eyes brightened with gratitude and hope as he shook Rafe's hand. '*Bonne chance*, Seigneur de Densmore.'

Rafe nodded, then headed off down the street, hearing the laughter spill out of the hell as the Frenchman pulled open the door and hurried back inside.

Rafe quickened his pace, eager to reach the

safety of his rented rooms and avoid any more unfortunate encounters tonight. He would need all the luck Monsieur Fournier offered. Mr Smith was right about the state of his finances: there wasn't a creditor or friend in England likely to lend Rafe enough to repay the moneylender. All the rents from Wealthstone tenants went to pay the mortgages and, despite his luck in finding the spoons, he didn't think he'd be so fortunate as to find another valuable missed by his father.

Curse the fool. Even the windfall from selling out his country to the French hadn't been enough to save his father from debt, and death.

Rafe stomped in a puddle of water. It splashed up the side of his boot and dripped in to wet his stocking. He hadn't escaped becoming an anatomy lesson in France only to end up in a medical theatre in London. Nor was he about to lose what little remained of the Densmore legacy, to see his mother evicted from her home and cast on the charity of some distant relative who'd do nothing except sneer at her misfortune. His father might have lacked the presence of mind to secure a future for his wife and child, but Rafe would, even if it meant crawling into bed with the enemy.

If Cornelia planned to increase her widow's portion using the register, then it was time for him to share in the wealth. If she thought she could ignore him and their past, she was mistaken. She needed him as much as he needed her and he would make her see it.

He had no choice.

Chapter Three

Cornelia watched the swan glide down the canal, the water trailing behind it forming a V spreading out to touch each shore. Despite being nearly noon, all good society was still asleep, leaving the park quiet except for the governesses tending to their small charges. She watched the water flowing through the canal, the steady current reminding her of the river behind Hatton Place and the way the ducks used to swim to the opposite shore as she and Andrew played beside the banks.

She sighed, wondering if he'd outgrown the French shirts she'd sent him for Christmas. She hadn't seen him since before she and Rafe had set sail for Paris in search of the riches to be gained from the Peace of Amiens. She'd visited him at Mr Higgins's school where he stayed during the school terms, comforted to know he was somewhere safe while she was across the channel.

She picked at a small knot in the wooden handle of her parasol. If only she had the money to pay the tuition and keep Andrew there over the summer. She lowered the parasol, fluffing the lace along the edge. She'd have the money soon enough and school would begin again in a few weeks. Hopefully, her empty-headed stepmother wouldn't do anything foolish between now and then. Once Andrew was back at school she could see him. She wasn't about to travel to Sussex and face the vapid woman or listen in person to the many demands for funds Fanny felt the need to waste paper sending.

Cornelia settled the parasol back on her shoulder, shielding her face from the morning sun as she focused on the rippling water. Closing her eyes, she listened to the gentle slosh of small waves against the bank, letting the rhythmic sound sooth her the way it used to when she was a girl. She'd spent so many hours playing by the river, her ill-fitting dress muddy as she wandered shoeless through the reeds, imagining the stalks to be the sturdy walls of a castle where a handsome prince waited to rescue her, and her mother was still alive.

Foolish dreams.

She opened her eyes and gazed across the grass at a woman holding a small child's hand as it tottered about on unsteady legs. None of her girlish dreams had come true: not a peaceful life, a happy marriage or a future with Rafe.

What happened between us?

He'd been so different from all the other men, smiling at her from across Lord Perry's card party as if he understood her humiliation and worry over her father's mounting losses. He hadn't laughed like the other men when Lord Edgemont had goaded her weak father into wagering her hand. Nor had he leered at her when old Lord Waltenham won.

Then, in the garden, as she'd fought Lord Waltenham's clawing hands, cursing him and her father for what was about to happen, Rafe had stepped out from behind the box hedge. He'd thrashed the lecher, sending him fleeing into the house, and everything had changed.

No one had cared or noticed when the daughter of an obscure baronet and a penniless Baron ran off together. It wasn't love, but curiosity which had led her to accept Rafe's proposal to join him in London.

A man and woman working together can win more than gambling alone, he'd tempted her and she'd followed him, wanting to see the world as he'd painted it. He'd taught her to play cards, to carry and dress herself like a lady, and to charm men away from their money with nothing more than a promise. Then, in their rented rooms one night, their winnings piled high on the table, he'd taught her the secret pleasures shared between a man and a woman.

She gripped the parasol tighter, her breasts growing as heavy now as during the first night she'd lain next to him, anticipating his touch with curious excitement and trepidation. The memory of his thick voice in her ear as he explained everything each finger did and all the new sensations they awakened inside her, stole through her body once again. Beneath him, his dark brown eyes pinned to hers, she'd experienced a need deeper than the press of their skin and the urgency of their kisses, one which spoke to her soul.

Or so she'd once believed.

She shifted the parasol to her other shoulder. He'd made it clear from the beginning their arrangement wasn't permanent, but she always thought she'd meant more to him than a partner at the tables and in his bed.

How could I have been such a fool?

A figure in a cherry-red coat appeared on the canal bridge, pulling Cornelia from her memories. She closed the parasol, rested the tip in the soft grass and laid her hands on the upturned handle. Guilt snapped at her, but she kicked it away. She shouldn't take advantage of the Earl, but she had no choice, not if she wanted to save Andrew.

The Earl paused in the centre of the bridge, looking over the park before spying her. He hurried down the near side and over the grass, rushing to where she stood.

'I received your note,' he announced, his brass buttons straining to stay fastened over his thick middle as they stretched and relaxed with each wheezing breath.

Cornelia extended her hand. 'My lord.'

He knocked her hand aside and grabbed her around the waist, his fleshy stomach pressing against hers. He was two inches shorter than her and she could see the beginning of a bald spot in the middle of his head. 'I've thought of nothing but you since last night.'

The smell of port and beef on his breath made

her stomach churn as he stood up on his toes to claim her mouth.

She arched backwards, pressing her hands against his soft chest to keep his puckered lips from touching hers. 'My lord, I think you misunderstood the meaning of my note.'

'I don't believe so.' He tried to kiss her again, his weight in danger of toppling them both. If they fell, he'd crush her.

'Yes, you have.' She shoved hard, stumbling free of his grasp before regaining her footing. 'Do you really believe I'd debase myself in a public park?'

'There are many places we can go for privacy.' He lunged for her and she snapped up the parasol, poking the end into his chest to keep him at bay.

'It's not privacy I seek, but a moment of your time. We have business to discuss.'

'Business?' He knocked the parasol away, then flicked blades of grass off of his coat. 'What business could we possibly have to discuss?'

'The motive behind your father's retreat at the Battle of Saratoga.'

'You summoned me from my bed at this early hour to discuss that tired old rumour?' His nose wrinkled as if he smelled something foul.

'It's no rumour, my lord.' She lowered the umbrella point back to the ground and adjusted the strings of her reticule on her forearm. 'I'm in possession of a document that confirms your father was paid by the French to turn traitor.'

A faint red began to spread up his neck. 'No one would believe you.'

'I assure you, my proof is irrefutable.'

'What proof?'

'Mrs Ross's register.'

'But it doesn't exist,' he sputtered. 'It was destroyed in the same fire that killed the old courtesan.'

'No, the rumours were true—it was her maid's body they found. Mrs Ross survived and has been hiding in a small house near Gracechurch Street, scarred by the fire and living off all the money she earned from the French for making men like your father betray their country.' He paled and for a moment she felt sorry for him. 'She was killed two weeks ago in a carriage accident. I have since purchased the register from her estate.'

'A very convenient tale to scare little lords with, but you won't frighten me.' His fingers gripped the edge of his coat, undermining his confident words.

'Then let me tell you a better story, one which is sure to frighten you. It comes straight from

Mrs Ross's book. Your father accepted five thousand pounds from the French to flee at the Battle of Saratoga and help deny General Burgoyne his victory. He received an additional five thousand pounds once news of the defeat was known. It seems your father wasn't as competent an estate manager as your mother and possessed some heavy gambling debts he needed to repay.' She stepped closer and the Earl's Adam's apple bobbed as he swallowed hard. 'The Bill of Attainder is still in place, my lord, and Lord Twickenham is eager to unearth evidence of treachery and avenge his brother who died in that disaster of a battle. If I show him the register, he'll relish the chance to invoke the bill and seize your lands and title.'

The Earl's pudgy cheeks sagged. 'You can't.'

Flexing her fingers over the parasol handle, she steadied herself, thinking of Andrew as she pressed on, despite her disgust with herself. 'I will, unless you deliver to me by Friday the sum of one thousand pounds.'

He clutched his chest. 'One thousand pounds!'

'It's a very small price to pay to keep your lands and standing, and only a tenth of what your father received to betray his country and place you in this difficult position.'

He tugged on the knot of his cravat. 'And if I make the payment?'

His genuine fear and the hard way she pressed on made her stomach churn. This wasn't who she was or who she wanted to be and with each step down this path she felt herself becoming more like her stepmother, or worse, Lord Edgemont. 'I will maintain my silence.'

'How do I know you won't come to me at some future date and demand more?'

'You don't.' She wished she could give him some assurance, toss aside this callous mask and walk away from the ugliness of it all, but she couldn't, not with Andrew's fate hanging in the balance. 'Nor are you to discuss the matter with anyone, not your man of affairs or your mother.'

Enough people already knew about the register, the wrong sort like Rafe and Lord Edgemont. She didn't need the Earl wailing his woes about town and having more people learn of the book.

'Of course I won't tell my mother,' he spat. 'The shock of it would kill her.'

Given the number of scandals she'd already weathered, she doubted the Dowager Countess would die of shock, but Cornelia was happy to know the threat carried weight with her son. 'Then we have an agreement. You will pay the specified sum and no one, not even your mother, need ever know the register exists.'

He turned a large sapphire ring on his thick forefinger, his lips lengthening with his frown. 'I'll arrange to secure the money at once.'

'Good.' She opened her parasol again and laid it over one shoulder. 'Then I expect to receive it at my town house in Golden Square by Friday morning.'

'Yes, you'll get it.' He whirled on the heel of one highly polished boot and stormed off across the grass.

Cornelia waited until he was nearly over the bridge before she let out a long breath of relief. By Friday, she'd have the money and Andrew would be safe. She'd even pay Mr Higgins a few extra pounds to ensure Fanny didn't do anything to Andrew without Cornelia knowing about it first. She felt sure the kind vicar would help.

In the meantime, there was one more man to put the screws to.

Lord Edgemont.

She closed the umbrella and swung it once, then a second time, eager to see Lord Edgemont suffer for everything he'd done to her. It was a far more savoury endeavour to look forward to than this morning's nasty business.

Rafe entered the theatre lobby, looking over the sea of feather-bedecked turbans for Cornelia. He guessed she might be in attendance tonight, an old habit left over from their first months together in London when they used to sneak into unoccupied boxes and stand in the shadows while Rafe pointed out all of London society. In the beginning, she'd known nothing and no one knew her, accepting their fabricated story of her brief country marriage and subsequent widowhood. While the actresses on stage titillated the audience in their breeches roles, he'd tutored Cornelia on who was lacking in funds or who couldn't hold their wine at the tables. She'd proved an eager student with a sharp memory. It'd served them well in Paris, where almost all of London society had rushed during the brief peace between France and Britain.

He wound his way through the crowd, grumbling at the new craze for long trains. They lay all over the floor like wrinkled rugs and Rafe toed more than one out of the way to keep from tripping. Avoiding the new fashion distracted him from searching for Cornelia. He peered over the heads of the crowd, recognising many former opponents from Madame Boucher's, but not seeing Cornelia. Hopefully, she wasn't already seated. With the Comte's money, she could hire a box and take advantage of the semi-privacy to look over society and choose her victims.

At last he spied her on the staircase. Her black silk dress shot with red swayed with her hips as she took each step, teasing Rafe with just a hint of the round *derrière* beneath. While he admired the curve of her long back and the white flesh of her shoulders above the dark silk, she paused on the centre landing to look over the assembled guests.

He ducked behind Lady Treadaway and the tall ostrich feather protruding from the top of her turban.

'Is there something I may help you with?' Lady Treadaway turned, scrunching her eyes at Rafe, the wrinkles in her thin face hardening with disapproval.

He offered her a low bow and a rakish smile. 'No, my lady, your plumage has benefited me enough this evening.'

Her pinched expression softened into an amused smile. 'Lord Densmore, you are too much.'

He took her hand and clasped it to his chest,

warming the thin skin with a small squeeze. 'And you, Lady Treadaway, are perfect just as you are.'

He pinched her cheek and she swatted him away, her faded eyes twinkling with the playfulness of a green girl after her first stolen kiss. 'A tease, just like your father.'

'I assure you, I'm serious in all my compliments.' With a wink, he released her and bowed back into the crowd before making for the stairs.

At the top he paused, looking up and down the long hallways before catching the black train of Cornelia's dress as it disappeared into the third box from the end.

He followed her, the actors' voices echoing through the hallway as he pushed open the curtain and stepped inside. 'Good evening, Cornelia.'

She whirled in her chair to face him, her full lips forming a tantalising O before tightening into a scowl. 'What are you doing here?'

'You know how much I adore the theatre.' He looked out over the audience, the story on stage not nearly as gripping as the one taking place in the box across the way. He snatched Cornelia's opera glasses from her gloved hands and held them up. In the dim glow of the footlights he could just make out a couple intertwined in the shadows, engaged in a performance of their own. He struggled to see their faces, but Cornelia grabbed the glasses back from him.

'I believe your seats are further down, near the orchestra,' she hissed, then turned to the stage, her back stiff.

'How very kind of you to ask me to join you.' He slid into the empty chair behind hers and leaned over her shoulder, the curve of her neck so close to his lips. 'I've been considering your plan. You need my help.'

Her skin pebbled beneath his breath, but still she refused to face him. 'No, I don't believe I do.'

Rafe brought his lips next to her ear, aching to slide his teeth over the tender lobe. 'He won't pay you.'

She turned her head, her almond-shaped eyes hooded and seductive as she peered over one smooth shoulder at him. Her lips parted, moving in a tantalising rhythm to form each whispered word. 'He's already agreed to pay me.'

The shock struck Rafe like cold water.

'You met with him?' More than one head in the audience turned and looked in their direction. He dropped his voice. 'When?'

'This very morning.' Her lips, so tempting before, now chafed with the way they curled up in a triumphant smile. 'By the end of the week, I shall have a tidy sum in my possession.'

He took her arm, the warmth of her skin beneath his fingers rattling him before he regained his focus. 'You shouldn't have met with him alone. It's dangerous.'

'As you can see, I escaped the meeting unscathed.' She whacked his knuckles with her fan. He pulled back his hand, more annoyed by her flippant attitude than his stinging knuckles. 'If all goes well tonight, I shall continue to prosper.'

She nodded across the theatre.

He followed her gaze to Lord Edgemont. The square-jawed man sat in his box watching them, not bothering to conceal his interest. 'No. It's one thing to toy with your dolt of an Earl, but not Edgemont.'

'You needn't bother trying to protect me. My welfare is no longer your concern.'

'You have the register. That makes you my concern.' He leaned in close again, trying to ignore the way the heat of her skin heightened the notes of her verbena perfume. 'I needn't remind you what Edgemont is capable of.'

'Which is exactly why he deserves to suffer,'

she hissed, her calm mask sliding. 'I want to see him squirm.'

'I agree, but when you threaten a man like him, you make him desperate. You can't underestimate a desperate man.'

'Like I underestimated you?'

Rafe jerked upright, surprised by the venom in her accusation. 'What did I do in Paris to give you such a low opinion of me?'

'I'm sure if you think very hard, you'll discover the source of it. For the moment, I have no need of your assistance, so leave, or I'll make such a fuss the whole theatre will rally to my defence.' She shifted around to face the stage, raising her glasses to watch the performance.

Rafe moved to say something, but caught the glint of more than one lorgnette turning to study them from across the theatre, including Edgemont's. Having no desire to set society's tongue wagging with gossip, he rose and pulled aside the curtain, leaving the curtain rings to clank against the rail as he stormed into the hallway.

Impudent wench. He hurried along the upper level of the theatre and down the main staircase, banging the banister with his fist as he descended into the nearly deserted foyer. Whatever wrong she thought he'd committed in Paris, it'd taken a stubborn hold in her mind. For the life of him, he couldn't say what he'd done except try to help her, and this was how she chose to repay him? Dismissing him like some servant and then blaming him for her actions in France.

He stepped outside, ignoring the hackneys waiting by the kerb and letting his anger carry him towards a less respectable part of London. Cornelia would be nowhere without him. He shuddered at the memory of her and Lord Waltenham in Lord Perry's garden and what might have happened if he hadn't followed them. After the old man insulted her, her father probably would have wagered her away again, or sold her to some moll for a few sovereigns. She certainly wouldn't have become a Comtesse with a generous inheritance.

Rafe halted in the middle of the pavement, ignoring the inviting calls of a doxy lounging in a doorway across the street. Despite his former misgivings about her morals, it still seemed strange a rich widow would want to dabble in blackmail, not with all those diamonds dangling from her tender ears and caressing her pretty breasts. They'd twinkled with her current good fortune, or were they there to hide the lack of one?

No matter what Cornelia might have done to him in France, if the Comte's riches were as rickety as his legs then it was a revenge not even Rafe could have designed.

He whirled around on one heel and headed back towards the theatre. If Cornelia wore her finest baubles to distract society from any scent of money problems, it might offer his last hope to reel her in and remove his father's name from the register.

Cornelia tried to focus on the play, but the actress's sing-song voice grated on her nerves as much as Rafe's sudden appearance tonight. When he'd gripped her arm, she'd nearly bolted from the box. The Comte used to curl his gnarled fingers around her and try to drag her to their bedroom, his ragged nails biting into her skin before she'd shake him off. After their first horrid night together, when he'd tried to rally his body enough to violate hers and she'd shoved him away, she'd refused to let him near her again. It'd stopped his amorous advances but not the cruel insults he'd taken sport in constantly hurling at her.

She stamped down the nasty memories and rubbed her arm, trying to feel Rafe's warmth, but the skin was cool. His warning grasp was nothing like the Comte's rough handling, but strong and reassuring. Until he'd pressed his flesh to hers, she hadn't realised how much she missed the comfort of it.

Apparently, Rafe didn't miss her quite as much. If she didn't have the register, he wouldn't even be troubling with her, just as she wouldn't deign to acknowledge Lord Edgemont.

She peered through the glasses across the theatre.

Lord Edgemont sat deep in the shadows of his box, his staunch nose made more prominent by his high forehead and close-cropped hair. He was the one man in London she hated more than Rafe. She could still hear his mocking voice at Lord Perry's card party, encouraging her drunk father to wager her hand, laughing at her father's desperation and hers. Then, in France, he'd tried to play her, believing she was as weak and gullible as her father.

He'd regret thinking so little of her.

The audience broke into wild laughter and Cornelia shifted in her chair again, eager to leave but determined to stay. She'd spent more than she should have to hire the box for the evening. It galled her to think the expense would only result in a stinging rebuke from Rafe. What she needed was society's notice of her and her new title, and the invitations to card parties it might garner. If the Earl found a way to delay his payment, gambling was her only chance to raise enough money to live on or pay for Andrew's school.

It wasn't just society's attention she needed, but Lord Edgemont's. Despite the uncomfortable weight of his narrow-eyed stare over the audiences' heads, she wanted him to come to her. If he approached her tonight, in a box in front of a theatre full of people, it would make blackmailing him a touch easier and safer.

For all her bravado in front of Rafe, she was wary of the thick-necked Baron.

Cornelia jumped as the actress let out a high-pitched laugh on stage.

Hang Lord Edgemont. She stuffed the opera glasses in her reticule and quit the box, determined to find a better, cheaper place to ensnare him.

Hurrying down the quiet hallway, she descended the stairs to the main lobby, passing only one or two other people and a footman carrying a note upstairs.

Outside, she watched from the top of the portico as the last hackney pulled away from the kerb.

Hopefully, it wouldn't be long before another appeared.

A breeze blew through the open row of tall columns. Cornelia wrapped her arms around herself, wishing she'd thought to bring a shawl, but she'd expected the evening to be warmer. She could go back inside, enjoy the comfort of her box but she decided to wait. She wasn't in the mood for any more play-acting tonight.

'Good evening, Comtesse.'

Cornelia whirled around at the sound of Lord Edgemont's voice. Anger filled her as he approached, his movements slow and easy like a snake, but with enough hint of danger to make her shiver. She flicked a glance over his shoulder at the empty foyer, the chance someone might happen on them offering her slim protection.

She dropped her arms, ready to face him. He looked as sure of himself tonight as he had on the wharf in Calais when he'd approached her with his bargain and started this ridiculous game. If she hadn't been so desperate to escape France, and seen the opportunity to harm him in the offer, she wouldn't have accepted his proposal.

'Lord Edgemont, what a pleasure it is to see you again.'

His eyes glinted at the thought of his power over her. Little did he know, she now held the upper hand. 'And how are you coming on our little matter?'

'I've succeeded.' She touched her necklace, noting with triumph the way it drew his attention to her chest. 'You have no idea how easy it was for me to purchase the book.'

He arched one surprised eyebrow. 'You've always been resourceful. It's what I admire most about you.'

'Is admiration what you feel? I always thought it was something more base.'

'And to think, you could have chosen me over Lord Densmore, with a comfortable little town house in Mayfair and all your needs provided for.'

'Thankfully, your losing hand of cards spared me from such an illustrious fate.'

He crossed his arms in front of his thick chest. 'Enough pleasantries. If you have the register, why haven't you delivered it to me?'

'All in good time.' She wasn't about to give him what he wanted, only what he deserved. 'You see, I've decided to make a small alteration to our agreement.'

His slick smile dropped. 'There'll be no altera-tions.'

Rafe's warning rang in her ears as the shadows around them seemed to darken before she steadied herself. This was like any gamble and now was no time to lose her nerve. 'Your father's name is in the register, more than once. If I show it to Lord Twickenham, it will be the end of the illustrious Barony of Edgemont.'

His expression sharpened into an edge which cut through her. 'Are you threatening me?'

She met his hard stance, despite the cold fear creeping up her spine. 'It was kind of you to pay my passage back to England.'

'In exchange for the register.' He jerked his thumb to his chest. 'My register.'

'The one you weren't man enough to acquire on your own.'

His hand lashed out and grabbed her wrist, and he pulled her away from the entrance and into the shadow of one tall column. 'You will give it to me.'

'Never. You thought you could manipulate me like you used to manipulate my father but you were wrong.' She twisted her arm, but he held fast, crushing the edge of her bracelet into her wrist.

'You have nothing over me while I have the ability to destroy you.'

'Do you really think I'll let you get away with this?'

'You don't have a choice.'

'Oh, I do.' His lips pulled back in a sneer. 'You see, everyone has their weakness. Don't think I won't find yours.'

'I'll destroy you before you can.'

'You ungrateful little whore.' He shoved her back against the stone column, pressing his body hard against hers. The two of them were nearly matched in height, but his shoulders were wide and his neck thick, the veins bulging out with his anger. 'You will give me the register.'

'Let go of me.' She pushed hard against him, but he didn't budge. Her wrist and chest stung and the rough stone of the column scratched at her exposed shoulders.

A shadow rose up behind him and the flash of a blade appeared at Edgemont's throat.

'Do as the lady says,' Rafe demanded.

Edgemont stiffened before his hand on her wrist eased. Cornelia wrenched free and slid out from between him and the pillar.

'That's no way to treat a Comtesse. Now, apologise,' Rafe growled.

'She can dress herself in all the diamonds and titles she wants, but she's still not worth the blunt her father used to gamble with,' Edgemont spat.

Rafe jerked the knife up higher under Edgemont's jaw and the man winced. A small drop of blood formed above the blade, then slid down the smooth surface to stain his cravat. 'Your apology. Now.'

Edgemont hesitated and Cornelia doubted he'd speak.

'My apologies, Comtesse,' he muttered, to her surprise.

'Now, that's more like it.' He shoved Edgemont aside and came to stand beside her, sheathing the knife in his boot.

She reached up to take his arm, her fingertips grazing the wool jacket before she pulled back. She wasn't about to cling to him like some Gothic heroine. Instead she stepped closer, drawing from his steady presence to replace the courage rattled out of her by Edgemont's outburst.

'I should have known where there is one of you, there is the other.' Edgemont touched his throat and grimaced at the blood on his fingers. 'You always possessed an unusual soft spot for this little whore. She must possess quite a tongue to keep you so enamoured.'

Rafe rushed at Edgemont, grabbing him by the lapels and shoving him hard against the wall. Surprise and height gave Rafe the advantage over Edgemont's sturdiness and he tugged the Baron up by his coat to face him. 'Say one more word to the lady and I'll call you out.'

'You wouldn't dare,' Edgemont spat, his wide hands puling at Rafe's.

'Would you like to bet on it?'

Edgemont's lips curled to reveal his crooked front teeth, but he stayed silent. A long moment passed, the quiet broken by the jangle of equipage as a hackney pulled up to the kerb.

Finally, Edgemont's hands relaxed and dropped to his sides, signalling his surrender.

Rafe released Edgemont. The Baron straightened his coat, then fixed them both with a look of venom before skulking back into the theatre.

Cornelia rubbed her aching wrist, the darkness not deep enough to hide her trembling hands.

'Are you all right?'

She faced Rafe, ashamed of her fear and weakness. 'Yes, I'm fine.'

'Good. Then let's get you home.' He took her by the arm and drew her towards the hack, but she pulled back.

'I don't need your assistance.'

His hand tightened on her arm, not threatening, but steadying. 'Then simply enjoy the pleasure of my company.'

He started forward again. Pride told her to pull away, to make an exit worthy of a Comtesse, but instead she followed his lead, his gentle coaxing a relief after Edgemont's bullying.

He opened the hackney door and helped her in, the firmness of his fingers missed as she settled against the worn squabs.

'Where do you live?'

She hesitated, not wanting to reveal her address. He'd know it wasn't a fashionable enough area for a rich Comtesse. However, with him standing in the open doorway, she couldn't sit there like a stone and say nothing. 'Number Eighteen, Golden Square.'

Whatever his thoughts on her residence, his face didn't reveal them as he stepped back to call instructions up to the driver.

She waited for him to bid her goodbye, to close the door and leave her to the privacy of the carriage. The tight darkness might weigh on her as it had during the many lonely nights as a child, and again at Château de Vane, but it was preferable to the embarrassment of appearing so vulnerable in front of Rafe.

To her dismay, he climbed in and settled across from her, his knee tapping hers as the vehicle rocked into motion. She jerked away from him, tucking herself as far as she could into the corner. Rafe said nothing, but the rhythm of his breathing punctuated the steady clop of hooves on the cobblestones.

He sat with his long body curved to keep from hitting his head on the low ceiling and she smiled to herself. The world was not accommodating for a man of his height.

'Do you still have your duelling pistols?' she asked, more afraid of her own thoughts than Rafe's overwhelming presence.

He picked at a spot on his breeches. 'Alas, no.'

'Pawned?'

'But Edgemont needn't know that.' He flashed a wide smile, as if all the cares of the world never troubled him. It warmed some of the cold creeping through her. If only she could be so optimistic in the face of adversity. It was his gift, the light which had first drawn her to him, the thing she'd missed the most after she'd married the Comte.

She tapped his boot with one slippered foot. 'But you still have your knife.'

'There are some things even I can't afford to part with.'

I'm not one of them. Outside the dark city passed and not even the moonlight glittering off the windows of the buildings could soothe her. She might parade through London as a Comtesse, but deep inside she was still the common country girl, unloved by her father and wanted by no one, not even a destitute Baron.

'Don't let anything Edgemont said trouble you.' Rafe's voice soothed from across the darkness. 'He's no better than we are. He simply has more blunt. Though rumour has it, he's sinking in debt.'

'Good, I hope he drowns in it.' Edgemont's words sat hard on her chest, not because they were vile, but because they were true. She was no better than a whore. She'd sold herself to the Comte for the promise of his money, nothing more. How the old fool must be laughing at her from hell. 'If Edgemont values his land and title, he'll shortly have even less money while I shall have more.'

'And what of my land and titles?'

She shifted against the squabs, guilt making her back ache more than the hard seat. After what he'd done for her tonight, it seemed petty to hold the threat over his head, but he still needed to answer for Paris. 'I haven't decided if you'll keep them.'

'I can't help feeling, since you haven't already rushed to Lord Twickenham's office with the register to crush me, you won't. At least not until you get what you want from me. I wonder what it could be?' There was more teasing amusement in the question than curiosity. Despite all the uncertainties of their situation, the fickleness of their fortunes, with him it always seemed as if nothing could touch them. What she wouldn't give to know such calm confidence.

'For a man with a sword held over him, you seem awfully sure of yourself.'

'It's a charming hand holding it.'

'I could drop it on you at any moment.'

'Yes, you could.' His smile vanished, his sudden seriousness unsettling. 'Why did Edgemont hire you to get the book?'

The direct question startled her. He must have overheard her and Edgemont before he'd intervened. She let the silence drag out, the rattling hack and the laughter of men on the street filling it. She struggled to come up with a suitable answer, but her mind turned to mud and nothing, not one clever lie came to mind.

'Cornelia?' The entreaty was soft, like when he used to coax from her the extent of a loss, not to punish or rail at her, but simply to know the truth and plan their next move. Only this time, she wasn't about to tell him the truth.

'After the Comte died, I had trouble getting out of France. I had the money to leave, but not the connections to secure a passage in the rush.' She hoped the darkness hid the lie. If he discovered her lack of money, it wouldn't be long before he found a way to use it against her to get to the register. 'He knew a captain willing to bring me home.'

'In exchange for what? I'm sure he didn't do it out of the generousness of his heart.'

'He asked me to get the register for him, using any means necessary. Who knew it would be as easy as walking into Mrs Ross's and buying it.'

'Easy for you,' he said, his voice turning serious again. 'Why didn't he get it himself?'

'It seems I'm not the only one with a grudge against the man. Mrs Ross wanted to punish him, though he never said why.'

'Probably something his father did. The old

Baron was the woman's protector at one time. They parted badly.'

'It must have been horrendous given the price she demanded for the pages with his father's name on them.'

'With Edgemont's mounting gambling debts, I suppose he thought having you get the book was easier than paying her price. He probably intended to use the tome to increase his coffers through a little blackmail.'

Cornelia shifted uneasily in her seat, hating to think she'd lowered herself to Edgemont's level. Unlike the Baron, she had a more noble reason, but it didn't make the swill of it any easier to swallow.

'So you accepted Edgemont's help, but you had no intention of giving him the book,' Rafe observed as the hack made a turn, leaning heavily on one set of tired springs before righting itself.

'He thought he could order me about like he used to order my father. Now he's the one who'll dance to my tune.'

'Was that your tune the two of you were dancing to when I interrupted?'

She didn't answer, irritated at his reminder of her misstep tonight.

He reached up and took the strap above the door,

his jaw tight with the same worry she saw when the Peace of Amiens began to fail and word of the impending blockade had reached Paris. 'You shouldn't have approached him alone. You underestimated him, almost to your detriment.'

'Are you worried about me or about losing access to the register?'

'Both.'

Hope hung heavy on the word, threatening to snare her as it had in Lord Perry's garden. Rafe's deep brown eyes watched her and she curled her fingers over the edge of the squabs, resisting the loneliness pushing her to cross the floorboards, press herself into his chest and beg him to make her forget France. She couldn't cross the emptiness separating them and cling to him like some forsaken mistress, abandoning her pride just as he'd abandoned her in Paris.

The hackney rocked to a stop in front of her town house, the horse whinnying as the driver waited for them to climb down. It was time to go, to leave him behind and face her troubles alone. She reached for the door handle.

He rested one hand on her waist, stopping her from fleeing.

The air in the hack evaporated, just as it had in

Mrs Ross's house, leaving her struggling to breathe as she met his piercing eyes.

'There was a time when we would have done this together.' Concern for her sat hard in the thin line of his lips and all hint of the carefree gambler was gone. 'You need me, Cornelia. Let you me help you. Think of what we can accomplish together.'

His hand on her waist was like an anchor in a storm offering her a safe harbour. How easy it would be to lean into him, just as she had so many times before, draw from his strength and share his belief that everything would be all right. Only tonight, his siren call sounded more like a lure to draw her on to the rocks so he could plunder the wreck.

She laid her hand on his, curling her fingers underneath his smooth hand. If there was one lesson her father had taught her, it was to trust no one. She'd already made the mistake of ignoring it.

'No, Rafe, our days together are over.' She lifted his hand from her waist and let go, her chest tightening as she pushed the door open and stepped out. To her surprise, he followed her down onto the pavement. 'I told you I don't need you.'

'I know, but I haven't the fare to pay for my ride home.'

She narrowed her eyes at him, then dug a few coins from her purse and handed them up to the driver. As the hackney pulled away from the kerb, she expected Rafe to say more about the register or his desire for a partnership. Instead, his eyes darted around the square and she swallowed hard. He was appraising the street the same way he appraised a card room, looking for his opponents' weakness. Her hands tightened on her reticule for she knew the semi-darkness couldn't hide the chipped paint and dirty stone evident on most of the houses.

He hooked his thumbs in his waistcoat pocket, the serious man from the hackney gone, replaced by the gambler she knew too well. 'A rather modest section of London for a widowed Comtesse.'

He knows. No, he only suspects and she would confirm nothing. 'My return was so hurried, I didn't have time to secure lodgings in a more fashionable neighbourhood.'

'An error you will no doubt rush to fix.' He smiled like the devil, increasing her irritation, but she was careful not to show it.

She strode past him to the front door, annoyed to find it closed and the windows flanking it dark.

'I am, at this very moment, enquiring into a more suitable house.'

'At this very moment.' He leaned against the railing, watching her as he always did when she sat down to a hand of cards.

Fishing her key out of her reticule, she silently cursed her useless maid for not rushing to open the door. If the girl hadn't been so afraid of Napoleon, she would have left her in France. 'Goodnight, Rafe.'

She unlocked the door and pushed it open, ready to leave him on the street when his voice stopped her.

'When you finally realise you need me, you may find me at Mrs Linton's, just off Drury Lane?'

She stopped, her hand on the knob. 'What happened to your town house?'

He shrugged, his smile never faltering. 'It went the way of my pistols.'

'Does nothing ever trouble you, Rafe?'

'Goodnight, Cornelia.' He tossed her a wink and pushed away from the railings.

She watched him walk away, rolling her wrist against the lingering pain of Edgemont's grip. It was her move now. Rafe had helped her and offered her a partnership. Instinct and a stinging bruise urged her to accept it, but for the moment she decided to stay. Despite what had happened tonight, she held the register and therefore the stronger hand. With so much to gain, she wasn't about to trust her future or her heart to Rafe again.

Chapter Four

The next evening Cornelia watched the hackney drive away, leaving her on her dark doorstep. Daylight had slipped from the sky hours ago and there were at least another five to go before it appeared again. She wished it would hurry. There was something oppressive in tonight's darkness, as if any number of dangers might slide out of the shadows and strike her. If they did, who would care? Maybe Antoinette, her French maid, but only because she hadn't been paid since they'd landed in Dover. If the little madam opened the door in the morning to find Cornelia dead on the step, she'd probably run back inside to steal anything left of value before seeking employment elsewhere.

Rafe would be the next one to rush over her stillwarm corpse to get to the register.

She sighed. Once all these pariahs were done

picking at her bones, there wouldn't even be enough to sell to keep Andrew at school. There wasn't enough now. She'd pawned her gold wedding band this morning to raise enough to play at Mrs Drummond's. Her meagre winnings would keep the roof over her head until Lord Daltmouth paid. If he paid.

Cornelia tugged open the strings of her reticule to fish out the door key. There was no sense lingering in the darkness waiting for tragedy to strike, though she doubted the candles in her bedroom would succeed in pushing back the heaviness any more than the chandeliers hanging over Mrs Drummond's gaming tables had. As she searched the silk sac for the key, the lightness of her winnings deepened the darkness. The gapped-toothed old crone who'd sat across from her had proven more cunning than she'd first looked in her wide brocade skirt and wrinkled mob cap. If Cornelia hadn't been so distracted by Rafe and all her other problems, she might have noticed how the old hag toyed with her garnet ring whenever she held a good hand. The sign only became obvious during the final game, soon enough for Cornelia to win back her money, and a little more, but not much else.

If Rafe had been there, he would have instantly recognised the old woman was more cunning than she looked. Then he'd have picked out the weakest player and Cornelia might have come home with a heavier purse.

She pulled out the key and shoved it in the lock, turning it with such force she thought it might bend. Having Rafe at her side wouldn't have made tonight a success. He'd have only pointed out the obvious, speaking to her as if she were still fresh from Sussex with no talent of her own. He might have been her tutor and partner once, steering her towards weaker opponents or warning her about cheaters, but she'd been the one to play the cards and the weak men filling the tables. She owed Rafe nothing. Even if she did, his abandonment in Paris cancelled the debt.

As she closed the door behind her, the thick shadows of the high-ceilinged entrance hall made her shiver. It reminded her too much of the hallways of Château de Vane and her ears sharpened, listening for the old man's disgusting voice yelling his insults for all the servants or guests to hear. She balled her hands at her sides, fighting the crushing loneliness pressing in on her. When his valet had found him dead on his bedroom floor, she couldn't arrange the funeral fast enough. She'd enjoyed one day of peace before all the problems of his debts and escaping back to England had overwhelmed her.

She spied the tin heraldic shield hanging over the fireplace in the sitting room. The de Vane crest glittered in the faint light of the single candle burning in a brass holder on the mantel. Hate made her fingers tighten on the reticule strings. She should have chucked it in the Channel, but she was determined to have this symbol of her title, the one and only thing of value she'd gained from the marriage.

It wasn't enough to repay her for everything she'd suffered under the old man.

Marching into the room, she snatched the crest from the wall and threw it to the floor. It clattered against the wood, tearing the quiet of the house.

She hoped he burned in purgatory.

'Madame, est-ce vous?' Antoinette's shaky voice called from upstairs, probably startled awake by Cornelia.

She kicked the shield across the room where it clanged to a stop against a chair leg. *'Oui, c'est moi.'*

Weary with sleep and memories, she made her way to the stairs. Candlelight flickered in the hall upstairs, growing brighter as Antoinette's hurried footsteps drew closer. Something in the glow of it made her think of Rafe and the single candle they used to burn on the bedside table each night in their room. In the dancing light, he'd kneel across the crinkled sheets from her, running his fingertips up her outstretched arms before tugging her down into the bed, covering her body with his and driving away all thoughts except her desire to be one with him.

She paused, clutching the banister. For all the foreignness of those simple lodgings, they'd never felt as cold and unwelcoming as this house or Château de Vane. With Rafe, even the smallest garret felt like home.

Antoinette appeared at the top of the stairs, her eyes as wide and white as a porcelain faro chip. 'Comtesse, we've been robbed.'

It took one brief flicker of the flame for the words to sink in. Cornelia rushed up the stairs, pushed past the maid and raced down the hall. She threw open the door to her room, then stopped. The reticule dropped from her hand and hit the floor with a thud. She didn't need to search to know what was missing. The top of her desk lay splintered and broken on the floor next to a shattered ink jar. The papers strewn across the floor fluttered in the breeze coming through the open window. In the centre of the mess, her black jewellery box sat tipped on one side, the necklace and earrings spilling out from beneath it, their facets sparkling in the wavering candlelight.

It was gone. The register was gone.

'Did you see the thief?' She whirled on the maid. 'Did you see who it was?'

Antoinette shook her head and her blonde braid bounced back and forth. 'No, *madame.* I heard a noise, but by the time I rose to see what it was, the thief was gone.'

Cornelia pulled in first one breath and then another, struggling through the panic to stay focused. She could bluff the Earl into payment, and maybe Edgemont, but it wouldn't last. Once the thief stepped out of the shadows and made his own demands, her game would end and with it all chances of keeping Andrew safe.

Her mind raced to identify the culprit. There were only three men she'd told about the register. The Earl and Rafe knew where she lived. Of those men, just one was underhanded enough to resort to thievery.

Rafe.

* * *

Rafe tossed aside the burnt edge of his bread, frustrated at the meagre fare in front of him. Even in London he ate little better than he did at Wealthstone. At least there he enjoyed fresh vegetables from his mother's garden, not this wilted cabbage. He shoved the plate away and leaned back in the uncomfortable, turned-wood chair. It creaked beneath him, threatening to give way as he undid the ties at the top of his shirt. He slid onto one of the other mismatched chairs around the scarred table, kicking the old chair aside. It knocked up against the sagging sideboard, making the wine bottle, pewter goblet and cup on top rattle. Watching the goblet come to rest, Rafe wasn't sure which he detested more, these shoddy lodgings, his cheap homespun shirt or his inability to scrape together enough blunt to keep his mother from sullying her once-fine hands with the demeaning work of growing food and sewing his shirts.

Curse the bastard, he muttered as he pulled off his boots. They'd once been his father's best pair, purchased with the blunt he'd won the night before they found him in the gutter outside his favourite hell, his throat slit and his purse gone.

He dropped the boot to the floor, then pulled off

the other one. His father had been one of the most respected men in the House of Lords before he'd fallen prey to the cards. To think he'd been foolish enough to succumb to Mrs Ross and her French agents. It grated on him as much as Cornelia stealing the register out from under him.

A commotion in the hallway, followed by Mrs Linton's shrill voice, caught his attention. The voices grew louder until at last the door to his rooms flew open, banging against the wall behind it.

Cornelia stood in the doorway.

'Speak of the devil,' Rafe muttered, pushing himself to his feet.

Their eyes locked, the tension between them riveting her to her place. He tried not to smile as he admired the flush of her cheeks and the rosy hue sweeping across the sweet curves of her breasts. The faint pink echoed in the glittering facets of her diamond necklace. Moist, parted lips, red with heat, stirred his blood. It brought him back to the night after their first win at Madame Boucher's when he'd slid the yellow dress from her shoulders, traced the curve of her waist down across the roundness of her hips and worshipped at her temple.

He pressed his lips together and shifted against his stirring manhood. Even when staring at him with all the fury of a Bonfire Night blaze, she was stunning.

Something of their past rippled through her, too. He caught it in the subtle movement of her fingers at her side and the long, stroking look which paused at his open shirt before continuing to his face. Her rage simmered down into something more potent. It reached out to him like a secret signal made across a card room—a simple gesture everyone might see but only they understood.

'Good evening, my dear.' He forced himself to bow, then straightened, severing the subtle connection before it made him forget how much he disliked her.

'Where is it?' Her fury returned, blotting out her interest in his current state of undress as she marched into the room. 'What have you done with it?'

Behind her, Mrs Linton clutched her wrapper tight to her neck, her nightcap askew over her wild red hair as she glared at Rafe. 'I run a respectable establishment, Lord Densmore. I won't have such scenes in my house.'

'Mrs Linton, allow me to introduce the Comtesse de Vane.'

'Oh, I'm sorry, Comtesse.' Mrs Linton swayed a little as she slid one heel behind her and genuflected to Cornelia. 'If you'd made yourself known, I wouldn't have interfered.'

Cornelia didn't turn around or acknowledge the woman, her ire fixed on Rafe.

'Thank you, Mrs Linton. I'll see to the Comtesse and I assure you there'll be no more scenes.'

'Thank you, my lord.' Mrs Linton reached in and grasped the doorknob, pulling it shut as she backed out of the room.

'My dear Cornelia, can I assume you're here to accept my offer of a partnership?'

'It's not Cornelia, it's Comtesse.' Her heels knocked over the uneven floorboards as she advanced.

'Of course.' He fixed on her oval face, determined to avoid looking at her breasts, which rose and fell fast enough to tempt a dead man back to life. 'But I'm sure you didn't come to see me at this hour merely to emphasise your title.'

'Give it to me.'

'My dear...' Rafe struggled to keep a smile from

spreading as he motioned to the table '…I haven't even finished eating.'

She swept her hand over the table, sending the pewter and food crashing to the floor. 'You're finished now.'

Rafe stood perfectly still, not allowing himself, or any part of him, to rise to her challenge. 'Careful, Comtesse, your country roots are showing.'

She snatched the pewter knife from the table and held it up between them. 'Give it back to me before I impale you like a sausage.'

The light from the rushes in the centre of the table slid down the length of the blade. Rafe slowly raised his hand and placed it over hers. He slid his thumb down her fingers, trying to soothe her and the violence threatening them both. Her breasts paused in their rapid rise and fall, before first one long breath and then another stilled the tremors in her hand and the mesmerising cadence of her diamond-bedecked *décolletage*.

'Before you impale me, might I know exactly what it is of yours you believe I have?' With gentle pressure, he pushed her arm to one side. He wasn't sure the dull implement could pierce his shirt, but he didn't want to find out the hard way.

'The register. You stole it and I want it back.'

His fingers tightened on hers, all amusement gone. 'You mean it's gone?'

She struggled against his grip to raise the knife. 'I mean you stole it, you conniving weasel of a—'

'Please, let's dispense with the flattery.' The tension in her arm radiated up through his, heightening the unease of her unexpected appearance. The register was out there with the power to destroy him. 'I didn't steal it.'

'You dare deny it?' She tried to jerk her hand away, but he held it tight, drawing her a little closer. Her fiery eyes smouldered with outrage and something he remembered too well. Uncertainty.

'Threaten me with all the knives in the room, I can't return what I don't have.' He cocked his head slightly and arched one eyebrow with the same seriousness he used to pin her with when warning her about a cheat at her table.

She studied him and he waited for her to see it, to recognise their old signal. Her pulse raced beneath his fingers like it had the night he'd led her from Lord Perry's garden to the safety of the stables. His own pulse threatened to bolt as the heat of her skin against his spread through him. He focused on the small hairs of her eyebrows, shaped into an arch above her eyes, struggling to maintain the cool composure which always served him so well.

Then, the muscles beneath his palm began to relax and the pace of her pulse against his fingertips slowed.

She believed him.

Cautiously, he took the knife from her and tossed it on the table. He led her to the worn sofa near the small fireplace, whirling her around so her back faced the sagging thing before he let go. 'Sit down and compose yourself.'

Her lips screwed together in annoyance, but she said nothing as she pulled out the sides of her skirt and lowered herself with all the poise of a princess onto the faded chintz. She laced her long fingers together in her lap, the nails short and clean and buffed to a subtle shine. He heard the slow intake of breath. It rattled through his own chest as she exhaled and the wild Amazon from the doorway drew into a composed lady worthy of the title Comtesse.

'Well done,' Rafe congratulated, heartened to know she remembered something of what he'd taught her. 'Now, tell me what happened.'

'I was gambling at Mrs Drummond's and I came

home to find my bedroom ransacked and the register gone.'

He walked around the back of the sofa, tracing the rounded wood with his fingers, resisting the desire to stretch one out and circle the small freckle on her shoulder.

'I'm flattered to know you'd think of me first,' he offered drily as he dropped onto the opposite end of the cushion.

The faintest hint of red coloured the apples of her cheeks before she set her jaw against it. 'Who else could have stolen it?'

'Edgemont. Or your Earl.'

'I doubt Lord Daltmouth associates with housebreakers.'

'No, but he knows about the register and he knows you have it. Perhaps he didn't wish to pay your fee.'

'I don't think an Earl would stoop so low, but Edgemont might.'

He shifted off the spring digging into his thigh. 'Then you believe it wasn't me?'

She adjusted one hairpin at the back of her head. 'Perhaps I was a bit irrational to accuse you so quickly.'

He suspected this was as close to an apology as she would come.

'If Edgemont found out where I live, it wouldn't be hard for him to hire a man to break into my house,' she continued. 'After all, he cavorts with as many shapers and questionable men as you.'

He didn't like the comparison, but he couldn't deny its truth. He knew something of Edgemont's acquaintances. They were practically the same ones as Rafe's and just as crooked. 'And if he has it?'

'I'll get it back from him,' she announced, her determination charming, if not naive.

'How?' Rafe crossed his arms over his chest. 'By scattering his supper on the floor?'

Her even breathing paused, the fury threatening to rise up again before she dragged in first one deep breath, then another. Her breasts swelled over the edge of her bodice with the effort, drawing his eyes down before he caught his mistake.

Her eyes widened, then narrowed in wicked delight.

Damn. He hadn't caught himself fast enough.

'I have my ways.' She tilted her head, parted her sweet lips and considered him through feathery dark lashes. He didn't know whether to congratulate her or kiss her for mastering the look they'd worked so hard to perfect. It was innocence and experience melted together and tempting enough to raise even an old man's staff.

'I don't doubt you do.' He commanded his staff to lie still. Now was no time to be fuddled by feminine charm. 'But mine are less obvious.'

'I don't need your help.' Her tongue slid over the fullness of her bottom lip, sweeping through him like her crisp verbena perfume swept over his senses.

'Oh, I think you do.' He held steady as he leaned in, matching her enticing look with one of his own, refusing to let the student best the master, no matter how tight his dark breeches grew. 'Why else would you invent such a dramatic reason to call on me?'

'You flatter yourself.' Her fingers swept her chest, the little half-moons of her fingernails matching the high curve of her breasts.

'And you can't recover the register without me.' He shifted closer, the wood beneath him creaking and almost covering the slight hitch in her breathing. He laid one hand on top of her knee, the curve of it filling his palm. 'You need me.'

She laid her hand over his, her fingers light and teasing against his skin. 'Need is a very strong word.'

'Phrase it however you prefer, but without my help, you'll never see the register again.' He slid out from beneath her grasp and pushed the small curl dangling near her cheek behind one ear.

'And when you discover it, you'll take it and cheat me out of my share.' Her lips moved before him, red and beautiful like berries against delicate snow.

'You know I'd never behave in such an unchivalrous manner.' He stroked the soft curve of her shoulder, following it down to her neck. As he caught the faint flicker of her pulse in the tempting hollow, his hand stiffened along with his loins, but he held steady. The game was not won yet. 'To show you just how chivalrous I am, I'll let you keep Daltmouth and Edgemont. Only give me a few hundred pounds to pay my creditors and the page with my father's name on it.'

'Pages,' she whispered.

His hand froze above the small hairs at the nape of her neck. 'What did you say?'

'Pages. His name is in there more than once, in fact a number of times over a few years.' The desire in her eyes faded into sympathy. It reminded him of the look in his mother's eyes the morning after his father's death, when she'd told him exactly how poor his new estate and title really were.

He jumped to his feet, treading back and forth in front of the sofa, his father's failings and betrayal mocking him. 'He was collecting money for all those years while leaving me and my mother in poverty at Wealthstone? The selfish bastard.'

'I'm sorry, Rafe.'

'Are you?' He turned on her, the pity in her azure eyes making him sick. 'Or does it delight you to lower me more than my father already has?'

Indignation wiped away her pity. 'You aren't the only one threatened by the register.'

'Why? Did your father manage to rise from the tables long enough to learn something of value to sell to the French?'

'Of course not. He didn't know anything except how to drink and lose at cards.'

'Then how can you be hurt? Please, soften my heart with your tender story. I'm eager to hear it,' he jeered, sensing her weakness and aiming for a cutting blow, wanting her to share the pain of his predicament.

'Not me. Andrew.' Her courage wavered with her voice as she laced her fingers tightly together in her lap. 'I need the money from Lord Daltmouth to pay his school fees. If I can't, Fanny will send him to her brother's plantation in the West Indies.'

Rafe crossed his arms, failing to see the urgency of her plight. 'Maybe he should go to the West Indies. He might learn how to properly run an estate. It's more than your stepmother is likely to teach him.'

'It'll kill him.' She jumped to her feet. 'Many grown men die from fever in their first three months there. What chance will a seven-year-old boy have?'

Rafe lowered his arms. He hadn't expected this. 'Why would Fanny risk her own child?'

'Because she doesn't want him any more than my father wanted me.' Her eyes glimmered with threatening tears.

Rafe wished he could hold her and chase away the pain pulling down her shoulders, but he couldn't, not yet. 'Does the twit understand Andrew is your father's precious heir, and if he dies, the estate will go to another?'

'She doesn't care. She'd rather have her widow's portion and a house in London where she can catch another fool than a crumbling estate tethering her to Sussex.' She twisted the diamond ring on her finger. 'If I don't secure the money for Andrew's school by the start of the next term, she'll send him away.'

Rafe settled against the edge of the table, studying her, the truth he'd suspected since last night slowly revealing itself. 'The Comte must have left you the means to pay the few pounds for Andrew's education.'

She blinked once, slow and deliberate. Nothing else about her changed, not her breathing or the stiff set of her shoulders. He silently applauded her composure and knew every word she was about to speak would be false.

'The war has delayed the payment of my funds.'

'Then why not sell your diamonds to raise the money?'

She righted the ring on her finger and, in the pause, he felt her concocting a lie.

He didn't have the patience for deception. 'I want the truth. All of it.'

She shifted on her feet, as uncomfortable as a gentleman caught out with an ace up his sleeve. He expected her to lash out, to snatch up another knife and threaten him but she didn't move.

Outside, the bell of St Martin-in-the-Fields rang once, twice, then a third time.

'I'm poor.' She exhaled at last and he knew no

amount of breathing would hold back the truth now. 'The Comte had debts, hundreds of them from the years he spent abroad after fleeing the Terror. What little money he had when he returned to France he spent to buy back his château. Like us, he haunted the tables in the hope of regaining his wealth, but he never did.'

'And the diamonds?' he pressed, already suspecting the answer.

'They're fake.' She tugged the ring from her finger and flung it to the floor. 'If they weren't, I'd have sold them ages ago, but they're worthless.'

He picked it up, the thin metal still warm from her skin. She was as trapped by her circumstances as he was. The knowledge faded some of the anger he'd nurtured since Paris, but it didn't extinguish it completely. 'Why you? Why not some wealthy merchant's daughter looking for a title?'

'He thought I was rich. I guess our charade fooled someone.' She clutched her arms across her chest and stared down at the floor. 'And it wasn't just money the disgusting old man wanted.'

'Did he—?' He had to know. For some reason he felt responsible.

'No, thankfully, but he tried and learned the mistake of taking a young wife. I could move faster than he could.'

He reached out and stroked her cheek with the back of his fingers, the pain in her eyes tearing at him. 'I'm sorry things didn't turn out as you wanted.'

She knocked his hand away. 'Are you? Or do you feel yourself revenged now?'

'No. I wouldn't wish what you've been through on anyone.'

The tears she'd struggled to suppress slid from her eyes, streaking down one cheek and then the other. 'I can't lose him, Rafe. He's the only person who loves me. The only person I've ever loved.'

He tossed the ring on the table, then cupped her face in his hands, brushing away the tears with his thumbs. As much as the words stung, he understood. He'd gone to great lengths to protect his mother and would go to many more if it meant keeping her safe. 'Don't worry. We'll find a way to get the money.'

'In another card game?' She shook her head free and stepped back, wiping her eyes with the back of her hand. 'A win might pay this year's tuition, but what about next year and all the years after until he's old enough to assume control of Hatton Place?'

'Don't think of the future, focus on now.'

'I can't. I don't want to live by the cards any more, or trust Andrew's fate to luck. I want to have enough so I never have to worry about losing him. It's the whole reason I tried to blackmail the Earl. I didn't want to, but I didn't have a choice.'

The exhaustion dragging at her words echoed deep inside him. This wasn't how he wanted to live either and the reason he'd let her go with the Comte instead of chasing after her. He couldn't give her the safety she craved for herself and her half-brother. All he could offer was another game, another chance to win, or lose. It wasn't a way to live, but it was the only way he knew.

He strode to the sideboard and poured himself a cup of wine, then splashed some in the goblet for her. He walked back to her, holding out the peace offering. 'From what I see, there's just one solution. We must find the register. Together.'

She eyed him more than the drink, suspicion blanketing her vulnerability.

He waited, arm stiff as he held out the goblet. He wouldn't ask again, or beg or remind her of their predicaments. No, she must weigh the options and come to the partnership on her own, even if it left him waiting until the wine turned to vinegar.

Her eyes never wavered from his, matching his intensity as though trying to call the bluff. He wasn't bluffing this time. The game was too serious.

With a subtle frown she reached out and took the goblet.

He raised his cup in salute to her and with relief drank. He knew he held the stronger hand, but, like any game, one could never be sure until all the players knocked.

Over the rim of his cup, he watched her eyes close with relief as she drank. Then she lowered the goblet, the Comtesse gone, the trusting girl from Lord Perry's in front of him once again. 'How will we find it? We don't even know who has it.'

'Our fat solicitor friend might know.'

'I doubt it. He didn't even know what the register was.'

'He knew exactly what it was. I'd bet Wealthstone on it.'

'Then why did he sell it to me? Why didn't he take it and use it to his advantage?'

'To avoid having his cheap coat ruined by a set of carriage wheels.'

Her goblet paused midway to her mouth. 'You think Mrs Ross was murdered?'

'She leaves her house for the first time in over twenty years and is run down by a carriage. Too much of a coincidence, don't you think?'

'But who would have known where to find her?'

'Once she began writing to people and revealing herself, it was only a matter of time before someone with a great deal to protect discovered her whereabouts.'

She stared into the goblet, the furrow between her brows deepening.

Rafe took her cup and returned it and his to the table. 'Now, it's late and we have a lot to do tomorrow. My bedroom is through there. You'll find a clean nightshirt in the trunk.'

She gaped back and forth between where he pointed and him. 'If you expect me to indulge you, you're very mistaken. I'm hardly in need of any more of your tutoring.'

He moved forward, towering over her despite her height. 'What I expect is whoever stole the register may have an interest in silencing permanently those who know about it. So unless you wish to have your pretty throat slit while you sleep, you'd better stay here.'

She touched her throat, then straightened her necklace. 'Of course. Goodnight, Rafe.'

Walking with all the grace of a Comtesse, she swept into his room, closing the scratched door behind her.

He stared at the distressed wood, following the arch of a small dent near the bottom, probably the boot heel of some ex-tenant who'd expected an open door from his mistress. At one time he could have followed her into the bedroom and received as much as he gave. Not tonight.

He rubbed his thumb over his forefinger, searching for evidence of her tears, but the skin was dry. He knew the depth of her love for Andrew, and the lengths she was willing to go to protect him. Sending him money had always been her first thought whenever they'd split their winnings and she'd insisted on visiting him at school before they'd left for Paris. He tapped the table, sending small waves vibrating through the puddle of wine in the bottom of her goblet. He stared at the deep red, seeing her lips pressed tight in worry, the blue of her eyes deepening with the sting of tears. Dipping his fingers into the goblet, he turned them over to balance one small drop of wine on the tip. The candlelight caught in the drop as it had in the fake diamonds glittering around her neck. He looked at the ring lying on the table. He didn't doubt the sincerity of her worry. He hadn't doubted it in Paris either, failing to spot the con until it was too late. Judging by what she'd told him tonight, in the end, she'd been just as duped as he was.

He shook the drop from his hand, snatched up her goblet and finished off the wine.

'It's a good thing I'm not a man for revenge.'

Cornelia stood beside the bed, watching the flame of the tallow candle fatten, then lengthen on the wick. Across the tidy sheets, the light danced in the lines of the white wainscoting, catching the small specks of old gilding the painters had missed. The shadows seemed a poor substitute for company, but the solitary darkness was a welcome relief from Rafe's company.

Reaching up, she unhooked the heavy necklace, drawing it from around her neck to droop across her palm. She'd embarrassed herself tonight, crying like some scared girl and revealing the weakness of her hand.

She tossed the necklace on the bedside table, the draught making the light wink in the facets. Everything she'd wanted to prove to him, the superiority of her new title, the security of money and good fortune, had died with the Comte.

It never existed to begin with. She sagged down onto the side of the bed.

She'd been so desperate and terrified when the Comte had arrived at her door, too ready to believe his feigned affection and concern, just as she'd once believed Rafe's. He'd lied to her about his money and the safety a marriage to him could offer. If he hadn't died so suddenly, she wondered what other falsehoods time might have revealed.

The sound of Rafe's boots hitting the floorboards as he paced made her look to the door and the faint light sliding in underneath it.

The Comte had told her he'd overheard Rafe laughing with the men at his card table about leaving for London on the next ship, without Cornelia. Watching Rafe's shadow move across the gap under the door, she wondered if the Comte had lied about that, too.

No. She banged her fists against her thighs, making the bracelet wobble on her wrist. The note the old woman had delivered after Rafe left for the card room was in Rafe's hand, his words ending their partnership, expressing his laughable regret and the pathetic hope she might find a way back to

England without him. The Comte had only taken advantage of a bad situation, turning it to his advantage to gain a young, and what he thought wealthy, wife who could warm his bed.

Undoing the clasp of her bracelet, she pulled it off to reveal the neat circle of bruises left by Edgemont. Rubbing the dark marks, she felt the pressure of Rafe's thumbs on her cheeks and the confusion his gentle caresses raised in her heart. He could have been cruel in the face of her tears, gloated over his victory or sneered at her like Lord Edgemont, but he hadn't. Instead, he'd demonstrated the same compassion as he had in Lord Perry's garden, convincing her to hope for the best even when everything seemed lost.

She laid the bracelet next to the necklace, baffled by Rafe's concern. For a man who'd so callously left her in France, he'd been kind tonight, and last night he'd been so quick to come to her aid.

It's only because he wants the register.

She rose and struggled with the buttons of her dress, loosening enough of the top ones to slide the silk over her head. Laying it carefully over the back of a threadbare chair, she reached behind her to undo the laces of her stays. When the tightness eased, she slid it down over her hips. Out of habit, she checked the small pocket sewn into the front, calmed to find the last of her money still tucked safely inside. There wasn't much left and it would be a stretch to make it last until they found the register and Lord Daltmouth paid her fee. Assuming he did pay. Come Friday, he might demand to see proof of her threat. Without the register, she had nothing.

She clutched the stays in panic. If she couldn't make the Earl pay, then what little money she possessed would have to be risked at the tables.

Hopefully she'd win.

She chucked the stays in the chair with the dress and snorted at the ridiculous thought. The same foolishness has almost sunk her father and countless others here and in France. She wanted to leave this life, not fall deeper into its debt. Deeper into Rafe's.

Pulling off her few remaining layers, she stood naked in the chill of the room and glanced to make sure there was no view from the keyhole. Only light peeked in through the small opening. She rounded the bed to the sagging trunk at the foot, opening the lid to find a stack of neatly folded shirts inside.

She lifted one from the top of the pile, took it by

the shoulders and shook it out. Despite the goose bumps rising along her skin, she hesitated, almost afraid to slip the garment over her naked body. It frightened her to be this close to Rafe again, to need and trust him and place her future, and this time Andrew's, in his hands. There were no assurances he'd see this through, or not abandon her again once he had the register, leaving her and Andrew to fend for themselves just as he had in France.

Another chill gripped her and she pulled the shirt over her head. The coarse material caressed her taut breasts and flat stomach before dropping down to swish along the tops of her thighs. She shivered, the memory of the homespun against her bare skin, Rafe's arms around her after a night in the gambling halls, the two of them tumbling into bed to explore each other's bodies stealing over her. If they'd won, he'd sleep soundly beside her. If they'd lost, she'd lie in bed pretending to sleep, her body warm and languid as he rose from the bed to pace.

She slipped beneath the thin coverlet, unable to escape the tawny scent of Rafe. It permeated the shirt and sheets and not even the black smoke from the tallow candle could mask it. Snuggling down beneath the covers, the thin mattress hard against her back, she caught the shadow of Rafe beneath the door. It moved back and forth, matched by the muffled fall of his feet.

She closed her eyes, listening to the steady rhythm of his footsteps. Despite the door and everything else separating them, she could still see him, his dark hair falling over his forehead as he strode across the room, arms crossed, shoulders hunched, head down in search of another strategy to turn their luck around. The steady thud of his footsteps soothed her and, despite all attempts to harden herself against him, his strength gave her hope. He would find a way around their current dilemma. He always did.

Chapter Five

'You shouldn't riffle through his things,' Cornelia chided.

Rafe looked up from where he bent over the solicitor's desk, a folio open beneath him as he perused the papers inside. Cornelia sat in the small chair on the opposite side, dressed in the simple white day dress they'd sent Mrs Linton's maid to fetch from Cornelia's lodgings before leaving for Mr Nettles's office. The cotton flowed over the curve of her knees to sweep the tops of her calf-skin boots. A light, short-sleeved spencer sat snug against her round breasts, the plum-coloured material nipping in just beneath their fullness and teasing him as much as if the flesh were uncovered.

'If he doesn't want people poking through his business, then he shouldn't keep them waiting in his office.' He winked at her. 'Besides, it's a very dull matter.'

She rewarded him with the subtle rise of one side of her red lips, her eyes sparkling with delight instead of last night's fury. Whatever had turned her against him in Paris, it hadn't won out completely. Her desire for him was still there, lingering just beneath the surface like the winning queen sitting in the deck, just under the deuce.

His finger traced the hard edge of the folio as heat rushed through him, bringing back the dreams which had kept him awake last night. There were times, lying on the lumpy sofa in the sitting room, when he'd thought he'd heard the subtle flow of her breathing. It teased him in the darkness, sweeping over him like the faint flowery notes of her perfume, sliding through his body until he couldn't turn over for fear of impaling himself in the threadbare cushions. Late at night, as his aching member pulled him from yet another vivid dream of her naked, her hair tumbling over her shoulders, the dark ends curling just above the pointed tips of her breasts, he'd risen and thrown open the windows. The cool air skimming his damp skin had done nothing to ease the hardness gripping him. He had enjoyed only a few hours of fitful sleep when the morning noise of the streets rudely awaked him.

Through the closed door, Mr Nettles's thick voice sounded as he called out to one of his clerks.

Rafe straightened and flipped the folio closed, disturbing a neat stack of papers beside it. He rounded the desk to stand next to a tall bookcase close to Cornelia's chair. He propped one elbow on the clean top, amazed at the clear reflection of his arm in the highly polished wood. For a man who took no care with his dress or person, Mr Nettles's narrow office was a shining testament to cleanliness and order.

The door opened wide, stopped by a black iron dog before it hit the arm of Cornelia's chair.

'Good morning, Comtesse.' Mr Nettles sucked in his belly and puffed out his chest, drawing attention to the threads escaping from his buttonholes. He reached for Cornelia's extended hand. At least the solicitor had the decency to keep his eyes on hers as he bowed, not stroke her entire body with them. 'I'm so sorry to keep you waiting.'

'Thank you very much for agreeing to see us on such short notice. You remember Lord Densmore?'

Mr Nettles followed the sweep of her hand, his smile dropping at the sight of Rafe.

'Good morning, Mr Nettles.' Rafe's cheerful salutation failed to unpurse the man's thick lips.

'Lord Densmore,' he mumbled as he squeezed himself behind the desk. He paused, throwing Rafe a suspicious glare as he neatened the stack Rafe had disturbed. Satisfied his papers were in order, he lowered himself into the creaking chair and looked to Cornelia, his gracious smile returning. 'How may I assist you?'

'We need some information about your late client, Mrs Ross,' Rafe stated.

'Really? Because when we last saw one another, I was dismissed as of no more use to you.' He pinned Rafe with the innocent look of a hound dog, but Rafe heard the low growl.

It didn't bode well for extracting information from the man.

'Surely Lord Densmore was mistaken,' Cornelia interjected with the charm of a songbird while sliding Rafe a warning look.

'I was very mistaken.' Rafe offered an apologetic if not shallow bow, not enjoying this little taste of humility. However, if it meant getting the register back, he'd eat his fill. 'It seems you may be able to help us after all. We're in need of information about who else Mrs Ross might have contacted about the little book the Comtesse purchased.'

'You mean the register with the names of all the traitors in it.' Smug condescension replaced the innocent canine look. 'Yes, Lord Densmore, I know what the book is and why you wanted it.'

'Then why were you so quick to part with it?' Rafe stepped up to the desk, all pretence to apologetic grovelling gone.

'Because the thing is a curse to anyone who owns it,' Mr Nettles blurted out, eyes round with fear. 'What happened to Mrs Ross wasn't an accident. She was killed, run down in the street because someone found out she was still alive and ready to exploit the register. I can't tell you how glad I was to see it leave. I'm only sorry it might have put the Comtesse in danger.'

'Not sorry enough to stop you from selling it to her,' Rafe countered.

'What choice did I have?' He mopped his shining forehead with the worn sleeve of his coat. 'I have family to protect, too.'

'If you wish to protect your loved ones, then help us now.'

Mr Nettles's head practically bent back as he looked up at Rafe. 'Why should I risk my hide for someone who, despite not having a penny to his name, still looks down on me?'

Rafe was about to tell the man where he could go when Cornelia sat forward in her chair, her soft voice luring them both down from their indignant perches.

'Mr Nettles isn't to blame for putting me in danger. After all, he didn't foist the book on me. I sought him out and asked for it, didn't I?' She smiled up at Rafe, the demand for him to step aside clear in the faint, tense lines around her eyes.

'Yes, of course,' Rafe mumbled.

She smiled at the solicitor with so much honey, it made Rafe's teeth ache. 'Didn't I, Mr Nettles?'

The solicitor's face eased along with his conscience. 'Yes, you did.'

Rafe moved back to the bookcase, relinquishing this game to her. Today, she was the better player and he silently applauded her for keeping her head after he'd foolishly lost his.

'You were such a great help to me the other morning. I do hope you can assist me once again.' She moved to the edge of the chair and laid one curving arm on the front of the desk, careful not to disturb the pens arranged in a straight line along the top of the blotter. 'All I need is a list of who else Mrs Ross might have contacted about the register. If I have their names, then I can engage them in a discussion about the book's fate and it would give them no reason to pursue you.'

The man poked at the edge of the line of pens, disturbing, then straightening them. The struggle between pleasing Cornelia and protecting himself played out in the frown dragging down his jowls. Cornelia tilted her face to him in silent encouragement, reaching out her long fingers to straighten the two ink bottles in front of her. As though mesmerised by her charm, Mr Nettles's frown eased and he produced a smitten grin.

Rafe watched, impressed by the deft way she played the solicitor. It was a subtle reminder to not let her play him with such skill.

At last, Mr Nettles sat forward, ready to share. 'When I first received your note about the book, I had no idea what you were referring to. Mrs Ross's house was such a mess, papers and things everywhere. I asked the butler about the matter. Strange man, been with her for years. Told me a great deal about her past. He wasn't fond of the book either and was eager to see it go, especially with his mistress laid out in the sitting room. After you both left that morning, I asked him if anyone else might come for it. He told me Mrs Ross sent letters only to Lord Densmore and Lord Edgemont.'

'Why just them?' Cornelia asked.

'After nearly dying over twenty years ago in the fire and hiding herself away for so long, she knew it was dangerous to reveal herself, but she was desperate for money. She seemed to think, since both gentlemen skirt the bounds of respectable society, they might be more trustworthy.' Mr Nettles glared at Rafe. 'Some idea about honour among thieves.'

'And she sent no more letters?' Cornelia rushed on before Rafe could tell the man where to shove his honour.

'I found drafts of other letters to more prestigious families among her personal papers, but the butler said they were never sent.' He rubbed his chins. 'She should have been more cautious in her dealings, as should you, Comtesse.'

'I assure you, I will be very cautious.' Cornelia rose. 'Thank you, Mr Nettles, you've been most helpful.'

Outside, Cornelia's simpering smile dropped like the sad geraniums in the window basket of the shop next door. The summer sun hung high above the street, radiating off the pavement, the buildings and even the pastel-coloured dresses of the women pushing past them. As much as Cornelia detested the dark, she'd rather have the dim of a haberdasher's shop than this July glare. She'd even settle for the quiet of Hatton Place where the sunlight draped the creamy stone and thick grasshoppers jumped between tall blades of grass. Cornelia sidestepped a woman carrying a small dog, regretting the vow she'd made to never return home. It meant relinquishing the still of the country though even there she'd never truly known peace. What little she remembered had faded with her mother's death, dying completely when Fanny arrived.

The nasty woman.

Cornelia toyed with the idea of visiting, if only for the chance to watch Fanny scowl in envy as she curtsied to the Comtesse de Vane. It would be a little revenge against the shallow woman whose willingness to put her interests above those of her child was partly to blame for Cornelia's current predicament.

'Well played, my dear,' Rafe congratulated, his voice rubbing up against her irritation. 'You chose quite a charming way to obtain the information we needed.'

'With you coming at Mr Nettles like a bear in a pit, how else did you expect to get information from him?' She rubbed one tired cheek, annoyed at having to charm yet another man. However, it seemed the only way to ever get anything of use out of them.

'I'll admit, it wasn't one of my finest moments, and, as much as I'd love to discuss my manners, there's still the matter of the missing register and who stole it.'

She followed the steady flow of his body through the crush of people streaming past the shops. His stride was short and heavy and she sensed, if they weren't in the crowd, he'd cross his arms and bow his head to chew over everything they'd just learned. Instead he stared ahead, his seriousness increasing the unease seeping steadily through her since Mr Nettles's warning about the book.

She eyed the tangle of carriages and carts in the street. The drivers sat hunched in their seats, tugging at the reins. None noticed her as they went about their work, yet their disregard didn't stop her from wondering if, at any moment, one vehicle might break from the pack and run them down. 'It seems Mr Nettles shares your opinion on Mrs Ross's demise.'

'Good, it'll keep him from any further involvement with the register.'

'And the butler?'

'He's as afraid of it as Mr Nettles. If he wasn't, then he'd be the one blackmailing Lord Daltmouth, not you.'

She grabbed his arm, bringing him to a stop on the pavement. 'Then whoever killed her is still out there.'

'And they could be our thief.'

A whip cracked, followed by the loud shout of a driver. Cornelia flinched as a carriage rushed past in the street, oblivious to them. Rafe took her by the arm, the width of his grasp nearly covering the entire length of her upper arm, the pressure of his fingers both soothing and distracting. She moved a touch closer to him, coming within the shadow of his tall body as they watched the hurried carriage rattle down the road.

'Or, it was just an accident.' Rafe's lips tilted into a flippant smile as annoying as it was reassuring. At least he wasn't going to jump at shadows.

He drew her back into a walk, his firm grip keeping her close to him as he sidestepped a cart of books outside a shop.

'If it wasn't an accident, do you think Edgemont could have arranged it?' She touched her right hand, her wrist still sore from the encounter with the Baron.

'No, it's too subtle for a man like him and I doubt he possessed the time or means to manage it from Paris.' A basket of bright flowers hanging over the entrance to a tavern made Rafe duck. 'Either way, a runaway carriage doesn't scare me as much as the register lingering out there with the ability to ruin me.'

Her heart dropped and whatever comfort she'd taken in his touch faded as he guided her around a barrel outside a wine shop. Despite the concern he'd shown for her last night, their present arrangement had nothing to do with her, but his own selfish ends. Though she couldn't be too put out since her desire to find the register had nothing to do with protecting his family, but safeguarding her own. It seemed they were both selfish in this pursuit. 'Then what do we do now?'

'I think I have a way to discover if Edgemont is our thief. I happen to know his butler steps out in the afternoons for a quick drink at a tavern near his town house. Who knows what he might reveal after a tankard or two.'

'Why would he tell you anything?'

'Because he likes me.' He puffed out his chest in mock pride. 'He has since I was a boy and I used to visit the Edgemont town house with my father so he and the old Baron could discuss bills. Our fathers hoped we might become friends, especially since our estates are so close.'

'I see it was a futile endeavor,' Cornelia teased, his lighter mood easing some of her apprehension.

'The ugly boy who used to tell me all the nasty rumours about my father wasn't exactly a welcome playfellow. He didn't endear himself to his servants either.'

'And where will I be while you carouse with Edgemont's butler?'

'Back in my rooms. Mrs Linton will make sure you're safe, if only to keep her best lodger happy.'

'Her best lodger?'

He stuck his chin out over his cravat. 'The widow is awed by my title.'

'Then she's the only one in London.'

'The only one who matters since I have no desire to see my things tossed into the street,' he agreed with a sly wink.

Jealousy shot through her as she imagined what Rafe and Mrs Linton might have got up to in his rented rooms. She knew it shouldn't matter, nor did she want it to, but still it pricked at her like a forgotten pin in a dress.

'And what have you done for the widow to make her so enamoured of you?' The question was only half-teasing.

'Nothing.' He slowed them into a pace more suited to ambling through Hyde Park than weaving through the crowded streets. His fingers loosened on her arm, but he didn't let go. 'She thinks I lend an air of respectability to her lodging house.'

'If only she knew the truth about you.' Though even she couldn't discern it. Until last night he'd been the gambler she detested, now he was her partner again, like before.

A group of women surged towards them and they parted to let them pass. As the last one's walking dress fluttered by, they came back together, but Cornelia didn't press into him and he made no move to retake her arm.

No, this was nothing like before. They'd never been this distant or awkward with each other, not even during their first days in London when they'd known almost nothing about one another.

Loss weighed her down as much as the heat. There'd been a moment in Mr Nettle's office when the silent signals, the ebb and flow of the game as they each took a turn playing it, had revived something of their happy partnership in France. The moments were startling in their intensity and how much they made her crave those lost days. She didn't want to be this close to Rafe, to feel for him even a small measure of the respect and awe she'd once shown him as an ignorant country girl dazzled by the kind, worldly Baron.

They made the turn on to Mrs Linton's street. Their pace slackened as they approached the simple stone building squeezed in among the others at the end. She looked forward to reaching the rooms and being left alone to rest and think while Rafe discovered what he could from Edgemont's butler. Assuming he decided to return.

She subtly studied him from the corner of her eyes. His focus remained straight ahead, his features fixed to reveal nothing. Whatever he was planning, she wouldn't learn about it until he chose to reveal it.

With a sigh, she stared at the town house, burying her own emotions behind her gambler's mask. The days of easy faith in him were gone. All she could do now was hope he didn't make her regret trusting him again.

* * *

Cornelia stepped out of Rafe's bedroom, her bare feet relishing the cool of the wood as she rubbed her stiff back through her robe and chemise. She blinked against the late afternoon sun filling the sitting room, before the shadow in front of the window brought her to a halt.

'Did you sleep well, Comtesse?' Rafe's voice slid through the thick summer air.

'Rafe, I didn't hear you return.' She jerked closed the robe to cover her damp chemise. The cotton clung to the perspiration sliding between her breasts, the stickiness of it having pulled her from her rest.

'I've been back for some time, but I didn't want to wake you.' He stood at the window, one arm raised to lean against the jamb, the other in a fist on his hip. The sun fell over the dark waves of his hair, turning the mahogany colour almost black. She felt his hot stare as much as she saw it in his shadowed eyes and her toes pressed down hard on the planks as she anchored herself against the pull of him. His coat was off, laid over the back of the sofa, and the sleeves of his shirt hung loose about his long arms.

'And?' she choked out. The languid curve of

Rafe's waist highlighted through the homespun by the light behind him proved distracting and tempting.

'Eat and I'll tell you.' He waved one large hand at the meagre supper of cheese and bread on the table before sliding an appreciative look along the curve of her body. 'I remember how famished you used to be after a good rest.'

'Only when I was up all night.' Her cheeks stung with the unintended slip.

'I must admit, I was up most of last night as well.' With a suggestive grin, he snatched a piece of bread from the plate and tore off a chuck with his perfectly straight teeth.

She pinned him with a disapproving look as though chastising Antoinette in the dressing room, not facing the one man alive who knew what she looked like naked.

Striding to the table, she was just about to reach for the chair when he stepped up and pulled it out for her. He towered over her, the sultry heat in his eyes making her robe and chemise stifling. Sweat matted down the hair on his exposed chest and the firm skin beneath teased her as much as the small bead of moisture running down her back. She could drop the robe to her feet, let him see the hint of her breasts beneath the damp fabric, tantalise and tempt him as she had during the first sweltering summer day in Paris when they'd nearly crushed the gilded dining table with their lovemaking.

She doubted this rickety table could hold them, but she was almost willing to take the chance. Almost.

'I should dress,' she mumbled, eager for the safety of the dim bedroom behind her and the layers of clothes inside. She feared this pull of him, the way her body answered it and the weakness it implied.

'Eat first,' he urged, more tenderness than temptation in the request.

She clutched the robe tight around her, more to stop herself from flinging it aside and falling into his embrace than to protect her modesty. This was how he'd won her heart before, with little considerations and unfettered compliments.

Lowering herself onto the sagging caning, she inhaled as his fingers brushed the backs of her arms as he slid the chair forward to nestle beneath her buttocks. Lingering behind her, he let out a long breath, the caress of it against her damp neck making her shiver. She pulled the robe tighter around her to hide the tight points of her breasts as she waited for him to walk away.

At last, he circled the table to drop into the seat opposite hers, twisting himself to one side to keep his knees from banging against the underside.

Forcing all of her body to relax, she reached for the food, helping herself to a generous portion of bread and cheese. 'Did the butler remember you fondly enough to tell you his master's secrets?'

'I didn't go to the tavern. I went to Edgemont's town house instead.'

'You did what?' She slapped her hands down on either side of her plate, making the pewter rattle against the wood.

'I paid a call on our old friend.' He broke off a piece of cheese and tossed it in his mouth, unapologetic. 'I've dealt with Edgemont enough to know the most direct approach is the best.'

'And was it?'

'He wasn't home. He left for Darringwood early this morning.'

She took a bite of food, chewing it slowly. 'Rather suspicious of him to depart so suddenly for his estate.'

'Which means he could well be our thief. We have to get to Wealthstone. Darringwood is only five miles from there and we can concoct some way to steal the register back.'

'Housebreaking. I think our situations have sunk to a new low.' Cornelia huffed, not relishing getting so close to Hatton Place or Edgemont.

'Our situations were never high to begin with.' Rafe sighed.

He picked at his plate while she ate, the silence between them punctuated by the clink of pewter or the cries of hawkers outside. Cornelia tried to think of something to say to make them laugh or bolster their spirits, but nothing came to mind. Conversation didn't roll from her tongue like it did from Rafe's and she abandoned the effort as quickly as she'd taken it up. Words came easily to him because most of them were lies, or elaborate screens woven to keep people at bay.

'While I was out, I took the liberty of collecting your things,' he said at last, pointing past her. She turned to see two large trunks and a small portmanteau stacked beside the door. 'Your little French maid was quite helpful.'

'And she let a stranger just come in and take my things?' She'd dismiss the girl the moment she saw her next.

'She practically foisted them on me. And I'm

to tell you she's taken another position with Lady Mailor as French maids are much in demand and she's tired of not receiving her wages.'

Cornelia scowled at the trunks, wondering what the French woman had stolen as payment before she'd packed up her things. It couldn't have been worth much since almost everything of value had been sold the moment they'd arrived in London.

'Now, back to the matter of business.' Rafe pushed his plate away and leaned back in his chair. 'We need enough to buy two places on a coach to Sussex. Mr Smith was kind enough to relieve me of my money. What do you have tucked into the sweet little pocket in your stays?'

He pointed at her chest and the open neck of the robe. Her breasts tightened again and she covered the hard tips by propping her elbows on the table and resting her chin in her hands. 'Not enough to get us both to Wealthstone and back.'

'Unless you're willing to let me go alone.'

She crossed her arms over her chest. 'No.'

'Then we must raise more. Is what you have enough for both of us to open a game of Commerce or *vingt-et-un*?'

Cornelia eyed him warily, seeing at once what he had in mind. 'It is.'

'Good.' He rose and stood behind the chair, his long fingers curling over the wood and sliding through a frayed hole in the caning. 'The Dowager Countess of Daltmouth is having a card party tonight and she made it quite clear at her salon she'd be delighted by my presence.'

'I doubt the Earl will be pleased to see me there.' She lowered her hands to the table, trilling her fingers over the rough wood. 'If he defied my instructions to not tell his mother, I have no desire to be publicly thrown out of the Daltmouths' house.'

'Even if the Dowager Countess knows, neither one of them is likely to make a scene. Remember, they're trying to avoid scandal, not create it. If he's kept silent about the deal, then your presence will emphasise the seriousness of your threat. After all, if you're bold enough to attend his mother's party while blackmailing him, you're bold enough to make good on your promise to ruin him.'

The idea of facing him in his own house after what she'd done made her uneasy. She didn't want to threaten him, but she didn't want to lose Andrew either. 'Not a very pleasant business, is it?'

'No, but don't think of it as an opportunity to threaten a man.' He leaned forward on the chair.

'Think of it as a grand affair where two talented people could take the tables by storm.'

A tingle of anticipation shot through her at the sound of the old phrase and her toes curled with excitement. It was wrong to take delight in out-playing others, but it was they who chose to sit and challenge her, they who decided how much to wager and when or when not to walk away. The only thing she could control was how well she played, how she read her opponents, what cards she discarded or kept. It was no way to live, no talent to revel in, but it was hers and if it brought her one inch closer to protecting Andrew, she'd use it to its full potential.

'What do you say?' he pressed.

As much as she hated this life, the old thrill for the game and the possibilities it carried were too tempting to resist.

'It sounds exactly like our kind of affair.'

Chapter Six

Cornelia opened her fan stick by stick as Rafe escorted her into Lady Daltmouth's card room. Porcelain counters clinked together, punctuated by the soft whir of shuffling cards and the rumble of conversation. Tall footmen moved through the room, offering refreshments to the guests who groaned or cheered with the tide of play. She waved her fan, making her reticule swing on her arm, the bag heavy with the counters she'd received from Lady Daltmouth's man in exchange for her few remaining pounds. The eagerness to play heated Cornelia's skin, pushing aside the disappointment of the past few days.

'You can smell it, can't you?' Rafe inhaled beside her, flexing his fingers, as impatient to hold the cards as her. 'The heady scent of luck.'

'A most glorious perfume.' This thrill hadn't existed at Mrs Drummond's when each bet had felt like a task instead of a challenge. No, this moment radiated with possibility just like their first night together in Madame Boucher's. 'Almost as sweet as a silver coin in your hand.'

'Not quite the sweetest thing I've ever held.' Rafe drew her a touch closer to him and a different heat swept across the tops of her breasts. He leaned close to her ear, his breath tripping across her skin and disturbing the earring dangling from the lobe. 'Tell me what you see.'

Cornelia steadied herself, glad for the focus his question demanded. She took in the players, noting the smiles and chatter of those closest to them. 'The tables near us are for those here to enjoy themselves. The stakes are too low and the laughter too high.'

'And those in the back?' His voice tickled her ear, as troubling as it was tempting.

Height gave her the advantage and she peered over the crowded front tables to scrutinise the faces of those seated at the ones furthest from the door. She recognised many from the card rooms of Paris or her night at Mrs Drummond's. They were the more experienced players who jealously guarded their hands, their expressions stony with calculated uninterest, but she could still read them.

'Lady Thrifton is having a good night, but Mr Edwards is losing a great deal and, judging by his heavy eyelids, dulling the sting of his losses with Lady Daltmouth's port.'

'Lord Hawkstone's estate is mortgaged almost as badly as mine. Nothing to gain by playing him.'

'Avoid the old woman in the mob cap,' Cornelia warned.

'Then who shall we play?'

She studied the remaining guests, her interest alighting on Lady Daltmouth. She was the strongest player at her table, calm when the thin man across from her was red with the effort of hiding his frustration. Lady Daltmouth's serene face shone like the painting of an ancient queen while the silver-haired woman to her left smiled too much, revealing crooked teeth. The Dowager's long fingers picked up a card and discarded another before searching out the pearl earring dangling from her small lobe. Despite the mask she wore for the game, Cornelia caught the whisper of the Dowager's solid hand in the gesture.

Then Lady Daltmouth slid a look at the door, meeting Cornelia's scrutiny.

Cornelia continued to fan herself as she waited for the woman to react to her presence, but Lady Daltmouth only nodded in greeting before returning to her cards. Obviously she knew nothing about Cornelia blackmailing her son.

'Our hostess is enjoying a good night.' Cornelia exhaled in relief.

'My thoughts exactly.' He motioned to the table across from Lady Daltmouth's. 'And the Earl?'

Lord Daltmouth dealt *vingt-et-un,* a respectable stack of winnings piled before him. He looked up, his hand pausing over the deck as his small eyes met Cornelia's. Her fan stopped and she waited for him to rise and make a scene. He didn't. Instead, he pursed his pudgy lips together and returned to dealing, practically flinging the cards at the other players.

Cornelia closed her fan. 'He's filled the table with worse players than himself.'

'And since your presence has rattled the concentration out of him, I think it's time for me to turn lady luck against him.'

He slid his arm out from under Cornelia's fingers, catching them in his hand and raising them to his lips. The heat of him streaked through her, threatening to unleash the more carnal feelings she struggled to suppress. He straightened to his full height, making her breath catch as he stood over her like one of the sturdy pillars holding up the long room. *'Bonne chance,* Comtesse.'

He smiled at her like the devil and she was glad they weren't playing against each other.

'Good luck, Lord Densmore,' she murmured through parted lips, her mouth barely able to form the words.

She gathered up the train of her yellow dress and started in smooth steps towards Lady Daltmouth's table, watching the players as she approached. The turbaned woman sitting across from the Dowager nodded at her cards. The peacock feather sticking out of her headdress bounced in agreement. The thin man sighed as he added his counter to the pile in the centre, discarded a card and chose another. Then it was the Dowager's turn. She laid down her counter and exchanged one card for another, her fingers searching out the earring before something over the head of the thin man caught her attention. Her fingers lowered to stroke the strand of pearls draped around her neck, the hint of desire softening the stern set of her grey eyes.

Cornelia followed the line of her gaze to where it fell on Rafe as he moved down the opposite side of

the room. He stood a head taller than the tallest liveried footman waiting against the wall, his confidence unmistakable as he circled Lord Daltmouth's
table. He took no notice of Lady Daltmouth, too
focused on the Earl to see the Dowager's frank
appraisal.

If it'd been the old lady in the mob cap, Cornelia would have laughed, but Lady Daltmouth was
a different woman. She might have over twenty
years on Rafe, but she was beautiful enough to
suggest danger and with a fortune deep enough
to snare a desperate man. He might pride himself on not stooping to woo rich old widows, but
Cornelia knew how fast convictions could change
under pressure. She'd once vowed never to wed an
old man in exchange for money. Then one night,
in fear for her life and safety, she'd betrayed herself. If Rafe's debts increased, if the register cost
him his title and lands, he might choose the same
loathsome path.

Along the edge of her vision, she caught Lady
Daltmouth scrutinising her. She turned back to the
table and the Dowager's eyes dropped down to her
cards. If Rafe and Cornelia's connection bothered
the Dowager, she was careful not to reveal it. Instead, she called for her opponents to knock, wait-

ing until the others revealed their hands before she showed hers and won the game.

The players offered limp applause as the Dowager Countess collected her winnings. Cornelia clapped with more enthusiasm, refusing to let the Dowager's ogling of Rafe distract her. There was nothing to fear in the Dowager's admiration. After all, a woman of Lady Daltmouth's questionable social standing could hardly afford the scandal of a dalliance with a man like Rafe.

The players chatted as the Dowager Countess gathered up the cards. The thin man accepted a glass of wine from a passing footman, saying something to make the woman with the turban and feather laugh. The silver-haired woman bade the players good luck and left.

Cornelia slid into the still-warm chair, fluffing her skirt about her legs.

'Good evening, Comtesse.' The Dowager shuffled, the steady swish of cards sharpening Cornelia's desire to play. 'I understand you're a talented Commerce player.'

Cornelia waved away the footman offering wine. 'Like any player, I enjoy the occasional streak of luck.'

'Come now, don't be modest.' The Dowager

dealt, laying the cards neatly in front of each player. 'After a number of lacklustre games tonight, I'm eager for some spirited play.'

Cornelia picked up her hand. 'Then I'll do my best not to disappoint you.'

Counters clicked together as players bought new cards and discarded old ones. Over the top of the king of spades, Cornelia watched the Dowager, waiting to see if she touched the earring. Lady Daltmouth made no move for the jewel. Instead, her long fingers swept the strand of pearls falling over her large breasts, her nails clicking over each orb as she looked past the thin man.

'I see Lord Densmore escorted you here tonight,' Lady Daltmouth remarked with more purr than politeness. 'Why didn't he join us?'

'He prefers to play *vingt-et-un*.'

'Pity. He'd have been a most delightful opponent.' She flicked a counter into the centre of the table, licked one finger and slid a single card out from between the others. She laid it on the green baize before selecting another from the top of the deck.

Cornelia pushed a counter into the centre, then discarded the deuce and chose another card. Her toes curled inside one slipper as she slid the queen of spades in next to her king. For the first time in months, she felt in control again, even more so than when she'd held the register.

'You and Lord Densmore have known each other for some time?' Lady Daltmouth asked as the turbaned woman traded cards with the thin man.

'We were thrown together quite a lot in Paris.'

'Yes, you two seemed as thick as thieves when you entered.'

Cornelia took a deep breath and focused on the black-and-white rose in the queen of spade's hand, allowing the Dowager's little dig to slide away. The Dowager was trying to take advantage of Cornelia's interest in Rafe and use it to rattle her. She wouldn't allow it to distract her or try to end the Dowager's interest in him. Let the woman drool over the man like a broke player over grand odds. It created a diversion and increased Cornelia's odds of winning.

The Dowager took her turn, selecting and discarding one card, then arranging it with the others. She neither reached for her earring nor fondled her necklace and Cornelia suspected she was struggling.

Cornelia held on to her counter, waiting for the next round to discard her three of hearts.

'With the cards sitting so temptingly in the centre, just begging to be revealed, how can you resist trying for a better one?' the Dowager asked as the play continued.

'An experienced player knows when to resist temptation and when to embrace it.'

'Quite right, and we're both very experienced players. Shall we increase the stakes?' Her long fingers curled around two counters, her rings clinking against the porcelain. She tossed them in the centre, then discarded and selected another card.

'Why not?' Cornelia picked up two counters and, with the confident flick of her wrist, tossed them in the centre. Laying down the three of hearts, she selected another card. Both feet curled in her slippers as the jack of spades revealed himself to join his king and queen.

'You ladies are certainly making a rich pot,' the thin man laughed.

'Rich for some, perhaps not so much for others,' Lady Daltmouth observed in a haughty tone. 'Knock.'

Lady Daltmouth revealed her cards and the others groaned at the strong hand.

'And your hand, Comtesse,' the Dowager ordered.

'It's the winning one.' Cornelia laid the cards down one by one.

'Congratulations.' The thin man slapped the table in his delight, making the counters jump. The turbaned woman's laughter joined his, carrying over the card room and drawing Rafe's attention.

Cornelia flicked her top teeth with her tongue as she rose, heady triumph filling her as she tilted over the table to draw in the counters. Rafe's deep-brown eyes dropped to her winnings, then rose up her yellow dress to caress her breasts before finally meeting hers. Something sparked in the air between them, as if this were in Paris and they were lovers again. Her hands froze over the counters at the memory of him from across Madame Boucher's, desire smouldering in his proud smile and fuelling the faint hope he might truly make her his.

One of his opponents drew him back to his game, breaking the connection between them.

Slowly she lowered herself into the chair, the old disappointment dimming the lustre of her win. He hadn't made her his, instead he'd left her to another man.

'A well-played game, Comtesse.' The Dowager slid from her chair and stood over Cornelia, her rosewater perfume as sharp as her displeasure.

Cornelia shook off the old memories to beam up at Lady Daltmouth. 'Thank you, I thoroughly enjoyed it.'

'Though as one player to another, I might advise you to snap up Lord Densmore before someone else does. A woman of means would do well to have such a handsome figure on her arm.' Lady Daltmouth strode away, as regal tonight as in the large portrait over the fireplace, her hair powdered and high as was the fashion in her youth.

Cornelia brushed the top of one smooth counter with her thumb, noting the way the blue ink feathered into the white ceramic beneath the glazing. In the older woman's warning lay the very real threat of losing Rafe, though he was no longer hers to lose. He never was.

She watched Rafe play. He sat low in his chair, his posture easy and languid, but she caught the intense focus of his eyes on the other players. He'd looked at her like that once, his hunger for her as strong as his need to win. It was more than lust back then, more than his willingness to tutor her in the ways of the world and the rhythmic dance between a man and a woman. In the flickering candlelight of their rented rooms, she'd caught the first faint spark of love.

She dropped the counter on top of the others, then pressed them into an even stack. Love had never been part of the bargain. Despite Rafe's delicate caresses, it had all been nothing more than a game. It still was, only this time there were too many opponents, too much at stake. She'd fold if she could, but she had to play or risking losing everything.

A shadow moved over her and the red-haired Lord Rollingham appeared at her side.

'May I?' He motioned to the empty chair.

Cornelia took two deep breaths, centring herself as she peered up through her lashes to meet his green eyes, the desire to play returning. It was time to forget Rafe and focus on the game.

Lord Daltmouth slouched in his chair, his round belly protruding beneath his slumped shoulders as Rafe slid yet another pile of counters towards himself.

'I think I've had enough for one night.' The Earl tossed down his cards as he rose. 'If you'll excuse me, Lord Densmore.'

'Another hand, my lord?' the dealer asked as he collected the cards.

'No, I'll sit this next one out.' Rafe scraped the counters off the table and dropped them in his pocket. 'I need to stretch my legs.'

Rafe's lower back smarted as he rose, the pain easing as he walked away. For a woman who liked tall footmen, Lady Daltmouth seemed exceedingly fond of diminutive furniture.

He leaned against one of the plaster pillars holding up the ceiling and watched the play at Cornelia's table, admiring the curve of her legs beneath the pale yellow dress. It was the same dress she'd worn their first night in Paris. He couldn't see her feet, but he guessed by the sure way she held her cards her toes were curled in triumph. The memory of her feet arching as he stroked her hips, his lips pressed against her stomach as he trailed kisses lower and lower to join his fingers, teased him. He rubbed one cheek, almost able to feel her silken thigh against it as she laid it over his shoulder, her lips parted with excitement. She'd been so responsive, her innocence turning to experience beneath his caresses as she gave herself to him, embracing his lessons on pleasure, just as she'd grasped all his hard-learned lessons about human nature and society.

During those long nights together, as he'd rested beside her, the candlelight deepening the subtle pink tips of her breasts, he'd caught the hint of something more in her embrace. If he'd asked her to marry him, to share a life of poverty governed by the cards, she'd have accepted. She'd believed in him back then and all his schemes to ensure their survival.

Something of that trust had returned tonight when he'd asked her for her money and she'd willingly given it. He wondered how much further her trust might extend.

Another player called the knock and everyone revealed their cards. Lord Rollingham was especially gracious about his loss as he leaned in to congratulate her, practically batting his light eyelashes at her.

Why doesn't he just lay his head on her lap and ask her to read him poetry? The man's dramatic fawning disgusted him. It reminded him too much of how the Comte used to behave.

He wondered how long it would be until he came home to find her driving away in Lord Rollingham's dark green town coach.

A footman passed by with a tray of wine and Rafe plucked one glass from the silver and took a sip. The fine vintage lingered on his tongue before he swallowed it, his next sip more deliberate than the first. He wasn't about to gulp it down and fog his brain. That was the sure path to the gutter.

Cornelia laughed at something Lord Rollingham said, the high notes of her voice clear, but not the words. It grated on his nerves, making his shoulders tighten. Watching the two of them together, he wanted to curse Cornelia to the devil for sneaking out on him, but much to his ire, he couldn't. He'd made enough questionable choices in search of security, only to watch it elude him every time like a ship in the fog. Even protecting himself from the threat of the register had proved more illusory than he'd imagined during the week he'd spent at Wealthstone struggling to raise the blunt to buy the pages with his father's name.

Wealthstone. He pushed away from the pillar and continued along the edge of the tables, unsure whether to curse or congratulate his grandfather for giving the tumbledown pile of brick such an illustrious name. He certainly cursed his father for driving it into ruin with all his neglect and debt.

He glanced at the painting of Lady Daltmouth in

her youth hanging over the fireplace. His mother had once dressed in such fine silks, her head held high as she curtsied to the King and Queen. His father had stood beside her, unashamed to show his love for his beautiful Baroness. It'd all changed when his father's rabid love affair with the cards had become too much to hide, his mother's spirit and pride dimming beneath each new humiliation.

The proud Baroness who'd stood before the Queen disappeared completely the night his father was murdered.

He indulged in one last taste of wine, drinking just enough to dispel the dryness of his throat before depositing the half-finished glass on a table. It didn't stay there long before an oak of a footman took it away. Rafe watched the bewigged and liveried young man carry the drink through a far door, marvelling at his efficiency. The Dowager's help, besides being tall, was very well trained.

The subtle swish of silk and the heady aroma of rosewater slid up beside him.

'Are you enjoying yourself tonight, Lord Densmore?' Lady Daltmouth clasped her hands in front of her and tightened her arms against either side of her magnificent breasts, raising the mound up just a touch.

'I am.' He rewarded her effort with a quick glance, more interested in staying in her good graces than slipping into her bed. 'You're an excellent host. You have an eye for every detail, except one.'

'And that would be?' Her arms relaxed, lowering her chest.

'The chairs. Dainty seats flatter a petite woman like yourself, but they don't suit a man of my stature.' He offered her the flirting smile he usually saved for Mrs Linton on the days the rent was due.

'Indeed, they do not.' She stroked his body with her eyes. 'Nor do your present circumstances.'

The comment nearly curdled his smile. 'The same might be said of yours.'

'Yes, we've both been left to deal with the mistakes of others,' she conceded as if they shared some deep connection of which he was not aware. 'I know something of what it is to struggle with the past.'

'Do you?' An almost imperceptible idea brushed the back of his mind. Maybe Edgemont hadn't stolen the book. Maybe it was someone else, someone more resourceful with even more to lose than Rafe.

No, it couldn't be her or she'd have never let us in here tonight.

'More than you realise.' She fingered her pearl earbob, making it swing below her sculpted ear. 'Surely you have no desire to follow your father down such a ruinous path, not when you have so much more potential.'

'Suffering is good. It builds character.'

'And how much character do you need?'

'According to some, quite a lot.'

'No, Lord Densmore, what you need are resources. With the proper financial backing and the right connections, you could become the man your father could have been.' She flicked a glance to his breeches. 'Raise up the Densmore name, so to speak.'

'With the proper backing,' he repeated flatly.

'You have only to ask for it and it will be granted.'

'That's quite a gamble to take on a man you hardly know.'

'I'm not afraid of risk,' she said breathily, as pleased with herself as Rafe was disgusted.

He leaned down and her lips parted as though she were about to suck a cherry from its stem.

'You should be.' The edge in his voice cut the surety from her face, but didn't slice it away completely. 'A woman like you could stand to lose a great deal in the wrong investment.'

She touched the pearls again, her enthusiasm dampened, but not her confidence in the proposal. 'When you're ready to discuss the investment further, send word. You'll find me a most willing listener.'

She slid away from him like a grey cat on a carpet, silent, elegant, yet ready to scratch any mouse unfortunate enough to wander into her path.

If he were a different man, he'd accept her offer and declaw the wicked feline.

Laughter and muffled applause erupted from Cornelia's table and he watched her rise, the swirl of yellow silk caressing her round *derrière* as she bent over to collect her winnings. Lord Rollingham noticed, too, taking in the roundness with an appreciative smirk. As she lowered herself back into her seat, she pinned Rafe with a smile as bright as his mood was dark.

I hate this life.

He strode from the room and out on to the adjoining terrace without returning Cornelia's smile or answering the question in the slight arch of her eyebrow. Let her wonder, he owed her no more explanations than she'd given him in Paris.

Outside, he paced back and forth over the stone, passing in and out of the squares of light made by the windows. Through the smooth panes, he glimpsed the other guests, their ridiculous feathers and lace ruffles making him as sick as Lady Daltmouth's revolting offer. He was no country boy to be bought and stuffed into livery for her amusement, nor was he about to hang on her arm before the bottom rung of society, led around on a tether like some stud stallion.

Though, for a moment, he wondered what other option he possessed.

He stopped in the shadows beyond the last window, peering out into the shapeless shadows of the garden. In the darkness, he saw nothing but a future of shady hells, of Wealthstone sold to some merchant with more money than lineage, his mother forced into even more degrading lodgings, joining him in a life of wandering and squalor.

No, it wouldn't come to that.

He whirled around to march back into the room, ready to fleece more fools, but halted.

Cornelia stood in the light from the French door, the yellow dress rustling over her slippers. The breeze stiffened, flattening the material against her long legs before the direction of it changed, billowing out the fabric to obscure them again.

'What did Lady Daltmouth want?' Cornelia

moved forward, the candlelight from inside playing in the small curls arranged at the back of her head and glinting off the fake diamonds dangling from each ear.

'It seems she's eager to add to her collection of tall attendants,' Rafe grumbled, the offer still chafing like a pair of poorly made boots.

'Only she wants you to do more than polish her silver.'

'It appears so.'

'I can't believe she's so vulgar.' She paced in front of him, the wind catching her dress and making it brush against his legs. 'What did she say when you rejected her?'

'I didn't reject her. She's offered me fair compensation and promises my employment with her will be very pleasurable,' Rafe needled, expecting a thimble of sarcasm from her, not a pitcher full of anger.

'You'd stoop so low, wouldn't you?' She flew at him, stopping short just beneath his chin. 'Let yourself become a kept man, a plaything to the old woman paying your bills.'

He leaned forward, his face inches from hers. The clear whites of her eyes deepened the blue irises and glistened with the candlelight from inside. Her sweet breath swept past his chin as she faced him, her neck arched, her body close enough to pull into the curve of his. He raised one hand to draw her to him, eager to kiss her and prove how likely he was to service some old woman for a few pounds. Then he forced his arm down. He wasn't going to lower himself, not for her or the Dowager. 'I wouldn't be the first to sell myself, now would I? For all I know, you're already plotting to pitch me aside for Lord Rollingham.'

She started, his arrow hitting the mark, but it didn't make him any happier to wound her.

'Why shouldn't I encourage Lord Rollingham?' she countered, recovering quickly. 'What promises have you ever made to me?'

'I promised to help you find the register and protect Andrew, or has Lord Rollingham's money already made you forget those?'

'I haven't forgotten,' she stammered. 'Only I—'

'Don't trust me,' he hissed, unmoved by her discomfort.

The shadow of experience darkened her eyes. 'You think you're strong enough to resist temptation, but you're not. When desperation finally grips you, you'll cave in just like anyone else.'

'Your faith in me is staggering. You'll excuse

me if I don't wish to revel in it any more tonight.' He stepped around her and back into the bright light of the card room. Let her have Rollingham or whatever decrepit old man she decided to fling herself at next. After they recovered the register, she was no longer his concern.

Chapter Seven

Cornelia lit the reed lamp in the middle of the table and the rising flame pushed back the darkness of Rafe's room. He closed and locked the door, his shadow dancing behind him on the panelling, the dark gangling version of him echoing his mood and hers. She cupped her reticule, the heavy bag a comfort, the only one she'd enjoyed since their spat on the Daltmouths' terrace.

Rafe slipped off his coat and draped it over the chair by the door. Without a word or an invitation to join him, he strode to the table and emptied his pockets. Coins bounced and clanked together as he dropped them on the wood before laying the notes next to them. His large hands moved fast to sort them by size and value.

Determined to appear as unaffected by their argument as Rafe, she dumped out the money in her reticule. The coins spread out in a rush. Rafe paused, then began to stack her coins and notes with his, blurring the line between what was hers and what was his. There seemed too much of this intermingling of their lives in the past few days, more than she wanted.

As he worked, she remembered other nights like this, when his laughter was as seductive as the glint of the coins. She'd playfully disturb the focus of his counting with a flash of flesh or a few words whispered over his shoulder, her tongue tracing the line of his neck until the blunt was forgotten for other games.

There was no laughter or sighs tonight, only the whisper of pound notes.

His hands stopped, the money arranged in two depressingly short piles. She could only imagine what they might have won if they hadn't quarrelled. It was some comfort to know it had disturbed him as much as her.

'Not our most lucrative evening.' He raked his fingers through his thick hair. 'But it's enough to get us to Wealthstone and back with a decent amount left over for each of us to spend as we see fit.'

'Our best night was the first one at Madame

Boucher's,' Cornelia recalled wistfully, tracing a white embroidered flower on her yellow dress. 'If only every night could be as lucky as that one.' *And as happy.*

'Yes, the same wish ruined both our fathers' lives.' He separated the money, making three small stacks before picking up one and holding it out to her. 'Here's your share.'

She opened her hand and he dropped the coins one by one, each holding the warmth his expression lacked.

He grabbed his share of the winnings, closing his fist over the lot and crushing the notes. 'Not exactly the astounding amount I'd hope to give Mother for the bills at Wealthstone.'

She frowned at her share, thinking it wouldn't go very far either. The more time she spent at the tables, the more she felt like a dog on a wheel turning a spit, walking and walking, but never getting anywhere.

He slid the money into his waistcoat pocket. 'A carriage leaves for Sussex at six o'clock every morning from the Bell Savage Inn in Ludgate Hill. You stay here, gather together what you need for the journey. I'll make arrangements and then return.'

He reached for the remaining money and she shot out her hand to clutch his. The steady beat of his pulse beneath hers startled her, but not enough to shake her from her purpose.

'You intend to leave me here while you make travel arrangements.' The irony of it almost made her sick. 'What assurances do I have you won't simply take the money and leave?'

He pulled his hand away, the only sign her words had struck home. Otherwise, he wore his usual cocksure smile and she wanted to slap it from his face. 'You have my things. If I don't come back, feel free to sell them and recoup your losses. I should be gone no more than an hour. I trust, unlike Paris, you'll still be here when I return.'

'I'll be here, waiting to see if it's you who returns or another old crone carrying your letter. This time, please do me the courtesy of actually paying the old woman you hire to deliver your parting note.'

He jerked back. 'What parting note?'

At least she'd found a way to rid his face of his cocksure smile.

Her fingers curled around the coins, the edges digging into her skin as she struggled to hold back the months of anger and hate simmering inside her.

She wouldn't rail at him like some fishwife, but face him with all the composure of a Comtesse. 'The one you sent me our last night together in Paris, the one informing me our partnership was over.'

'I never sent you a note,' he scoffed. 'And who are you to accuse me of ending the partnership? I arrived back from the gambling house to see you driving away with the Comte without an explanation or even a small show of gratitude for everything I'd done for you.'

'You expected me to thank you for abandoning me to the French?'

'I abandoned you?' He rounded the table on her. She didn't move, but stared up at him, determined to make him answer for what he'd done. 'While you were sneaking off with the Comte, I was trying to win our passage home.'

'I only went with him because of your letter.'

'I never sent you a letter.'

His growl vibrated in her ears, followed by the cold echo of the Comte's laughter. It spread through her, making her shiver as her anger dropped like a ballast stone into her stomach.

'If you didn't send the letter, then who did?'

He didn't answer, his shoulders settling as the

reality spread over him, too. She wondered if he also heard the Comte's mocking laughter, or felt the stab of bitterness at having been cheated out of something they couldn't win back.

On the table, the flame bobbed and weaved on its wick. She crossed her arms, wishing the flame would grow taller and push back the loss sliding through her. She'd let it burn the entire lodging house to the ground if it would warm the iciness cracking her heart or bring back the security she'd once known with Rafe.

'I fear, *madame,* in Paris we were both duped by your beloved husband.' He slid a coin off the table and rolled it over the over the tops of his knuckles, his expression hard and unreadable.

She watched the coin move, shining, whole, unlike their shattered faith in one another.

'But the letter was in your hand.' Her anger slackened like a sail without wind. Only the sour taste of loss remained, as strong tonight as it had been in Paris. She slid her wrist in the loop of the reticule strings, the weight of the bag on her arm pulling on her like the Comte had when he'd guided her up the church aisle. She sank into the wobbly chair, the Comte's plan so clear now. The timing of his arrival, the surety with which he knew she'd accept him when she'd dismissed him in the card rooms so many times before. 'At least it looked like your hand.'

It was impossible to tell now. She'd burned the letter.

He flipped the coin and caught it. 'You were very quick to believe it was from me.'

'You were the one who always said our arrangement wasn't permanent,' she insisted. 'How was I to know the letter was forged?'

'You couldn't have known.' The defeat in his voice was as heavy as when he'd told her they didn't have the money to escape France. 'Yet after all I'd done for you, you crawled into another man's carriage and drove straight to the church the first moment you doubted me.'

'How dare you blame me.' She slammed her fist on the table, making a pile of money slide. 'If I'd meant so much to you, you would have come after me, tried to stop me instead of leaving me to the Comte.'

'Given the abruptness of your departure, I thought it was what you wanted.'

His calm chafed. She wanted his temper to burn as hot as hers, but she knew it wouldn't. Theatrics

weren't his way. 'Apparently, we weren't as knowl-
edgeable about one another as we once thought.'

'So it would seem.'

The bells from St. Martin-in-the-Fields rang
twice.

Rafe laid the coin on top of an undisturbed pile.
'I have to see to our fare or we'll lose tomorrow.'

Tomorrow is already lost. 'Yes, of course.'

'You may come with me if you like.'

It was an offering, a feeble attempt to bridge
the awkward gap between them, but she didn't
know how to cross the divide. She'd been so angry
and hurt by him for so long and now he wasn't to
blame. 'No, I trust you.'

'That remains to be seen.'

'The same might be said of you.'

'Yes, you're right.' He swept the stack of coins
from the table and dropped them in his pocket.
'Try to get some rest while I'm gone.'

She nodded, fearing there weren't enough candles in the room to stop the darkness from keeping her awake while he was away.

He headed for the door, lifting his coat from the
back of the chair and pulling it on. 'And, Cornelia,
if anyone brings you a note written in my hand—
don't believe them.'

The grim set of his lips eased a touch, the faint traces of the cavalier Baron she'd once adored returning.

'What if it says you're in trouble, from Mr Smith or who knows what?'

'Then only believe it if it includes an invitation to a grand affair where two talented people could take the tables by storm.' He closed the door, his footsteps fading down the hall behind it.

She sat for a long time staring at the uneven door and its rusty hinges, trying to take it all in. He hadn't left her. He hadn't sent the note. The Comte had lied and nothing she'd believed about Rafe for the past two months was true.

She jumped to her feet, eager for something to do, any activity to distract her from the bitter confusion chewing at her. She went to the trunks and pulled the small one off the top, opening it to retrieve the portmanteau inside. The last time she'd packed this travelling case, at Château de Vane, she'd been as anxious as tonight, frantically shoving things in as she listened for the creditors to arrive. She'd just made it out the back gates to the cart and horse waiting for her when the dust from their creditor's carriage had begun to rise over the front drive.

She settled herself in front of the open trunk, trying to calm herself by sifting through the contents inside. She removed a few carefully folded dresses and laid them in the portmanteau. On the bodice of a simple white one, a round tearstain made her stop and run her fingers over the silk. There hadn't been time to see to the water mark as she'd packed in Paris, the fear of the looming war stronger than the fear of sharing a bed with the Comte, who paced in the sitting room, urging her to hurry. She'd ignored him, taking her time, hoping with each folded dress Rafe might change his mind and come back to her.

He didn't leave me.

If she'd dallied just a little longer, taken more time to pack, Rafe might have returned and exposed the Comte's wicked plot. Everything she'd suffered, all the loneliness, desperation and heartache might have been prevented. She and Rafe would have been true partners tonight, not wary and wounded strangers.

If only he'd returned sooner.

If only I hadn't left.

She loosened her grip on the dress and the stained silk drooped over her lap. Rafe was right. She'd been so quick to believe the worst of him, but he wasn't the first man to betray her. She could still see her father's remorseless face as he'd turned from the garden door while Lord Waltenham pulled her into the darkness. She'd called after him, but he'd done nothing except walk away. That night in Paris felt so similar.

Yet it wasn't true.

They'd both been duped.

She roughly folded the dress, hiding the stain.

I won't be blamed for Paris.

Rafe might have stepped in between her and Lord Waltenham when he'd known nothing about her, but after almost two years of their partnership and everything they'd been through, he'd let her go the first moment the opportunity presented itself.

She stuffed the wrinkled silk back in the trunk and pulled out a walking dress. It didn't matter what Rafe had or hadn't done. It was the past and nothing could change it or their strained faith in one another. She'd get on with Rafe as best she could until they recovered the register and Andrew was safe. Then she'd take her money from the Earl and set herself up in a house in a respectable part of London. Perhaps she'd even use her newfound wealth to attract a husband with more virility than the Comte and more money than Rafe, a man like Lord Rollingham.

She carefully folded the walking dress, trying to find comfort in the plan, but it didn't exist. Lord Rollingham was a tolerable enough opponent at the tables, but his good looks and shallow charm didn't move her. However, if she landed a man like him, she could finally offer Andrew a proper home and real protection free of the ugly stain of blackmail.

Exhaustion washed over her at the thought of gambling her future on another man, of waking the morning after the ceremony to discover if she'd made a better choice or placed herself at the mercy of a monster. For all Rafe's faults, at least he was honest. He'd never trick her with false promises or lure her into a trap purely for his own ends.

Too bad his faults kept getting in the way of his good qualities.

Rafe slipped a penny from his pocket and rubbed the dull brown metal between his thumb and forefinger. It was the only coin dark enough to keep from catching the attention of all the greedy eyes watching him from the doorways.

There was a safer route from his lodgings to Ludgate Hill, but this way was faster and he welcomed the darkness and the danger, it kept him from thinking too much about Cornelia.

She didn't dupe me.

The anger he'd cultivated since watching her ride away with the lecherous old aristocrat should have eased, but it didn't, it only shifted to Fate, adding points to the tally board he'd kept since his father's death. That wicked goddess was winning again.

He passed a noisy tavern, slowing to inhale the bread-like aroma of warm beer. The temptation to step inside and ease the tension in his gut with a few tankards nearly made him spend the coin.

Cornelia hadn't thrown him over for the Comte.

He ran into the more populated lane before slowing back into a steady stride. Cornelia might not be entirely to blame for Paris, but the whole unfortunate affair was a glaring reminder of the dangers of growing too close to someone. His mother had once made the mistake of loving her partner and look what it'd cost her.

What had Cornelia's marriage to the Comte cost Rafe?

He scraped one fingernail over the lion engraved on the coin. The truth took the bite out of his fury, but it didn't banish it completely. Maybe Cornelia wasn't at fault, but the speed with which she'd left him cut deeper than any of his father's deceptions. He'd expected the old man to let him down and he hadn't been disappointed. He hadn't expected the same of Cornelia.

She didn't run out on me.

He could repeat it a thousand times but it still wouldn't change one truth. He hadn't chased after her, not because he didn't care, but because he'd cared too much. There was no woman like her and if poverty hadn't sat so hard in his heart, she might have won it completely with her smiles and wit. He'd let her go because there was nothing more he could give her than a future of unpredictable card games and rundown lodgings. Even now there was nothing he could offer except retrieving the register. Once they had it, she'd save her brother, collect her money from the Earl and do with it what she pleased. He'd destroy the pages with his father's name, then return to the tables, growing old as he waited for the winning hand, the amazing game which would finally turn everything around.

The game he feared would never come.

He reached a crossroad, the direct route to the Bell Savage Inn to the right, the more circuitous route to the left. He shouldn't turn left, he should go straight to the Bell, but he ignored reason and started down the left lane. He kept a steady pace until the tall house next to the alley rose up in front of him. It looked like any other on this street except for the carriages waiting outside and the absence of riff-raff huddled in the doorway.

Rafe slowed as the building grew taller, stopping on the pavement in front of it. There was nothing special to mark it, nothing to advertise the temptations inside. A man had to know what he was looking for. Rafe knew. He stared at the brass knocker plate shimmering in the dark pool of the door. How many times had his father used it after gambling away his membership and good standing at White's? How many nights had he haunted the tables inside before some stranger gutted him in the alley?

Rafe's finger tightened on the penny, the edge digging into his skin. He'd never played here. He didn't need to sit through a few losing hands to know this wasn't a lucky establishment. Yet the house called to him, daring him to cross the threshold and stare his father's devil in the face.

As if the house wanted to taunt him, the door swung open and two gentlemen spilled out, grim faced and weaving as they staggered by. The odour of wine clinging to them was almost as nauseous as the stench of loss. The men wandered off, oblivious to Rafe, but the door remained open, offering a glimpse of the tables and players hunched over their cards. The ghost of his father sat with them, the last of his inheritance on the table in front of him.

He cringed to think what Cornelia would say if he lost the massive amounts his father used to lose. She'd rail like a banshee, not stand in stoic silence like his mother, who refused to speak ill of the man even as she laid yet another dinner of limp vegetables and stale bread before her son.

At last some butler inside noticed the door ajar and hurried down the hallway to close it. He spied Rafe and paused. 'Sir?'

'No. Not tonight.' *Not ever.* Rafe stormed away, the faint light from inside snuffed out by the closing door. There was no point staring into the past. Nothing could change it. All he could do was keep going forward, down one street and then another, leaving the past and everything it had stolen in the alley behind him.

Merrier sounds filled the street as the Bell Savage Inn came into view. Rafe stepped inside, the stuffy air as thick as the noisy conversation. The long trestle tables were full of people laughing and eating together. Others slept on the benches, their belongings tucked beneath their feet as they waited for the morning carriage. Rafe wound his way through the throng to the bar and paid the publican for two places on the morning stage, spending the extra money to secure them inside seats.

With the tickets tucked safely in his pocket, he ordered a tankard of ale. Cornelia was waiting for him, but he wasn't ready to return, not with the icy anger still clinging to him. He took a sip of the tepid brew, tasting the water thinning the mixture.

A man in a neat coat of fine wool leaned on the bar beside him. 'Hello, Rafe.'

'Hello, Rodger. How's my favourite sharper?'

'Much better now with all these rubes coming over from France. They can barely speak our language, but I speak theirs fluently.' He held up an ace slipped from his sleeve.

'Makes them easier to fleece, does it?'

'It helps facilitate the transaction.' He signalled to the publican. 'What are you doing here? You don't usually trouble with travellers, or are you considering a career as a sharp? A man with your breeding and connections could make a killing.'

'I'm not contemplating an occupation.' The publican placed another tankard on the scarred bar in front of them. 'I find myself in need of a respite from London.'

'And you're paying these prices for passage? I know a man who can get you a cheaper fare on another coach leaving from the Five Points.'

'One that will drop me at the crossroads just outside town after relieving me of my money? No, thank you.'

He placed one well-manicured hand over his heart. 'Rafe, you wound me.'

Rafe raised his tankard in salute. 'No, my good man, I know you.'

'Indeed you do, and, because you've been so pleasant to me in the past, I feel it's my duty to warn you. Mr Smith has been complaining a right bit about you. Said he has a mind to make an example of you to the other toffs who owe him money. Don't know what value he thinks you are to him dead. Dead men can't pay their debt.'

'Neither can this live man, but if he dumps my body on the Marquis of Baldwin's doorstep, it might scare him into settling what I hear is a very large account.' Killing a Baron, even one of Rafe's questionable standing, would send a chill through a certain section of society and many moneylenders might benefit from the rush to pay. The momentary lightness Rafe had enjoyed with his old friend faded like the ring of foam on the top of his ale. 'Thank you for the warning.'

'My pleasure.' Rodger gulped down his beer and set the empty tankard on the bar. 'Now, if you'll excuse me, I need to get some sleep before the morning coach arrives with all those wealthy, wide-eyed boys from the country eager to gamble their allowance away.'

Rafe watched Rodger cross the room, weaving around a tavern maid before passing a burly, wide-shouldered man sitting at a table. Rafe fixed on the man whose eyes dropped into his tankard.

It was one of Mr Smith's bulldogs.

Rafe's calf tightened in his boot, pressing against the steel of his dagger. He left his ale unfinished and made for the door, conscious of the man watching him. Outside, Rafe hopped over a pile of dung and ran to the dark shadows of the mews across from the entrance, careful to stay out of the low pools of lantern light hanging overhead. He waited in the darkness for some time, watching the tavern door and the people coming and going. The wide-shouldered man never emerged. Whatever interest he had in Rafe, it didn't extend to following him into the night.

Rafe set off for Mrs Linton's, taking the quicker path though the longer one was more tempting. He was in no mood to bump into Mr Smith and run the risk of meeting Cornelia's expectations by not coming back.

With any luck she'd be asleep by the time he returned, or at least pretending to sleep, then she'd hear him come in and stop worrying about whether or not he'd run off with their money.

He slapped a low shop sign, making it swing on its iron rings, the sting of his skin almost as nasty as the cut to his pride.

After everything he'd done for her over the past few days, she still didn't trust him, though he couldn't blame her for being suspicious. Life had taught her some hard lessons about trusting men.

Rafe clenched his fists at his sides, wishing it was the Comte and not Lord Waltenham whose face he'd bloodied. The old codger deserved a broken nose for what he'd done to her. She'd suffered too much under men like her father and Lord Edgemont to deserve the cold caresses of a lecherous old man hiding his debt behind the grandeur of a château.

I should have chased after the carriage or searched for her instead of leaving Paris.

Guilt hit him as hard as regret. If he could do anything to make her forget her time with the Comte, he would, but he wasn't sure how much it would matter. By letting her go, he'd proven himself as bad as the rest.

Even the truth about Paris couldn't redeem him now.

Chapter Eight

Cornelia took Rafe's hand as she stepped down from the seat beside the cart driver. Without thinking, she gripped his fingers hard, steadying herself against the barrage of old emotions encroaching on her already tangled and complicated present. It'd been two years since she'd been this close to Hatton Place. Two years since she'd met Rafe at the Red Lion Inn where the coach from London had left them an hour ago. Though Hatton Place was further east, closer to Edgemont's estate than Wealthstone, like Wealthstone it enjoyed the same rolling hills covered in fields broken by rows of low hedges and groves of tall trees.

When she was young, she used to wander these fields. More than once, she'd followed the paths too far, coming to the hill overlooking Wealthstone. She'd never wandered down to the house or done anything more than stare at it before travelling home. She'd known very little about the Densmore family then, except what gossip Fanny used to relay. Her father had only ever made friends with the Edgemonts. He'd been too lazy to cultivate more reputable relationships with his other neighbours.

Cornelia turned to face the familiar hill, the clouds moving in slow wisps behind it, the trees taller and fuller than she remembered. Behind it, five miles off, Andrew waited for the next school term to begin at Michaelmas. If she wanted, she could walk over and see him, sneak through the kitchen garden and slip up the servants' staircase to his room. She might steal an hour with him without having to face Fanny. It'd be more difficult than simply walking up to the front door, but after a night without much sleep, Cornelia didn't have the patience to endure Fanny's usual rant about money, the one which filled her nearly illiterate letters.

A cart full of hay moved along a distant lane, shivering under the weight of its load. The same carts used to creak over the lanes while she and Andrew played in the late summer fields. When they were tired, they'd lie back and watch the clouds, Andrew hugging her as she told him stories of knights and ladies, his blue eyes wide with amazement. Tears blurred the golden grass and green elms. It seemed like a very long time until Michaelmas.

'Are you all right?' Rafe squeezed her hand and she returned the gesture before remembering herself and letting go.

'Yes, of course.' She turned away from him, wiping her eyes with the back of her hand.

'Don't worry, we'll make sure Andrew stays safe.'

She brushed the dust from her dress, looking down to avoid the pull of his caring face, hating how easily he could guess her thoughts. She wished he would go back to being as aloof with her as he'd been after Lady Daltmouth's card party. Enduring his cutting quips was better than hovering in this strangling, awkward truce. The hours she'd sat pressed against him in the coach had been torture. None of the confusing thoughts, the questions about their future and the past could be addressed, not with the old couple sitting across from them and a vicar to her left. Yet, even in the stuffy air of the coach, she'd felt Rafe reaching out to her, offering her his shoulder when she could no longer keep her eyes open, seeing to her comfort as he had the night they'd run off to London.

His boots crunched over the gravel and she heard a few coins clink together as he handed them to the cart driver. The man's low voice called out to the horse before the wheels began turning in time to the animal's steady pace.

'Let's go inside. You must be hungry and you should rest,' he offered.

'You needn't concern yourself so much with my welfare,' she retorted, hoping to annoy him enough to send him storming into the house, leaving her here in the drive to think.

He didn't rise to her challenge, as calm and cool as always as he picked up their portmanteaus. 'You're my guest. It'd be rude not to see to your welfare.'

She said nothing, afraid to speak and reveal how much his kindness touched her. Instead, she drew up the hem of her pelisse and walked ahead of him over the uneven blue-limestone path. The rhythm of his boots on the worn stone kept pace with hers and to distract herself from him and all her warring emotions, she took in the front of Wealthstone. Ivy choked the front half-turret and the pointed slate roof, nearly covering in some places the narrow leaded windows. Hatton Place was no grand palace, but its old brick didn't look as tired or worn as Wealthstone's limestone.

The wide wood door in the half-turret opened and a woman with Rafe's sharp nose and dark brown eyes emerged. She wore a faded green dress with the low waist and full skirt popular a decade ago. A large smile swept the exhaustion from her fine features as she hurried out to Rafe, her wooden clogs clomping over the limestone walk.

Rafe dropped their cases and held out his arms to her. 'Good afternoon, Mother.'

'It's a great afternoon.' She threw herself into his embrace, holding him close.

Cornelia's chest tightened. Once, after a visit to her spinster aunt in Canterbury, her mother had met her at the door of Hatton Place with the same love and enthusiasm. She wasn't likely to get such a warm welcome from anyone there now, except Andrew.

'I wish you'd sent word you were coming,' the Baroness said.

'There wasn't time.'

'You did it then?' She clutched Rafe's forearms. 'You purchased the page and we're safe.'

Rafe moved out of her grasp, his smile falling.

'No. The situation has grown more complicated since I left for London.'

The Baroness laced her hands in front of her, drawing her lips to one side just as Rafe did whenever he was irked. 'Your father's troubles always had a way of doing that.'

'Don't worry. I have a plan.'

'I don't doubt you do.' She patted his arm before settling her attention on Cornelia. 'And you've brought a guest.'

Rafe escorted his mother to Cornelia and she braced herself. She'd never met the Baroness, but if Rafe had told his mother about his plans for the register, he'd probably told her about Paris, too. Hopefully, he hadn't told his mother too much.

'Lady Densmore, allow me to introduce you to the Comtesse de Vane.'

'The Comtesse de Vane?' the Baroness gasped in surprise.

Apparently, he'd told her enough.

'The widowed Comtesse,' Rafe clarified.

'Oh, I see.' The Baroness steepled her fingertips in front of her lips and eyed her son. 'It has grown more complicated.'

'The situation has become a regular Gordian knot.'

'It's a pleasure to finally meet you, Comtesse.' The Baroness smiled with poorly contained amusement, looking even more like her son. 'Rafe has told me a great deal about you.'

Cornelia took two deep breaths, centring herself before executing a dignified curtsy she hoped was as respectful as it was apologetic. They might only spend a night or two here, but she wouldn't have Rafe's mother looking down on her like some scheming woman, or worse. 'Thank you, Lady Densmore. It's a pleasure to finally see Wealthstone. Rafe always speaks so fondly of it.'

'I'm afraid it may not live up to your expectations. Rafe sees more potential in it than there is. A trait he shares with his late grandfather.' She linked her arm in Cornelia's and drew her towards the door. 'Now come inside and we'll get you settled.'

Rafe followed behind them, carrying the portmanteaus.

Inside, a tall wall of diamond-paned windows rose above the main staircase, letting in the bright afternoon sun and illuminating the dark wood panelling. The furnishings were sparse, with a scratched table tucked against the wall beneath the stairs and a yellowed set of antlers hanging above it. Despite the lack of furnishings, the entrance hall was clean, the antlers free of the cobwebs the antlers in her father's study usually displayed. She could only imagine the deplorable condition Hatton Place must be in now if her stepmother didn't even have fifty pounds to pay for Andrew's school. Even if she did, Cornelia knew she wouldn't spend it on anyone but herself.

'Mother, have you heard anything about Edgemont coming home?' Rafe asked as he closed the door behind them, dropping the portmanteaus next to the stairs.

'You didn't come all the way here to see him, did you?' The Baroness led them into a small sitting room, the one table by the window littered with fabric and paper patterns. 'I didn't think you two got on.'

'We think he has the register.'

Her face went pale. 'What happened?'

As Rafe relayed the events in London, Cornelia listened from the shadows beside the door, glad to be forgotten, especially when Rafe mentioned her connection to the register. He did his best to tell the story without making her look too guilty, careful to emphasise her desire to protect Andrew. However, Cornelia knew it wouldn't be hard for the Baroness to guess her real role in the loss of the register. She backed up against the wall, expecting Lady Densmore to rail at her for putting their title and house in jeopardy, but in the midst of her own troubles, she seemed to have forgotten Cornelia.

'I'm sorry it turned out this way, Mother,' Rafe added, finishing at last.

'Don't be sorry. It's not your fault.' The Baroness gathered up the cloth and patterns, arranging them into neat piles. 'I'll speak with Alice. The cook at Darringwood is her cousin and, from what I hear, not treated well by Lord Edgemont. She might know if he has the book and where he's hiding it, though such information may come at a price.'

'I have some money to offer her.' He snatched up a few bits of fabric and slapped them down on the pile, ruffling the pattern edges. 'Though I hate spending it to fix more of Father's mistakes.'

'If it means not losing the house or your title, then it's worth it.' Lady Densmore took up two spools of thread and set them in a wooden sewing box. Lowering the lid, she traced the Densmore crest inlaid on the top. 'I may not see the potential in the house, but it's still our home and I'm not ready to lose it.'

He laid his hands over hers. 'It won't come to that, I won't let it.'

'Just promise me you'll be careful.'

'I'm always careful,' Rafe foolhardily asserted.

'That's what your father used to say.' Her gaze wandered to something beyond Rafe, something now gone, her love for her husband evident in the wistful sadness haunting her eyes.

'My father.' Rafe snorted. 'The scoundrel got off easy dying and leaving us with this mess.'

She touched his cheek. 'I know it's difficult, especially right now, but try to remember the better times. Despite your father's mistakes, he did love you.'

'Not as much as the cards.' Rafe pulled back, not sharing her fond memories.

'You have every right to be angry, but some day you'll have to let go of it, especially when you realise it won't change anything except you.'

He didn't answer, but leaned against the wall beside the window, the sunlight wavering over his face as it fell through the uneven leaded glass.

Lady Densmore turned, suddenly remembering Cornelia.

'I'm sorry. Where are my manners?' Lady Densmore exclaimed, her demeanour as welcoming as it was unexpected. 'Please come closer. You must be exhausted after the journey.'

'Please don't trouble about me,' Cornelia protested. 'I'm used to looking after myself.'

'I don't doubt you are, but you needn't do so here.' She took Cornelia's hands and drew her to a chair near the fireplace. 'I know what it's like to worry over someone you love.'

Lady Densmore gently pressed her down into the chair and Cornelia didn't resist, craving the motherly gesture and wishing her own mother was still alive. If she hadn't died, then maybe none of this would be happening.

'Rafe, please see to the Comtesse while I speak with Alice,' the Baroness instructed, then left.

'I wish I had as much love for Father as my mother does.' He picked a loose sliver of lead off one of the panes. 'When he used to teach me to play cards in the winter, I thought it was because he wanted to be with me. It wasn't. He just couldn't get away from the gambling.'

'If he spent time teaching you to play, then he must have loved you.' She undid one button of her pelisse, his contemplative mood weighing on her. 'My father ignored me. I wasn't the boy he wanted.

Andrew was. Marrying Fanny after he got her with child was the only honourable thing he ever did.'

'Then curse the both of them.' He pushed away from the glass and came to stand in front of her, pensiveness replaced by a more convivial air, as if he was lord of a prosperous manor, not on the verge of losing everything. 'Now, shall I take you to find food or would you prefer the solitude of your room?'

Exhaustion tweaked the small muscles of her back. 'My room. I fear the long night and longer day are wearing on me.'

'Come, then. Your suite awaits.'

He held out his hand. She eyed the long lines crisscrossing the palm and echoed in the length of his fingers. They curled up slightly at the tips as he waited for her to take it. Touching him would be such a simple gesture, another small step to closing the gap Paris had opened between them.

Laying her hands on the chair arms, she pushed herself up and past his outstretched hand and made for the door. She didn't want to close the gap or follow him and risk opening herself up to more pain and fear.

In the hall she waited for him. He emerged from

the sitting room and, saying nothing, picked up her bag and led her upstairs.

The light was thick on the stairs and she paused on the landing to take in the long shadows beneath the trees outside. Night was only a few hours away and soon she'd be alone again in her room with her fears and memories. She traced one cold, glass diamond with her finger, understanding why her father had turned to drink. The oblivion would be a welcome retreat from her troubles, but the comfort was a false one and the habit more difficult to escape than a bad marriage.

Upstairs, the light faded the further down the dark panelled hall they moved, the small window at the end poorly positioned to catch the afternoon sun. Rafe walked in front of her, his wide body dampening what little light penetrated the shadows. She gripped the sides of her pelisse, reluctantly following him deeper into the house.

'You can sleep in the south-west guest room. It's brighter there during the day.' He stopped at a door and pushed it open. Sunlight spilled into the hallway and her grip on the cotton relaxed. 'Will this do?'

She slid past him into the room, examining the faded bed curtains and the chipped basin on the rickety stand against the wall. 'It's a palace compared to some of the rooms we rented that first year in London.'

'And as short on staff. If you need anything, you'll have to come find us.' Bitterness laced his humour.

'I'll be fine. I only need to rest.'

'As soon as I discover anything, I'll let you know.'

'I'm sure you will.'

He cocked his head at her. 'Does this mean you trust me again?'

After living with the idea of Rafe's betrayal, it was so hard to think clearly through the jumble of new truths and realities. He'd let her go once without a fight, proving how easy it was for him to walk away. There was no guarantee he wouldn't do it again. 'I don't know.'

'If you're here, then maybe you already do.'

Rafe closed the bedroom door behind him and started down the hall, the dim light grating. He threw open each door as he passed, trying to ignore the emptiness of the rooms as sunlight spilled into the shadows. If only banishing the gloom between him and Cornelia was as easy. For all the flooding of the truth into the blackness of Paris, it hadn't done anything to allay her doubts, or his.

She didn't trust him any more than he trusted her, but he needed her help as she'd proven at Mr Nettles's and again at the tables at Lady Daltmouth's. Even if he could manage without her, he couldn't afford to alienate anyone as he'd discovered to his near peril when she'd possessed the register. However, the thought of her wandering out of his life when this was all over made his stomach tighten. After all, the games weren't as fun without her.

He smiled to himself, but it faded as he dropped a heavy foot on each tread of the stairs. It might be a long time before either of them regained their confidence in one another. If they could learn to believe in each other again, then maybe some day they'd regain something of the friendship they'd lost in Paris.

His slammed his fist against the banister.

Some day. His whole life was one long string of some days. Some day he might make the Densmore name respectable again and ease his mother's burdens. Some day he might enjoy the warmth of a family and home. It'd be a refreshing change if some day ever became today.

He marched across the hall, pausing in the centre to take in the cracked plaster ceiling, the dry wood panels and the sheer emptiness of the space.

He'd thought nothing of its neglected condition when he'd sat on the bottom stair as a boy and watched his parents laugh as they practised the latest dances. With the snow piled high outside the windows and his father prevented from travelling, they'd move through each turn, touching and teasing one another as if they were newly married. The joy would vanish with the snow and with it all his mother's smiles and more pieces of silver plate.

Rafe banished the memories and made for the back of the house.

It was hard to remember the good in his father. It was too tainted by the bad.

The thick scent of baking bread led him down the stone passageway to where it opened into the large kitchen. Mother sat with Alice and both women turned to look at him as he entered.

Rafe could feel his pockets lightening.

Alice wasn't greedy and she'd been more than willing to stay through the thin and thinner of the Densmore fortunes, but, like Rafe, she'd learned to get what she could when she could. At the moment, it seemed her chances of getting something were excellent.

If only Rafe could say the same about his current situation.

Chapter Nine

Rest eluded Cornelia like luck as she tossed in a light sleep on the lumpy mattress. Dreams of Andrew, his hand in hers as they crossed the countryside, faded into the card rooms of Paris with Rafe by her side. He whirled them down the length of a mirrored ballroom, the two of them laughing and happy, the dance making her as dizzy as fine champagne. Then a wind whipped through the room, extinguishing the candles and his fingernails dug into her palms as his face faded into Edgemont's angry sneer. She tried to push him away, but he dragged her through the steps, tugging her along as she stumbled and tripped to the tune of a scratching violin. At last, he pulled her from the dance floor, his face melting into Lord Waltenham's as he led her into a dark garden where the sharp branches tore at her cheeks.

Rafe! Rafe!

This time Rafe didn't appear. Only her father and the Comte emerged from the shadows, laughing and jeering as Lord Waltenham pressed her to the ground and tore at her clothes.

Cornelia wrenched herself from the dream and sat up, struggling against the tightness of her stays to breath.

He didn't come. He didn't come for me. The words faded with the dream, but the anguish of the nightmare remained.

She swung her feet over the bed and gripped one post, focusing on the tree outside the window and the rich late-afternoon sun turning the leaves a deeper shade of green.

No, he did come for me at Lord Perry's, she reminded herself before another truth struck her. *He let me go in Paris.*

She went to the washstand, poured water into the chipped porcelain and splashed it on her face. Bending over, she watched the drops fall into the bowl, plunking one by one like the tears she refused to shed. Clutching the rough sides of the stand, she inhaled once, then again, trying to force back the pain.

Rafe let me go with the Comte.

She reached for the towel and scrubbed her skin dry, then straightened to examine her face in the specked and cracked mirror hanging over the stand.

Would he have stopped her if he'd known about the Comte's lie?

No, he didn't want me enough.

She touched one red cheek, her smooth skin no worse for lack of real rest, but some day the long nights would show, along with the emptiness of her life. It would hollow out her face and sallow her complexion as it had her mother's, darkening the very faint circles beneath her eyes. Who would want her then? Not even an old man like the Comte. She'd finish her days at the tables like the old woman in the mob cap, with nothing but another hand of cards and a few good memories to give her comfort.

She smiled a little to herself. There were good times with Rafe, many of them, but they hadn't been strong enough to make him step between her and the Comte or to make him love her.

Tears blurred her reflection before she blinked them back. She threw down the towel and whirled around to find her half-boots discarded next to the bed, disgusted by her self-pity. Wallowing in her troubles would help no one, especially not Andrew, and she wasn't about to abandon her brother like her mother had abandoned her.

She laced her boots and marched to the door. Despite her newfound resolve, she paused with her hand on the knob, bracing herself to step into the dark hallway.

Stop fearing shadows! She pulled open the door, stunned by the strong light on the other side.

He'd opened the doors.

She entered the narrow hallway, catching the dust motes dancing in the light falling out of each west-facing doorway. Moving through one pool and then another, the hardness she'd carried from the room began to soften and guilt needled her.

After how nasty she'd been about the register and her part in its disappearance, she didn't deserve his consideration. Yet he gave it along with his promise to help Andrew, showing her numerous small kindnesses since they'd become partners again.

Just like before. She paused at the top of the stairs, then started down.

They might never be what they were in Paris, but perhaps they could be friends again. Heaven knew, she needed as many as she could collect since at present she had none.

At the bottom, she paused and listened for people, but heard nothing. She headed for the sitting room, the only room she knew, and tapped once on the closed door.

'Come in,' Lady Densmore called from inside.

Cornelia pushed the door open and the older woman looked up from where she sat sewing in the window seat.

'I'm sorry to disturb you,' Cornelia apologised. 'I was looking for Ra—Lord Densmore.'

'He's with Alice. She's just come back from visiting her cousin at Darringwood. Hopefully, he'll have some news for us.'

'I hope so.' Though she was tired of hoping. It never did any good.

'Come and sit with me awhile. Tell me all the London gossip.'

'I'm afraid I don't know much. I've only been back from Paris a short time.'

'Then tell me what you know. It'll be nice to have some company for a change.' She patted the bench beside her.

Cornelia hesitated, then crossed the room to settle herself on the window seat. After all Rafe had done for her, she couldn't be rude to his mother.

'I'm glad to see you're back, safe in England,' the

Baroness offered. 'I was distressed when Rafe returned without you, then told me of your marriage.'

A shame stronger than when she'd lied to the priest in France about being Catholic so he would perform the wedding ceremony filled Cornelia. 'I didn't have much choice but to marry.'

'Yes, sometimes we must do what we must to make our way in life.' Lady Densmore nodded, more understanding than censorious as she pushed the needle through the fabric. 'I've often found work takes my mind off my troubles. Do you sew?'

'I can do simple stitches. It was all my mother ever taught me.' There seemed so much her mother had failed to teach her. Stinging tears made her blink as the loneliness from her room threatened to sweep over her again.

There was no time to humour the mood as Lady Daltmouth laid a small, half-sewn garment across Cornelia's lap. 'Simple stitches will do.'

The threaded needle hung from the fabric, each stitch tiny and neat. 'What is it?'

'A baby's dress for my woman-of-all-work's sister. She's expecting another child and they are so poor.'

Lady Daltmouth picked up another garment and set to work. Cornelia watched her, amazed how someone with so little would think of those with even less. She couldn't imagine Fanny making clothes for a servant. She'd only grudgingly given Cornelia her old gowns to wear because Cook, who wasn't afraid of anyone, had complained to the rafters about Cornelia's too-small dresses. Fanny hadn't even bothered to make sure they were altered to fit Cornelia's tall frame. It'd fallen to Cook's kindly mother to see to them and keep Cornelia from traipsing about the countryside in ill-fitting clothes.

Cornelia took up the needle, the slender metal awkward in her hands as she struggled to match the Baroness's even stitches and not stick herself and bleed all over the tiny dress. The busy work soothed her, as did Lady Densmore's steady presence beside her. It'd been too long since she'd sat so still and her worries faded with each pierce of the needle and pull of the thread.

After a time, the Baroness leaned over, inspecting her work. 'You're better than you think.'

Cornelia startled. 'Pardon me?'

'Your sewing.' She motioned to the garment, but the compassion in her deep-brown eyes hinted at something more and Cornelia's heart ached with the kindness. 'You only need a little more practice.'

'That's what my mother used to say.' Cornelia swallowed down the lump in her throat, wondering what about Lady Daltmouth reminded her so much of her mother. They looked nothing alike. The Baroness was lean but healthy, where her mother had been rail thin and sickly, even before she became ill. Cornelia wished her mother had possessed the Baroness's fortitude and serenity. Her mother, for all her loving ways, had let her bad lot destroy her. 'I'm afraid I don't have the patience to sit still for so long.'

'I never did either when I was your age. Time has made me more patient.' She took a small pair of scissors from the sewing case and cut and tied the thread before threading the needle with another colour. 'Now, tell me what you know of London society.'

Cornelia relayed the stories she'd overheard at the Dowager Countess of Daltmouth's salon. When she was done, the Baroness told her about the surrounding country families. To watch her speak, smiling and calm, one would think her fortune was secure and her son feted by all London.

The peace lasted until the thud of Rafe's boots in the entrance hall joined the crackle of the logs. Cornelia jabbed the fabric and caught her skin.

She pulled back her hand, shaking off the sting as Rafe walked in.

'Edgemont is home,' he announced, carrying in a tray of meat, bread and cheese. Cornelia cleared a space on the table while the Baroness lit the reed lamp and Rafe laid the food in front of them. 'Rumour is he has a country paramour, though Alice's cousin wasn't sure who. Probably a farmer's daughter. It seems to be the way in these parts.'

'Rafe, mind your tongue,' his mother scolded, though Cornelia caught the amused smile playing on her lips as she helped herself to some cheese.

'We'll pay a morning call on Edgemont,' Rafe announced, filling his own plate with bread and meat.

Cornelia rubbed her wrist. 'If your cook can find out where the book is, why do we need to see him?'

'As I said before, Edgemont isn't one for direct confrontation.' Rafe leaned back, stretching out his long legs, his breeches pulling tight over the thick muscle of his thighs. Cornelia stole a glance, struggling to choke down a piece of crusty bread and not let her eyes wander any higher than his knees. All she wanted from him was friendship, nothing more. 'The moment we ask about the register, we'll know if he has it or not.'

She stopped eating. 'What do you mean, *if* he has it? We know he does.'

He popped a chunk of cold meat in his mouth.

Cornelia shifted in her chair, unnerved by the stretching silence.

'We don't know for certain,' he answered at last.

'And you think to say this now, after we've spent the money to come here?' It was difficult to be friendly with such a frustrating man.

He glanced at his mother, who pretended not to listen as she finished her cheese.

'Rafe, perhaps you should show our guest the garden, while there's still light,' Lady Densmore suggested. 'It's bloomed beautifully since you were last here.'

'An excellent idea.' Rafe rose, swinging his arm towards another door at the far end of the room. 'My lady?'

Cornelia rose, uneasy at the idea of being alone with Rafe, but not wanting to argue or discuss their less-than-genteel business in front of the Baroness. She marched to the door as Rafe moved swiftly forward to pull it open and flood the room with the evening air.

Outside, the encroaching darkness from the setting sun pricked at the discomfort already filling her. Rafe's doubts were now hers. She possessed enough troubles without thinking they'd made such a calculated mistake.

'Edgemont has to have the register,' she insisted as he led her past the overgrown box hedges to the small plot of land behind the house. Rose-bushes bloomed full and heavy along the outer edges, standing guard over even rows of summer vegetables in the centre. The Baroness's patient hands were as much in the dark dirt of the beds as they were in the tiny stitches of the white baby dress. 'With the way he used to play my father like a harp, I can only imagine how it must have delighted him to try to play me in France. Which is why I know he stole it. He isn't about to let me win.'

'And by tomorrow, we'll know if our suspicions are correct.'

'We should have been certain before we left London, before we spent what was left of my money,' she replied sharply, the peace of the sitting room gone.

'Then perhaps you should determine our next move.' He tugged a yellow rose off a nearby branch. 'Then you won't be so disappointed when my plan fails.'

She chewed her bottom lip, regretting being so sharp with him. 'I'm sorry. I just wish you'd shared your doubts sooner.'

'I would have if I'd had anything to base them on, but I don't.' He picked the petals from the rose, flipping them to the ground, then flinging away the empty bud. 'It's just a feeling, a hunch.'

'Your hunches have been wrong before.'

His eyes snapped to hers, regret softening the small lines at the corners. 'Yes, they have.'

Was it their past or their current partnership he regretted?

Uneasy under his scrutiny, she focused on the end of the garden and the stone statue of a girl all but covered in creeping vines. The image of Rafe folding the pages with his father's name, sliding them into his pocket and walking out of her life flashed before her. They might be united in their goal now, but it didn't mean he wanted her in his life once this was all over. If he left, there'd be no one to help her, no one to care what man mistreated her. The ugliness of the world might destroy her and no one would notice but Andrew, assuming Fanny didn't send him to his death.

She took a deep breath, trying to steady herself against the aching loneliness, but no matter how much her chest pushed against the stays, there wasn't enough air to soothe her.

'Are you all right?' he asked, his voice as gentle as the evening breeze.

'I'm worried about Andrew.' It was only half a lie. 'I doubt Fanny has risen from her bed long enough to look after him. Cook will make sure he eats, she always did with me, unless Fanny has finally dismissed her. She was so old the last time I saw her and Fanny won't be kind to her the way your mother is with your servants.'

Rafe took her hand and with it her pain and concern as if they were his own. 'We can see him if you'd like, tomorrow after we visit Edgemont.'

'I want to, but I can't.' She clutched him tight, hanging on as if he might save her from all the dread threatening to drown her. 'If I see Fanny, she'll demand money. If I put her off or she senses I don't have it, I don't know what she'll do. I can't risk her sending Andrew away.'

'She won't send him away so quickly.' Rafe caressed her cheek with the back of his fingers, the gesture too familiar and comforting. 'If she does, she loses the only chit she has against you.'

'But I can't risk it.' Cornelia struggled not to bury her face in his palm, or press herself against his chest and cry like she had in Lord Perry's garden. 'I'm not just frightened of the West Indies, but of how he'll grow up. I want him to be a better man than my father.'

He tucked a small strand of hair behind her ear, his fingers warm and soft against her skin. 'With someone like you watching out for him, your brother will turn out better than any of us.'

She wished she possessed such confidence in herself. 'I don't know what influence a poor Comtesse with a talent for cards can have on a boy.'

He slid one finger down her jaw, caressing the tip of her chin. For a brief moment he was the lover who'd held her through the nights, protecting her from all her fears. 'You love Andrew and care about his welfare and he knows it. That alone will be enough to make him a better man.'

He lowered his hand. 'I wonder how I'll turn out in the end, when the debt finally overwhelms me.'

'You could sell Wealthstone and erase some of it,' she offered. She'd never seen him look so lost and it scared her. If a man like him gave up, then there was little hope of her overcoming her troubles.

'No, it's all I have left.' His fingers tightened around hers with determination, giving her a sense of the fight still in him. 'As long as it's mine, then there's some way to save it, maybe even restore it. I just have to find it.'

The memory of Lady Daltmouth fawning over Rafe at the card party rushed back to her and with it all the doubts created by the Comte's lies.

'Some day, you'll find a way,' she insisted, struggling against the past to see the true man who stood beside her.

'If it doesn't kill me first.' He grimaced. 'Like it killed my father.'

'You won't end up like him. You care too much about others to neglect them for your own pleasures.'

'Perhaps.' He stared at the setting sun, his concentration as focused on the rolling farmland as it was on the cards when he was late into a winning streak. 'But even a noble pursuit can destroy a man.'

She followed his gaze to the horizon as a flock of birds flew past the first few stars of night.

'When I was young, I wanted so much to be like my father.' Pain choked his words and tightened his grip on her hand. 'I'd read about his speeches in the House of Lords and pester him to tell me about them whenever he came home. He'd sit me down at a table and take out the cards, explaining what he'd done in the last session while he dealt. Then we'd play and he'd teach me what tricks to watch out for, how to read the other players, keep track of the cards, when to knock and when to wait. I absorbed it all, practising in my room at night, eager for any chance to show him how good I was. The first time he took me to Lord Perry's, I was so proud. You don't know how devastating it was the day I realised the man I idolised was a weak sap who didn't give a damn about me or Mother.'

'Yes, I do know.' She ran her thumb across the firm skin of his knuckles, the depth of his anguish making her forget hers.

'So many times I've thought if I could do things differently, act differently, I could change what he's done, but I can't. The man was too thorough when it came to ruin.'

'Ruin was the only skill our fathers excelled in,' Cornelia offered wryly.

'I suppose I shouldn't complain.' Rafe shrugged. 'Teaching me to gamble was more than Edgemont's father ever did for him.'

'And look how well he turned out.'

Rafe smiled, something of the good-natured Baron shining through, but the heartache lingering just beneath the humour weighed it down. 'Now, if you'll excuse me, I have to hear from the estate manager the endless list of problems I can do little to address.'

'An estate manager?'

'Mr Tidwell. I can't pay him and he's too old to go anywhere else, so he stays. He says it keeps him busy in his dotage. Some day, I'll find a way to thank him.'

'I don't doubt you will.'

'I'm glad to see you've regained some faith in me.'

He raised her hand to his lips and paused over her fingertips, his breath brushing the skin, the heat in his eyes keeping something of the sunlight in the sky. She curled her fingers over his and everything she'd ever craved from him came rushing back. He leaned in so close, all she need do was rise up on her toes to meet his lips, accept the full comfort of his embrace, trust him completely as she had during their first intimate night together in London.

She didn't move, fear and doubt anchoring her to the ground. She'd made the mistake of muddling the terms of their partnership before, exposing herself to a heartache unlike any she'd experienced since her mother's death. She couldn't do it again.

Recognising her hesitation, he straightened and released her hand. 'Sleep well, Cornelia.'

He turned on his heel and made for the house.

She didn't watch him leave, but looked to the statue, wishing she was as hard as the stone girl so she wouldn't feel any of the confusing emotions tormenting her.

Rafe isn't the only one who cares about me.

Nothing of Hatton Place or its lands were visible from here, but she knew it was out there and so was Andrew. She couldn't come this close and not see him. Once everyone at Wealthstone was asleep, she could slip across the old familiar footpaths along the fields to Hatton Place and sneak unseen into the house as she used to when her father was drunk. If Andrew was safe, it would ease her mind and give her one less thing to worry about until they had the register. If Andrew was in danger, then she'd find a way to protect him.

Rafe rounded the corner of the house, the scent of dry summer grass driving away the faint echoes of Cornelia's flowery perfume. Pausing on the lawn to take in the darkness blanketing the fields, he remembered the black water of the Channel as he'd stood at the railing during the night crossing. Watching the coast of France disappear into the fog, he'd wrestled with the demon of losing Cornelia, thinking he'd never see her again.

Yet here she was, back in his life, her desire for him heavy in her encouraging words and the longing in her eyes.

It was the sharp look of distrust, the easy way she'd turned on him when he'd expressed his doubts about Edgemont, which made him hold back just now. It wasn't just her apprehension keeping him from tasting her tempting lips. Even if he found a way to overcome the bitterness of Paris, he couldn't justify dragging her into a union of affection only to have the passion snuffed out by poverty and worry. He'd witnessed too much of his mother's suffering to foist such a fate on Cornelia.

However, the threat of her marrying a peacock like Lord Rollingham made him want to spit. He'd already lost her once, he wasn't certain he could face the torment of it again. After they found the register, maybe he could convince her to stay with him as his partner. Together, they might finally make a success in London, just as he'd promised her two years ago. Then he could offer her a future and the safety they both craved.

He pulled open the back door and strode inside, wondering what foolishness had come over him. Reviving their partnership on such terms was akin to playing against a cheat and expecting to win. He was a better gambler than that and so was she. She wasn't going to risk her future, or Andrew's on more of Rafe's grand plans, not after his old ones had already failed.

Recovering the register might restore some of her faith in him, but it wouldn't change the realities of his life or hers, or bolster his sagging belief in his once-grand plans to rebuild everything his father had destroyed.

Approaching the study, he caught Mr Tidwell's grey hair bent over the ledger through the cracked door. He slowed, wondering if Cornelia was right. Maybe he should sell Wealthstone, walk away with dignity before the creditors chucked him out on the drive.

No. Never.

He pushed open the door and strode in to meet his manager. Wealthstone was all he had left and he would cling to it until death peeled the deed from his dead hands.

Chapter Ten

The moon hung large against the horizon, casting an orange glow over the rolling land. It'd been years since she'd followed these trails leading to Hatton Place. The old sense of freedom came rushing back as Cornelia ran her fingers over the tall grass lining the packed dirt. If she could stay here wandering these fields like some wraith, free of the troubles of the past and the uncertainty of the future she would, except the living needed her more than the dead.

She jumped over a small brook and paused to listen to the sweet trickle of water over the rocks, the sound easing some of her guilt at having slipped away without telling Rafe. Perhaps it wasn't wise to go alone, but sneaking into Hatton Place would be easier without him and she hadn't encountered a soul since leaving Wealthstone. With the moon so bright, there were few places someone following her might hide and she saw nothing around her except fields and bushes.

Cornelia pulled herself up and over a stone wall, her foot finding a chink to give her leverage, the stones rough against her skin. She dropped down on the other side, a cold patch between the rock and the low ground making her shiver. Wealthstone was too far behind now to offer any comfort or protection. Hatton Place was just over the next rise and who knew what she'd find there.

I should have taken Andrew with me when I left two years ago. Leaving him had been the hardest part of running away, but he couldn't have come with her. The wandering life of a gambler was an unsuitable one for a child.

As she'd stood at the altar with the Comte, she'd thought of writing to Fanny and offering to take Andrew. The brief hope the dream offered had died in the night when the truth of her new home and husband had become painfully apparent.

There'd been little then she could do except write to Andrew, lying in every letter about her new life so he wouldn't worry.

'Drat,' she cried under her breath as she stepped in a small puddle, the water seeping in through the small hole between the leather and the sole. Drawing up the hem of her sturdy walking dress, a few drops hit her calf just above the boot as she shook the mud off.

She continued on up a small rise, cursing the dampness in her shoe before the view at the top made her halt.

Hatton Place.

Sweat spread across her back and her heart raced as if she'd run up the hill instead of walked. The last time she'd seen the house was on a night like this when she'd rushed through the front gates, her worn portmanteau dragging on her arm as she'd hurried to the Red Lion Inn to meet Rafe. The future wasn't any more sparkling now than it had been two years ago, but at least then she'd had hope, Rafe's hope. What she wouldn't give to have him beside her now, his large hand in hers smothering her trembles.

The moon was higher and smaller now, the light whiter and more clear, thickening the shadows beneath the trees. The house sat square and narrow in the middle of a grove of elms, the simple front punctuated by two rows of windows and a third row of smaller ones tucked beneath the eaves. The windows were dark except for the moonlight reflecting off the panes and washing over the pitted brick walls. She didn't expect to see light in the front windows. The rooms were draughty and the furniture too shabby to make them comfortable or inviting. If anyone in the house was up and about, they were likely in the warmer sitting room around the back, closest to the kitchen.

She picked her way down the hill, slowing as she approached the front gate and the blue-limestone walk leading to the tall front door. Nothing moved in the garden except the bushes and trees, the quiet rustle of leaves punctuated by the croaking of frogs in the nearby duck pond. Watching the shadows waver and change as the trees shifted with the breeze, she remembered the last time she'd paused here, dreaming of returning some day covered in diamonds and riches. She never imagined she'd return in the middle of the night, sneaking in like some mud-splattered thief.

She followed the cold stone wall around to the back of the house and the small iron gate sagging open on its rusty hinges. She stole across the wide kitchen yard, stopping once to listen to the low clucks of sleeping chickens and the snorts of the two field horses in the sagging mews at the far end.

The answering snort of a horse from somewhere

behind her sent a shock of fear racing up her spine. She thought it came from outside the wall, but the frogs were so loud, she couldn't be sure. Whatever it was, it wasn't as nerve-racking as the sliver of light peeking out from behind the drawn curtains of the back sitting room.

She gripped her arms tightly around her, thinking she heard her father bellowing from inside, his drunken voice slurred, his vicious words making her want to melt back into the fields and never return.

Swallowing hard, she fought back the old terror. Her father was dead and buried and the most Fanny would do if she caught her was whine and rail. She had nothing to fear and she wouldn't let stale memories keep her from seeing Andrew.

Creeping cautiously closer to the house, Cornelia passed a garden box filled with neatly clipped thyme and fat onions. She snapped off a twig of thyme and held it up to her nose, her shoulders relaxing under the spell of the familiar fragrance. Thyme was Cook's favourite herb and if it grew so neatly, then she must still be here. Without even venturing inside, she knew Andrew was at least being fed.

At last she reached the kitchen door and peered

through the window. There was no one inside. Cook's handiwork was evident in the clean counters and the neatly arranged white crockery catching the faint orange of the coals in the grate. Not wanting to dirty Cook's clean kitchen, Cornelia scraped the mud from her boots on the scraper next to the step. Laying one hand on the latch, she pressed her thumb down slowly, wincing for fear the metal might squeak. To her relief, it moved easily and she pushed open the door, slipped inside and closed it behind her.

The strong scent of ashes and lemons brought quick tears to her eyes. She'd spent so many lonely days in here, lapping up Cook's kindness after her mother died. If only she could see the sweet old woman tonight, too, thank her for everything she'd done and all she surely did for Andrew, but she was already risking enough to visit him. She couldn't sneak up to the servants' quarters, too.

Fanny's high voice, muffled by the thick walls, drifted in from the room next door, bringing Cornelia back to the present. Fanny wasn't likely to wander into the kitchen during the day, much less at night. She probably didn't even know where in the house it was situated. However, Cornelia didn't want to risk being wrong and encountering the woman.

Stealing across the uneven limestone floor, Cornelia started up the narrow staircase in the corner, trailing her fingers along the smooth plaster walls as she used to as a child. She moved fast, as much to reach Andrew as to outrun the memories pulling at her.

At the top of the stairs she paused, peeking out from the shadow of the stairwell to make sure the hallway was clear. With no one about, she stepped onto the long landing, keeping herself pressed against the wall as she made her way towards Andrew's bedroom. She stopped in the centre of the landing, near a threadbare chair positioned against the dingy and chipped rail. The door next to it led to her father's old room. She'd stood here the night she'd left with Rafe, her fingernails digging into her palms as she'd listened to him rail at Fanny at how Cornelia had embarrassed him at Lord Perry's. Afterwards, she couldn't flee from the house fast enough.

Tonight, the only thing she heard was Fanny's obnoxious laughter from the back sitting room. The grating sound was answered by the deep tone of a man's voice. She couldn't make out his words, but he sounded relaxed. He'd probably been well satiated by her stupid stepmother in her quest to land herself another husband. Cornelia hoped the woman employed better judgement this time. Who knew what might happen to Andrew if the wrong man married his mother?

This thought was enough to send Cornelia hurrying down the hall. Reaching the far stairs, she climbed them as fast as she could without her boots thumping against the treads.

In the upper hall, a small peep of light from beneath the far door illuminated the unadorned plaster wall.

Andrew.

It was all she could do to keep from running at it and the little boy waiting on the other side.

Reaching his door, she tapped on the wood.

Rustling greeted her entreaty and the light went out. Cornelia pushed open the door, looking to where he lay on the bed, pretending to sleep.

'You can't fool me, I know you aren't asleep,' she whispered, closing the door behind her.

Andrew jerked up in bed, his wide eyes sparkling in the moonlight filling the room. 'Cornelia.'

She rushed to him, throwing her arms around him and burying her face in his warm neck. He was so much bigger than the last time she'd seen him, but he still seemed so small and vulnerable.

'What are you doing here?' he whispered, his arms tight around her, as desperate for her affection as she was for his. 'Mama said you were stuck in France for good.'

'I escaped'.

'Like the princesses you used to tell me about?' He smiled, revealing the gap in his front teeth.

'Something like that.' Though it hadn't been a fairytale but a nightmare and it wasn't over yet.

'I wish I could escape back to school.' He slouched against his pillows with a huff, blowing up the hair hanging over his forehead before it fell down flat against his skin.

She reached out and pushed the wisp of hair off his face. 'It won't be long now before you go back. Only a few weeks.'

'But it's so dull here. There's no one to help me steal cakes from the kitchen like we used to do. I have to be very sneaky now because Mama gets cross when she thinks I've taken one.'

Cornelia shook her head, remembering Fanny's constant complaints about the grocer's bills. Yet there'd always been enough for real beeswax candles in her room and bread made from fine flour.

The selfish woman. 'Does Fanny still eat the cakes while lounging on her *chaise* in her room?'

'No, she saves them for her friend.'

'She has a friend now?' It was difficult to imagine Fanny entertaining the other country families, but if she wanted to find another husband, she could hardly stay cooped up here.

'A gentleman mostly.'

So Andrew knew about the man downstairs. Hopefully, he didn't know too much. She wanted him to stay young and innocent for as long as possible, longer than she'd been allowed to remain.

'Who is he?' Cornelia asked, trying to keep the concern from her voice. With a man sniffing around, her stepmother wasn't likely to want a child hanging on her skirts.

'Dunno. I never see him. He only comes after dark, but Mama says he'll be able to help me some day. I hear Cook complaining about him to the maids sometimes, but she always shushes me whenever I ask about him.'

Cornelia frowned. If Fanny was making plans for Andrew, they couldn't be good, especially if they included her current paramour.

'Is Cook making sure you stay clean while you're here?' she teased, ruffling his hair.

'I don't like the way she washes behind my ears. She scrubs too hard.' He rolled his wide, blue eyes in exasperation and Cornelia saw something of herself in the expression. She wondered if she looked as silly when she rolled her eyes at Rafe.

'You let her scrub you. As the baronet, you must know how to present yourself.'

'That's what she always says.' He scowled with something more serious than worry over the wash basin, as if all the responsibilities of an adult sat on his slender shoulders. 'I don't know how I'll manage Hatton Place when I come of age.'

She tapped the end of his nose with her finger. 'Don't worry, Mr Higgins will teach you everything you need to know to be a proper gentleman.' *If Fanny didn't find some way to ruin it before you reach your maturity.*

'Cornelia. Now that you're back from France, are you going to stay here?'

She stroked his plump cheek. 'No, I only came to see you for a little while, to make sure you're all right.'

'But why? This is your home, too.'

She struggled to keep her smile. This hadn't been her home for a long time. 'Your mother wouldn't like my being here.'

'Well, I'm the baronet and I say you can stay.'

If only he was old enough to make such decisions, but he wasn't and she could imagine her stepmother laughing at the boy for daring to assert himself. 'Some day I will, I promise, but not tonight.'

'But you'll come see me at school again, won't you?'

'Of course and often. Mr Higgins won't be able to keep me away.'

'I will go back to school, won't I? You won't let Mama send me to Uncle Homer.' He bit his lower lip in worry. 'I don't want to go to the West Indies.'

'No, I won't let her send you away.' She pulled him into an embrace, clinging to him as much as he clung to her, wishing she could shield him from all this ugliness. 'Don't worry, Andrew, I won't let anything happen to you. You'll go back to school and everything will be all right. I promise. You believe me, don't you?'

'I believe you. You always keep your promises.'

She squeezed her eyes shut against the tears, determined not to cry in front of him. She would make sure he stayed with Mr Higgins and learned to be a man of integrity, even if it meant marrying a hundred old Comtes. If she could do this much for him, give him stability and the knowledge he was loved, then maybe, when he was a young buck and all the temptations of town and the clubs were thrown at him, he'd have the strength to resist them.

When the threat of tears passed, she sat back, holding his small shoulders. 'Now, you must go to bed.'

'Tell me a story like you used to.'

'All right.' She settled herself on the pillow next to him, hugging him close as she told him about France and the château. She dressed up the memories with images of fairies, dragons and a maiden saved from one hundred years of loneliness by a valiant prince. His face brightened with excitement at each mention of the dragons or the brave knight fighting them. She lowered her voice as his small blinks grew longer and longer, ending her story when his eyes remained closed. Carefully standing so as not to disturb him, she tucked the sheet beneath his chin. She dropped a kiss on his warm forehead, wishing she could bundle him in the blanket and carry him back to Wealthstone, but she couldn't. Instead, she would see to it the school was paid and he was back in the warm rectory before the cold winter set in.

Leaving her heart on the pillow with Andrew, she stole across the room, slipping out the door without a sound. She moved through the dark hallways, feeling like a scared girl again as the shadows rose up the walls to engulf her. Pausing outside the closed door to her mother's room, she laid a hand on the wood. She could almost see her mother lying in bed, the window open to let in the summer air, an old shawl tucked around her frail shoulders.

Nothing inside was the same. Fanny had seen to it, practically throwing her mother's things at her grasping maid while claiming the pewter and crystal for herself. It'd taken a great deal of effort for Cornelia to save even a few of her mother's embroidered handkerchiefs. Her father never answered her questions about the miniature of her mother. He must have sold it in some pawn shop in London, turning the precious memento into a meaningless trinket to decorate some merchant's house.

Fanny's high-pitched laugh rose up from the sitting room, pulling Cornelia back to the present. Whoever the tart had with her tonight, she was working very hard to snare him.

Cornelia hurried back down the hall, grasping

the banister as she reached the servants' staircase. Descending into the darkness, she moved slowly to keep her footsteps from echoing through the stairwell. She'd climbed these steps so many times during her mother's final illness, carrying hot soup up the stairs and then back down again, hoping something, anything, might save her.

Cornelia stepped into the kitchen, remembering the morning when she'd realised there was nothing more she could do and death would win. Leaning against the wall, the ghosts pressed in on her and she rubbed away tears of anger, hurt and frustration.

She wouldn't lose Andrew like she'd lost her mother. She couldn't.

Suddenly, the door connecting the kitchen to the dining room swung open. Fanny walked in with a bronze candelabrum. Cornelia froze as Fanny jumped back with a squeak, nearly dropping the cumbersome thing.

'What are you doing here?' she demanded, her voice shaky with surprise as she set the candelabrum down on the wood counter.

Cornelia stuck her chin in the air, drawing on everything Rafe had taught her about carrying herself. 'I came to see Andrew.'

'By sneaking in the through the back door in the middle of the night?' Fanny sneered, crossing her round arms under her very large breasts. Despite her years at Hatton Place, she'd never lost the ruddy plumpness of a farmer's daughter.

'I'd hoped to avoid an encounter with an inferior,' Cornelia said, mimicking Lady Daltmouth's haughty scrutiny.

Fanny wilted under the look before regaining her nerve. 'Aren't you the high-and-mighty one to talk, sneaking around in a muddy dress and shoes, probably rustling through the dressers for something to steal.'

'We both know there isn't anything of value left to steal here.'

'That's because your father—'

'Your husband, the man you *chose* to marry.'

'He's the one who mismanaged the estate and left me with nothing but this rotting pile of stone.' Fanny's petulant pout increased, making her blonde curls bob around her ears. 'I can't even afford Andrew's school. Where's the money you promised?'

Cornelia was amazed at how little time it took for the fool to pounce on her favourite topic. 'Mr Higgins will be paid by the end of next week. Andrew can start at Michaelmas.'

'Or you could send me the tuition and a little more for his upkeep. Clothes and food aren't free, you know.'

'Neither are beauty powders and gowns.' She eyed the length of the woman's tawdry dress in a shade of pink too deep for a woman creeping close to thirty. 'I know the school wouldn't see so much as a farthing if I sent you the money.'

'If your father had been a better man, I wouldn't have to rely on your charity. I'd have plenty of money,' she whined.

'If my father had been a better man, he might have chosen a more suitable wife than the daughter of a drunken farmer.'

Her hazel eyes widened, then narrowed with venom as she marched up to Cornelia. Cornelia didn't dare flinch or back away as she looked down at the woman, almost pitying her. She knew what it was to choose a bad husband.

'At least he loved and wanted me. That's more than you can say.'

All her sympathy for Fanny vanished. The stupid woman deserved the consequences of all her poor choices. 'Why don't you ask your gentleman caller for money? Tell me, which country squire are you trying to trap this time?'

'Whom I entertain here is none of your business.'

She was about to tell Fanny the whole county would learn of her business if she wasn't more discreet when the man's voice called out from the adjoining hallway, silencing her.

'Fanny, did you find the ham or not? I can't wait all evening.'

Lord Edgemont strode into the kitchen and jerked to a halt. He wore no jacket, his dove-grey waistcoat tailored tight to his stocky middle. Surprise rippled through his eyes before they settled into their usual serpentine cool.

'Good evening, Comtesse.' Edgemont bowed, wicked amusement sliding along the greeting.

'What are you doing here?' Cornelia seethed, hating Fanny even more.

'I'm sure you can guess.' Edgemont leaned against the door jamb, more amused than irritated at this unexpected interruption in his evening's plans.

Cornelia's stomach churned at the thought of Fanny and Edgemont intimate together. She turned on her stepmother, not bothering to conceal her disgust. 'If this is who you've invited into your bed, then you're a bigger fool than I thought.'

'Don't you dare judge me,' Fanny snapped. 'You

think I haven't heard about you and Lord Densmore? He hasn't got two pence to rub together and you've thrown yourself at him.'

'He's a better man than any you've ever chosen. And you're mistaken if you think this one will marry you when he gets you with child. He hasn't enough of his own honour to save yours.'

'I think we've had enough cat fighting for one evening, ladies.' Edgemont approached them, his cultivated veneer of calm curling at the edges as the muscles of his jaw twitched. 'I'm sure the Comtesse has no desire to linger here any longer than we wish to detain her.'

'Please. The sooner she's gone the better,' Fanny spat, all but sticking her tongue out at Cornelia.

'Yes, I don't usually keep company with rats.' Cornelia turned on one heel and made for the door, her head held high. She might be poor, but she was better than these two.

Edgemont slithered past her, reaching the door first, his bulk blocking the way. 'Careful how you address me, Comtesse.'

'Or what?' she challenged.

Edgemont stared at her as he had at Rafe when he'd threatened to call him out. She waited for his clever response, for him to throw the theft of the register in her face and remind her of his superior hand. Instead he dropped his voice and continued in his warning vein. 'I don't know what game you're playing, but I want the register and you will deliver it to me immediately.'

He doesn't have it. It took the most severe control to keep the surprise from crossing her face. He didn't know it was missing. It was her trump card, the one trick she could still hold over him.

She met his menacing glare with condescension, refusing to let him get the better of her. 'I don't carry it with me on midnight country excursions, nor am I about to give something so valuable and damning to a man like you.'

He moved nearer and she opened and closed her hand, wishing she carried a knife in her boot like Rafe. If he pounced, she couldn't reach the rolling pin on the counter behind her and she doubted Fanny would come to her aid.

His lips curled over his crooked teeth and he tapped the edge of the counter with one thick finger.

'It seems we've reached an impasse.' He slid a glance over his shoulder at Fanny, who shifted on her feet trying to hear what they said. 'So, let me suggest another course. Give me the pages with my father's name and I'll consider our agreement fulfilled.'

'Or I keep the pages and the whole register, and you find some other woman besides Fanny to dally with.'

'Oh, you won't be rid of me so easily.' He shifted closer, his face nearly level to hers. 'Look here, if you don't give me the pages, I'll make sure your little brother is on the next ship to the West Indies. I'll personally pay for his passage.'

She'd call his bluff, careful not to reveal her own. 'Threaten him and I'll take the register directly to Lord Twickenham.'

'Not even Lord Twickenham in all his patriotic fervour can move the wheels of government fast enough to seize my lands before the little Baronet is packed off to the islands.' His lips pulled back into an ugly sneer. 'Ruin me and I'll spend every last farthing I have making sure your dear brother suffers.'

The flames bounced with a draught, making the shadows from the ceiling beams waver across the adjoining plaster. High above this room, Andrew slept peacefully in his bed, unaware of the danger hovering so close to him.

Cornelia took a deep breath and shoved down

the panic, refusing to let Edgemont see how his threat frightened her. 'Only you would stoop low enough to threaten a child.'

'I told you I'd find your weakness.' The dancing shadows shifted beneath his eyes and along the corner of his crooked smile. 'Now, will I have the pages by Thursday, or must I return to London tonight and enquire about the next available passage to Barbados?'

She looked down her nose at him despite wanting to double over in frantic worry. She could make a hundred threats, but without the register she couldn't make good on any of them. Edgemont could and he would if he somehow discovered she no longer held the book. All she could do was stall him and hope it gave her and Rafe enough time to find the register.

She settled her shoulders, addressing him as if he were a thief and not the man who held her brother's future in his filthy hands. 'You'll get the pages at my leisure, when I return to London next week.'

'Then I look forward to meeting you in town.' He reached past her to lift the latch and push open the door.

She swept out of the kitchen, holding her head high until the door swung shut and the night swallowed up the faint light from the kitchen. Then she ran, the darkness enveloping her like the fear tearing at her insides. She pulled open the gate, not caring who heard the screeching metal. Outside the garden, she fell against the wall, the stone disintegrating beneath her fingers as she clutched it.

Edgemont didn't have the book and neither did she and now Andrew was in more danger than before. In the distance, an owl hooted. She looked up at the moon nearing its zenith. She had to get back to Wealthstone and tell Rafe. He'd know how to find the register before all was lost.

Hopelessness gripped her and she slid to the ground, leaning her cheek against the cold stone. If Edgemont didn't have it, then who did? There were hundreds of names scrawled on the pages. Any one of those people or their relatives could be the thief.

The rustle of leaves in the undergrowth made her jump to her feet and she watched the dark bushes, waiting to see what emerged. Leaning down, she picked up a rock. If Edgemont had followed her, he'd get a bruised head for his efforts.

The bushes shifted and she raised the rock, ready to strike, when Rafe stepped into the moonlight. 'Are you all right?'

'Rafe.' The stone dropped from her hand as he rushed to her, wrapping her in his arms. She clung to him, Paris and all the tension between them meaningless beneath the weight of her worry and his firm embrace. 'He doesn't have it. Edgemont doesn't have the book. He still thinks I have it.'

Rafe listened as the entire story came tumbling out. He stroked her back as she spoke, but his chest beneath her cheek tightened, anger making each breath more shallow than the last. When he'd walked into her bedroom and seen it empty, Paris was his first thought before his rational mind pointed him towards Hatton Place. He never imagined finding her clinging to a wall in the darkness, terrified to tears by Edgemont. It was too much like the night he'd held her after Lord Waltenham's attack.

'I'll kill him for threatening you and your brother,' he growled when she finished. 'The bastard.'

He started for the gate, ready to storm inside and pound the sneer from Edgemont's face the way he'd wanted to for so many years.

She held tight to his arm, pulling him back against the wall. 'No, if you threaten him he'll hurt Andrew.'

'Not if I kill him first.' He reached for his knife, but she grabbed his hand.

'They'll hang you if you do, then where will I be? What'll happen to Andrew?'

His muscles softened and he straightened, drawing her to him. 'You're right. We'll get the register back, then we'll destroy him.'

She laid her cheek on his chest, her fingers clutching his lapel. He slid his fingers beneath hers and they released the wool to curl over his. He could feel the trust in her grip, asking, begging for him to help her brother the way she'd begged him to help them flee France. Only this time she wouldn't run off the moment he left. She'd stand by him and he'd prove his trustworthiness.

'You shouldn't have gone alone,' he gently chastised. 'If you'd asked, I'd have come with you and we could have both faced him.'

'I wish I'd brought you with me, but I didn't think it would be like this. I didn't know Edgemont was her lover until tonight.' She looked up at him, fear shimmering in her eyes. 'What are we going to do?'

He brushed the loose strands of hair out of her face, 'We're going to find the register. Just like we planned.'

'How?'

'I know a less-than-reputable gentleman with a thorough knowledge of housebreakers. He might be able to point me in the direction of our thief.'

'And if not?'

'We'll think of something else. Now, let's get home and get some rest.' He slid his arms from around her and led her into the small thicket of trees. 'We'll need it to face the coach ride back to London in the morning.'

'Where are we going?'

'My horse is over there.' Up ahead, beyond the duck pond, the soft whinny of a horse mingled with the steady croak of the frogs.

'You rode here?' She gaped at the stocky beast tethered to a sapling and standing as still as a well-trained footman.

'It was the fastest way.'

She approached the horse with hesitation. 'I'm not much of a horsewoman.'

'Good, because Captain isn't much of a horse.' The animal seemed to understand the remark and tossed his head. Rafe patted the horse's large neck. 'Steady now, you're the best plough puller in Sussex and I wouldn't trade you for all the thoroughbreds in London.'

The horse returned to its patient stance as Rafe pulled himself into the worn saddle. He leaned down and reached for her hand. She gave it and slipped her foot in the stirrup as he hoisted her in front of him, settling her across his thighs. She wrapped one arm around his neck and slid the other around his waist, pressing in against his chest.

He clicked twice and the horse set off at a slow amble.

She started at the motion, clutching his jacket tight.

'Don't worry, I won't let you fall,' Rafe soothed.

'I know,' she murmured.

Her grip eased, but not the weight of her buttocks against his member, her body rocking with each step of the horse. Rafe gritted his teeth against the hardening need. There was nothing else he could do about it. He wasn't going to hurry Captain and break his leg. Wealthstone was in enough trouble without losing its plough horse.

If Cornelia noticed her effect on him, she didn't reveal it, snuggling as close to him as she could. When Captain started down a hill, Rafe drew her tighter to him, leaning back a touch to ease the horse's burden. As the path levelled out at the bottom, Rafe let the reins drop slack in his hands. Captain knew the way and Rafe trusted him to get them home as much as Cornelia trusted Rafe to not let her fall.

It wasn't long before the steady rhythm of her breathing matched Captain's even pace and she relaxed in his arms, fast asleep.

He studied the top of her head, her dark hair shining in the bright moonlight. He'd be lying if he said he didn't want this peace with her every night. Dropping a small kiss on her forehead, he inhaled the faint traces of lemon, the scent as sharp as the nasty way Fate kept tempting him with what he couldn't have.

She might lean against him with all the confidence of a lover, but there was still too much distance between them, too many obstacles to happiness. He didn't even have the blunt to buy her a wedding ring. His mother might have found contentment living a simple life, claiming the industry of sewing and gardening gave her more purpose than any London ballroom, but Cornelia wouldn't. The constant grind and worries of poverty would wear her down, kill her spirit in a way all her father's neglect hadn't. He couldn't do that to her. The most he could do was help her and hope they came out on the other side of this debacle with even a small amount of the friendship they'd once known. It was the only hope he had to keep her in his life without dragging her down with him.

He balled his hand and banged it against his hip, the pain unequal to the one tearing at his insides. There was no point keeping her close to him and torturing himself with the constant reminder of everything he couldn't have. If it was in his power to give her and Andrew a home and safety, he would, but he couldn't, not with the likes of Mr Smith skulking around and the creditors hovering over Wealthstone like buzzards. He couldn't remove Andrew from the dangers of the West Indies only to drop him in the disease-infested street of St Giles.

Cornelia mumbled something in her sleep and Rafe hugged her closer, easing her back into her rest. He envied Andrew and her devotion to him. He'd enjoyed such devotion once, before the Comte stole it.

If the man wasn't already dead, he'd call him out for what he'd done and blow the wig from his head.

In the distance, the back of Wealthstone came into view, the house and grounds dark except for the moonlight glinting off the walls and the faint glow of a lantern in the stable yard. As Captain approached the mews, the stable boy rose from his resting place in a pile of hay, wiping the sleep from his eyes as he took Captain's reins.

In Rafe's arms, Cornelia continued to sleep, her face soft and peaceful, her long eyelashes dark against her pale cheeks. He hated to wake her and reluctantly stroked one cheek, then the other until her eyes fluttered open. 'We're here.'

'Already?' She straightened in his arms, blinking the sleep from her eyes.

'We are and you didn't fall once.'

'I'm sure it was thanks to your skill, not mine.' She stretched as best she could in the space of his body, her shifting buttocks making his member stir again.

He lifted her off his lap, helping her to slide down onto the mounting block before she could detect the effect she had on him.

He threw his leg over the saddle and dropped to the ground, handing the reins to the stable boy who yawned and scratched as he led Captain away.

'With a few lessons you could become quite a horsewoman.' He plucked the lantern from its hook, carrying it between them as they crossed the yard.

'I don't possess your confidence around horses.'

He pushed open the unlocked back door and led her inside. The lantern cast a wavering pool of light around them as they made their way across the empty dining room to the entrance hall and up the stairs.

'With a little practice you might gain confidence.'

'You've taught me a great many things, Rafe, but riding a horse will not be one of them.'

He led her down the hallway, holding the light high to push back the darkness. She followed at his side, her arm brushing his as they walked. It would be easy to slide his hand into hers, maintain some of the connection they'd experienced during the ride home, but he didn't. She eyed him as she had Captain, wary and unsure, and he didn't want to give her a reason to bolt.

Rafe peered down the hall to where the doorknobs of their rooms glinted. He didn't want to reach the doors or bid her goodnight. Despite all the new troubles her nocturnal excursion had uncovered, there was peace between them now, a comfort he hadn't known in a long time. He didn't want it to end or to think of the uncertain future.

'What will happen between us once we have

the register?' she asked, as if determined to make him face it.

He set the lantern on a chipped table between his door and hers. 'Perhaps we can be partners again, like in Paris, and take the tables by storm.'

'Always the optimist.' She tilted her head back to study him, her eyes sparkling in the low light before her amusement dimmed. 'But you know we can't. Two gamblers can't bet on one another.'

'No, but they can still play together.' He slid his arms around her waist, drawing her into the curve of his body. They fitted together perfectly, like a matched pair of dice, her supple chest against his, her mouth achingly close.

She drew in a sharp breath, whether out of surprise or to calm herself he wasn't sure and he didn't care. She was in his arms and not pushing him away. He wasn't going to let go.

His lips enveloped hers and she answered the need in his kiss, opening her mouth and accepting his tongue to caress it with her own. He drank in the taste of her and the heat of her body pressed to his, the desire in her embrace pushing back the cold isolation he'd felt ever since she'd left his life.

He dropped a line of kisses along her cheek, following it to the soft curve of her ear. Taking one lobe in his mouth, he tasted the tender flesh and she sighed as his teeth grazed the skin. The soft sound stroked his desire and offered the faint chance they might crush the obstacles standing between them, and his touch might make her forget whatever ugliness she'd suffered under the Comte.

Then she pulled away, her palms flat and firm against his chest. 'No, Rafe, we can't.'

'Why not?' He pulled her tighter against him, refusing to let her doubt reopen the chasm between them. 'Who else will have us but the de Vanes and Daltmouths of the world? Why should we surrender to them?'

'Why should we surrender to each other when we have even less than they do?'

He laid a silencing finger on her lips, caressing the tempting arch of them. 'Because even we deserve to be happy, even if it's just for one night.'

It was all Cornelia needed to hear to surrender.

The earthy smell of horse and leather graced his skin as she twined her fingers in the hair above his collar. Sweet bliss lay in the sweep of his hand across her cheek and the hard pressure of his lips against hers. Whatever sunrise brought, Cornelia would confront it, but for tonight, she was free.

She leaned deeper into his chest, the taste of him bringing back the thrill of their first days in London and all their time together afterwards. It'd been too long since then, the nights too lonely and desolate without him. She wanted to know again the excitement of his body above hers, the heady intoxication of his fingers reawakening all the secret places deep inside her.

She stroked the width of his shoulders, drawing her hands together at his cravat before working the knot free. She pushed the separated strands of linen aside and tugged opened the strings of his shirt, revealing the coarse dark hair and white skin beneath. Laying a firm kiss on the hollow between his neck and chest, she tasted him like a savoury dish she'd been too long denied.

With a groan, he pressed her back and began to remove her hairpins one by one. They plunked against the wood floor as he dropped them, sending lock after lock cascading down over her back and shoulders. Leaning forward, he buried his face in the mass of curls bouncing at her neck as he nipped the skin, making it tighten with shivers.

As his tongue swept small circles over her neck, she tugged his shirt from his breeches and slid her hands beneath it to stroke the long expanse of his stomach. His muscles rippled as she caressed him, his low groan vibrating through her ear as her thumbs circled his nipples.

He backed away, catching her hands and bringing the palms to his lips. He licked the small creases, his tongue hot as it followed each line, the sensation sliding through her and stoking the warmth building deep beneath her stomach.

Anticipation made her heady as he drew her to his room. At the door, a single question hovered in his smouldering brown eyes.

Are you sure?

'Yes,' she whispered, wanting him as powerfully tonight as the first night they'd come together in London. Back then she'd known nothing about the sensations melting her insides, but she knew what to expect tonight and how beautiful and safe Rafe would make her feel.

He pressed his thumb against her hand as he led her into his room and closed the door. The moonlight falling through the window turned the room silver and made the white sheets on the bed shine. There was no need for the lantern. With Rafe beside her, she didn't fear the shadows.

When the lock clicked shut she rushed into his arms, not wanting even the cool air to separate them. Too much had already kept them apart, plunging her into a solitude only his warmth and caring could drive away.

He caught her in his arms, his frantic kisses matching hers, primal and urgent, pulling her deeper into the fury of their need. In the rustle of wool and cotton, the tugging of laces and sliding of buttons, they tore at each other's clothes, discarding layer after layer until their damp bodies pressed together, his shaft hard against her stomach. He gripped her buttocks, pressing her against him, his chest firm beneath her soft breasts, both rising in unison with the rhythm of their heavy breaths.

With his length so deliciously close, she slid one foot over his, wanting to wrap her legs around his hips and join with him, to fill the emptiness of her body and her heart. She resisted the desire urging her on as she opened her mouth to take in his probing tongue. The taste of him was as potent as wine and she wanted to get drunk on it, to forget herself and everything in the deliciousness of his caresses.

His wide hand slid up the curve of her waist to cup one heavy breast and her nipple pebbled as his thumb stroked the sensitive flesh. He lowered himself to take one tender point between his teeth. His tongue flicked it, making her moan and she gripped his waist, clinging to him in the rising storm of her pleasure.

He laid his hands on either side of her hips, his fingertips firm against her skin as he knelt, his tongue circling lower and lower until it found the silken hair between her thighs.

She trembled as he tasted and sucked, the wanting ache spreading out from her centre and sweeping through her body with each teasing stroke. So many nights at Château de Vane she'd dreamed of this, her memories the only defence against despair.

'Rafe,' she gasped, her fingers digging into his shoulders as she steadied herself against the waves of pleasure threatening to break through her. She never thought she'd know the delight of his touch or the comfort of being this close to him again.

He rose and she laid her hands on either side of his neck, feeling the fast tempo of his pulse. He was with her now, young, sturdy, alive, standing over her with the strength of a ship steady in a harbour. Only he didn't wait, but sailed towards her, sliding his arms behind her knees and back as he lifted her from her weak legs and carried her to the bed. He laid her down and she relaxed against the cool sheets as he stretched out beside her.

'You're so beautiful,' he whispered, covering her body with his, the weight of him delicious and tempting.

He settled between her legs, his member hot against the inside of her thigh. Her back arched as he probed her folds, anticipation driving her beyond all sense until one sobering thought made her body stiffen.

She moved out from beneath him, laying a staying hand on his chest. 'I don't have my sponge.'

He took her hand, dropping a tender kiss on each fingertip. 'Trust me, I won't let you fall pregnant.'

She slid her hand from his grip, twining her fingers in his mahogany hair and drawing him to her. His warm lips smothered hers, his body sliding forward to join with her, accepting her invitation as she accepted his promise.

'I've waited so long for this,' he whispered as his thickness filled her, claiming her as she claimed him.

She closed her eyes and wrapped her legs around his waist, losing herself in his embrace until there was nothing but the tang of his sweat and the solid pressure of his skin against hers. Her hips rose and fell with his, following the pace of his strokes, surrendering to his lead just as she had the first time, every time. She kissed him with the same desperation she'd once used to search every face at the port in Calais, hoping she might find him in the crush. Tonight, he'd found her and he was hers again. Not even the shadows creeping around the bed could drive him away.

She opened her eyes to meet his, his steady breath marking the pace of each stroke and the even thrusts pushing her closer and closer to the edge of pleasure. She raced with him towards the cliff until she tumbled over it, clutching his back as she fell into bright waves of release.

He groaned as he pulled away, struggling against the pressure of her legs to withdraw and spill his seed beside her, keeping his promise to leave her without child.

They lay, bodies entwined for a long time, Rafe's rough cheek pressed to hers. When he finally slid to one side, Cornelia snuggled close to him, delighting in the sweep of his hand down the curve of her back. So many nights they'd lain like this, spent with the exertion of a night at the tables and more pleasurable dealings in their rooms. Sometimes they'd sleep afterwards. Other times they'd talk, making plans for the next night or dreaming of a future away from the cards. When he'd speak of winning the hand that might save them, she used to picture herself taking the Densmore name and finally leaving everything about her past behind.

It hadn't seemed like such a hopeless fantasy back then.

Reaching down, she pulled the sheet up over her, the room cooling with the fading ripples of her pleasure. Resting her head against his chest, she felt it rise and fall in a sigh, as if the same reality were settling over him, too, driving away the euphoria of their coming together.

'I'm sorry we can't dally here longer,' he whispered, stroking her hair. 'But the sooner we return to London, the sooner we can settle this and put it behind us.'

She raised her head to him. The moonlight softened the angles of his face, but couldn't hide the hardness of his jaw and the strain she used to catch in him after a long losing streak.

'And once this business is behind us?' She cringed, hating the neediness in her voice. She'd never pressed him about their future before. She'd been too afraid the question might drive him away. Tonight she had to know. He might hold her like there was no tomorrow, but the sunrise would come, forcing them both to look at each other and their situation in the fullness of reality.

'The morning will be here soon enough.' He cupped her face in his hands and drew her lips towards his. 'Tonight, let's leave the future to the future.'

Chapter Eleven

The heady spice of roasted beans mingling with the thick smoke of pipes struck Rafe as he entered the coffee house. They'd reached London in the late afternoon and he'd seen Cornelia back to Mrs Linton's before setting out for Seven Dials. Cornelia had wanted to accompany him, but he'd refused to risk her safety in such a disreputable section of town. This coffee house wasn't a polite place and the men didn't meet here to discuss stocks. Their business dealings were of a more nefarious nature.

He looked over the filthy heads of the patrons for Rodger, spying the man at the far end of the room, his blond head bent over a deck of cards. With any luck, the sharper might know where they could begin their search for the register thief. He and Cornelia had already wasted enough effort and blunt chasing Edgemont. With the Baron's threat hanging over Andrew, they didn't have time to chase down a dozen different dead ends.

Striding down the long line of crowded trestle tables, he held his left arm at an angle. The hard ivory knife handle pressed against his forearm, hidden beneath the wool of his sleeve. All he need do was lower his arm and the weapon would drop into his palm, ready to deter a man from picking his pocket or slitting his throat. He didn't expect trouble, but there was no reason not to be cautious.

Rafe stopped to let a thin woman carrying tankards bigger than her breasts pass before he reached the end of the furthest table and stopped.

'Back from the country already?' Rodger greeted him, laying down another card in his game of Patience.

'Events have changed unexpectedly since we last spoke.'

He slid a card off the top of the deck, waving Rafe into the chair across from him with the jack of spades. 'Don't they always?'

'Which is why I'm here.' Rafe took a seat, refusing the offer of wine from Rodger's half-empty bottle. 'Do you still maintain your connections with the thief takers?'

Rodger shrugged. 'I've been known to converse

with them from time to time. In fact, if Lord Rollingham is looking to recover his silver soup tureen, I might know where he can find it.'

'That's good to know.' Rafe rested his elbows on the table, glancing around to see if anyone was listening. In a place like this, everyone kept to their own business, but Rafe didn't want to put Rodger or himself in jeopardy. 'In your conversations, have you heard anything about a man of quality or someone connected with the better sort who's gentleman enough to move through Mayfair without notice, but thief enough to pry open a window for members of society who don't wish to sully their hands?'

'The quality hardly needs someone to steal for them. Not when the law lets them take from others without impediment.' Rodger dealt himself three cards, swiftly shifting the bottom one to the top with such a subtle move it was almost imperceptible, except to Rafe, who knew to look for it.

'I'm not talking about the usual tyranny, but housebreaking to steal something very specific.' The register named nothing but lords, it was only reasonable to suppose someone with a title might have stolen it. It was Rafe's best and only lead.

Rodger surveyed the cards on the table, then

frowned, dealing himself three more. 'Something of yours gone missing?'

'You could say that.'

'What?'

'I can't tell you.' He wasn't about to have another person knowing about the register, especially one with Rodger's shady connections. 'But I need to get it back.'

'And you think I might know the man who took it?'

'I think you might know of him and his employer and that's all I need.'

'There is one man who fits your description.' Rodger took up his wine and enjoyed a long drink, savouring the swill before lowering his cup. 'But I'm having the hardest time recalling his employer.'

Rafe removed a coin from his pocket and laid it down on top of the ace of spades. 'Will this help you recall the man?'

'Indeed it does.' Rodger pinched the coin with a well-manicured thumb and finger and dropped it in his pocket. 'Name's Mr Green. He's tall, nearly as tall as you, but not quite. Did a bit of housebreaking in his youth, was part of old Hagen's gang before the codger swung. Now he's a footman.'

Rafe leaned forward. 'Who does he work for?'

Rodger smiled. 'Who in town employs the tallest footmen?'

'Daltmouth.' Rafe leaned back in his chair, tapping his toe against the scuffed floorboards. If the Earl had the book, then there'd be no blackmail money to pay for Andrew's school. Things were growing more complicated with each new discovery.

'Rumour has it the footman polishes more than Lady Daltmouth's silver.' Rodger took up his deck again and dealt another three cards. 'But it is, after all, only a rumour.'

'And I'm indebted to you for passing it on.' Rafe rose, trying not to imagine the regal Lady Daltmouth in such a compromising position with her servant. 'I'll be sure to tell Lord Rollingham where to find you so you can get the reward for recovering his tureen.'

Rodger raised the king of diamonds to him. 'Thank you, my good man.'

Outside, the aroma of manure and the Thames made the coffee beans and smoke a distant memory. Rafe paused, his hands on his hips as he pondered this change in circumstance. So, it seemed the Earl was more resourceful than Rafe first thought and willing to resort to thievery to avoid paying blackmail.

What else might he be willing to do to keep his family secrets secret?

If only they'd learned he was the thief before the card party, when they'd had easy access to the Daltmouths' house. It wouldn't have been difficult for Cornelia to distract the Earl while Rafe searched for the register. It goaded him to know they'd missed the opportunity, sat so close to the prize while the piggy Lord Daltmouth outfoxed them. For someone resting on such a trump, he'd displayed remarkable cool while playing Rafe. He didn't think the man capable of such a bluff.

Whatever his skills, at least now they knew where to look. All they needed was another opportunity.

Rafe started down the street in the direction of Drury Lane, eager to be out of this neighbourhood before the last of the sunlight faded. He was brave, but he wasn't foolish enough to wander around this part of London after dark and hope to make it out alive. However, the dangers of Seven Dials were almost preferable to returning to Mrs Linton's and telling Cornelia the Earl was their thief. There was no way to deliver the news without it sounding like an accusation or dashing her plans to pay for Andrew's school before Fanny made good on her threat.

Rafe turned a corner, approaching one of the many public houses littering the street. The lamps hanging over the front door were just beginning to cast a faint glow over the darkening pavement as the entry door opened. Out spilled a cacophony of deep laughter and gruff voices along with Mr Smith and his two henchmen.

Rafe froze. If the roach was the worse for gin, he might stagger off without noticing him.

His luck didn't hold.

Mr Smith whirled on one heel, his narrow jaw dropping open before he pulled it closed.

'Welcome back to London, *Lord Densmore,*' Mr Smith tilted forward in a mocking bow, the stench of garlic and beer clinging to every slurred word. He staggered a touch as he straightened himself, then cocked one thumb at the wide-shouldered man next to him. 'John here saw ya at the Bell catching the early morning coach to the country. Made me think you'd left town to avoid me.'

Rafe lowered his arm and the knife handle dropped into his palm. In Rafe's experience, drink only made a man like Mr Smith more deadly. 'I wasn't exactly searching you out.'

'Ya aren't paying me back either,' the scum spat.

'Patience, my good man, and all will be resolved.' Rafe brandished the knife, waiting to see if the two bulldogs were any more courageous after a few tankards of ale. They weren't and they fell back, not abandoning their employer, but not protecting him either.

Not waiting for his men to act, Mr Smith pulled a pistol from his worn coat and levelled it at Rafe. 'I've been patient enough. Now I'm going to get what ya owe me one way or another.'

'Not tonight, my good man.' Rafe kicked him in the chest, sending him flying back into his companions.

Rafe took off in the opposite direction, followed by Mr Smith's curses. It wasn't long before the echoes of running boots replaced the shouts.

'When I catch ya, I'll kill ya, Densmore,' Mr Smith shouted as Rafe darted left down another street. 'Your title can't stop a lead ball.'

The endless rows of crowded and crumbling buildings blocked out the fading sunlight and every tall landmark Rafe needed to guide him back to Drury Lane. He paused at a cross street, looking frantically down one dirty length and then another. He knew the main roads leading home, but not the narrow warrens of Seven Dials branching off into the dusk.

'John, go that way, Peter, ya go the other. I'll take the main alley. He can't have gone far,' Mr Smith yelled to his men from somewhere behind Rafe.

Rafe headed left, running faster as the steady thud of Mr Smith's feet echoed off the stone.

'Ya can't get away from me, Densmore,' Mr Smith shouted, his footsteps following Rafe around each turn and twist. Mr Smith had the advantage in this warren.

Rafe ran down one side street and then another before stopping hard in front of a brick wall. He staggered back, his chest burning as he looked for a door, a window, anything he might crawl through to escape the dead end. There was nothing.

'Hell.' He slammed his fist against the brick, scraping the side of his hand before the slap of slowing footsteps made him turn.

'Well, well, well, where ya gonna go now?' Mr Smith blocked the entryway, a smile of wicked satisfaction splitting his face and revealing his rotted teeth. 'Ya thought you'd beat me, but I'll show ya who's beat now.'

He levelled the pistol at Rafe, the barrel as dirty as the roach's coat.

Rafe braced himself, hoping the moneylender's aim was as bad as his clothes. It was his only chance to get out of this alley alive.

A faint shadow moved behind Mr Smith, but Rafe didn't look away, too focused on the rat in front of him. He flexed his fingers on the knife handle, his father's knife. This must have been how he'd met his end, his mind in a fury for a plan that wouldn't come, regret sitting hard in every past choice leading to this moment.

It would crush his mother when news reached her. It'd shatter Cornelia.

Then the pistol dropped from Mr Smith's hand and the moneylender let out a howl. He grabbed the back of his head and whirled around, his fingers growing dark with blood.

At the entrance to the alley, holding a large stone, stood the street urchin from the boxing match. Another stone lay on the ground next to the pistol.

'Why, you little wretch.' Mr Smith staggered towards the boy.

'This way.' The ragamuffin waved for Rafe to follow him.

Rafe shoved Mr Smith aside and the moneylender slammed into the wall in a clamour of curses.

Rafe snatched the pistol from the dirt and followed the boy out of the alley, his long legs helping him keep pace with the urchin's quick sprint. They veered down an adjoining lane, jumping over the body of a drunk sprawled in the mud before the boy led him into the courtyard from the boxing match and through the narrow door of the building at the far end. Rafe took the creaking stairs two at a time, close behind the boy, nearly running into him when he paused to throw open a door.

'Mother, blow out the light,' the boy called to the woman inside.

She leaned across the table, puffing out the rushes in the centre. In the brief flicker of light before she extinguished it, Rafe caught the straight dark hair falling forward over her pale cheeks.

'Come on, boys, Densmore can't have got too far in this maze,' Mr Smith's voice sounded from somewhere outside.

Rafe moved to the window to look down on the empty courtyard. Behind him he heard the swish of skirts as the woman came to stand across from him, laying her arms protectively over her son's chest as he stood in front of her. Rafe saw himself in the boy, his mother standing behind him in the same position as they'd listened to the vicar deliver the terrible news of his father's murder.

'Thank you,' Rafe whispered. 'I don't deserve your help.'

'You let Paul go when all your friends would have seen him swing.' She spoke too well for the gutter and the nagging feeling he knew her came over him again. 'I don't forget such kindness.'

'I have some experience with struggling.' Though his poverty was nothing compared to theirs.

'Yes, I know about you, Lord Densmore.'

'And I remember you, Miss Allen.' And he remembered the stories. Her father dying and leaving her penniless, her taking up with a barrister, then bearing him a son he refused to acknowledge before he cast her aside.

Shame filled her eyes and she looked down into the courtyard as Mr Smith's boots thumped over the pavement as he and his men met up.

'Where could they have gone?' Mr Smith cursed, holding a dark rag against the back of his head.

The two men mumbled their excuses and apologies as they all inspected the alleys leading out of the courtyard.

'It doesn't matter. They can't have gone far in

this maze. John, you go that way, Peter, the other. I'll take the one in the centre.'

The men set off in their different directions, the scuffle of their shoes fading into the darkness.

Despite the empty courtyard, Rafe didn't leave the window. He'd lost Mr Smith, but it wouldn't be long before the moneylender found him again. For whatever reason, the roach was growing desperate. His other, less accessible clients must have holed themselves up behind the iron gates of their manors. By wandering into this part of London, Rafe made himself easy pickings and all in search of the damning register.

Rafe shoved the pistol in the inner pocket of his coat, the weight dragging it down. Curse his father, the scoundrel got off easy dying. It was everyone else who'd been left to suffer. They wouldn't, not any more. Rafe would make sure of it.

'I should go.' Rafe's voice echoed off the bare walls and floors. 'Thank you again for your help.'

'Are you sure there isn't more I can do for you?' The question left her lips as a whisper as she shifted her son to one side.

Rafe could imagine the levels this poor woman sank to each day to survive. If his own mother hadn't possessed a will of steel and a resourcefulness to impress even the most hardened street urchin, she might have fallen to the same sad lows. It would be Cornelia's fate if he was careless enough to get her with child and then get himself killed.

He stepped close to the woman and took one of her thin hands. Paul's anger from beside her radiated in the darkness and Rafe sympathised with him. He knew what it was to be too young and helpless to help his own mother. 'Your kindness is all I require tonight or any night.'

Rafe reached in this pocket for a coin and pressed it into her palm, wishing he could do more. He could send her and the boy to his mother, but she could barely feed herself or the few servants too old or loyal to leave Wealthstone. Rafe let go of Miss Allen's hand, anger burning up his back at his father for placing him and his mother in this position.

'Thank you, my lord.' She opened her palm to look at the coin and her eyes widened. In the faint moonlight making its way in the window, Rafe could see the promise of food in the sad look. 'Paul will lead you back to where you need to be.'

'No, just tell me how to get to Drury Lane from here and I'll find it. I don't want to risk him running into Mr Smith.'

Her lips lilted up into a wry smile. 'Mr Smith knows better than to linger in these streets too long after dark.'

'Afraid someone will cancel their debt?'

'Many are waiting for the day.'

She told him how to find his way out of the rookery and back to Drury Lane as she escorted him to the door.

Rafe paused on the threshold and levelled one finger at the boy. 'Take good care of your mother, and if you ever hear of my success or good fortune, I want you to be the first to find me, do you understand?'

'Yes, Lord Densmore,' the boy said, wrapping his arms around his mother's waist.

Rafe slipped out of the small room and back down the rickety stairs. At the door, he peered out into the courtyard, but saw nothing except the shadow of a rat hugging the far wall. Sprinting across the open, Rafe hurried into the nearest alley, slowing as the damp bricks closed in around him and scratched at his shoulders. There was little room to manoeuvre in the narrow space and Rafe trained the pistol on the darkness ahead of him. If he stumbled upon Mr Smith and his men, the pistol would give him the advantage.

Advantage, Rafe snorted. He'd never enjoyed an advantage. Bitterness rubbed harder than the bricks against his coat. He'd never enjoyed anything but bad luck alleviated by a few moments of good.

The image of Cornelia in her yellow dress at Madame Boucher's wavered in the darkness ahead of him. Their two years together were some of the best of his life. With her by his side, everything seemed less dirty and sordid. Her laughter and wit made even the dullest card room shine brighter. It wasn't just luck he enjoyed with her on his arm, but a pride he hadn't experienced since the last time he'd accompanied his parents to court. Unlike anyone else who'd ever flitted into his life, with her he could be himself, not the Baron one crisis away from becoming a sharper.

In the garden yesterday, the intimacy he once took for granted had returned. In the twilight, they'd been honest and vulnerable with each other, just as in France.

I should have gone after her in Paris.

He'd gone after her last night and for a few hours they'd recaptured even more of what they'd lost.

Then Mr Smith killed it in the alley, just as if he had blown open Rafe's guts.

Rafe's boot came down on a rat's tail and the animal screeched. He stumbled, then righted himself, pushing forward into the darkness as the rodent scurried away.

His life was dirty and sordid. Cornelia could hang on his arm until the end of her days and all they'd have to show for it would be debts, broken-down furniture and death. In the end, she'd hate him for ruining her life as much as he hated his father for ruining his.

Rafe cursed as his shoulder hit the crumbling brick at a place where the alley narrowed before making a sharp turn. Around the bend, one building ended, leaving a small gap between it and the next. Rafe stopped and looked up at the few stars shining in the sliver of visible sky.

This was what his father must have seen at the end.

A chill whispered across the exposed skin above his collar.

He'd come too close to sharing the same view.

He rubbed his hand over the back of his neck, trying to drive away the cold perched there. He'd nearly lost his life over the few hundred pounds he'd borrowed to keep Wealthstone's creditors at bay. If Mr Smith had pulled the trigger, it would

have been a parson and not some old woman visiting Cornelia tonight, breaking Rafe's promise to
return. He'd watched his mother suffer through
such a travesty once. He couldn't lay another devastating tragedy on her shoulders, or Cornelia's.

He kicked a discarded bottle and it shattered
against the wall, his boots crushing the shards as
he hurried around the next turn.

Ahead, the front of a tavern took shape, the rau-
cous singing inside rattling its dirty windows. He
hustled towards it, the voices and lights increasing
as the alley opened onto the street. The stench of
rotting vegetables permeated the air and he took
a deep breath, glad to be free of the narrow crush
of buildings. Brushing the brick dust from his
coat, he eyed the people around him. Mr Smith's
lanky frame didn't stand out among the riff-raff.
Rafe pocketed the pistol, keeping his hand on the
warm wood handle. Moneylenders weren't his only
worry here. Until he reached Mrs Linton's, he was
a target for all the pickpockets huddled in the doorways looking for an easy mark.

Rafe strode down the pavement, meeting square
on any man who eyed him as prey. It was enough
to keep the ruffians at bay until the torches on the
theatres in Drury Lane came into view and the

streets around him grew more familiar. He took his hand out of his coat, leaving behind the dangers of Seven Dials, but not the unease.

As he turned onto his street, he slowed. The lighted windows of his lodging house mocked him. Cornelia waited for him inside, trusting him to help her and Andrew and he would. It was the frail connection they'd struggled to reclaim last night he was about to betray.

Regret dragged at him, but he shook it off. Any pain she experienced tonight would save her from future grief and heartache. This was the best way, the only way.

He touched his chest, the memory of her head against it as they'd lain together last night lingering in the anguish gripping him.

In all their time in London and Paris, she'd never pressed him about their future. Last night, she'd hit him between the eyes with it. He hadn't known how to answer her.

Now, he knew.

Cornelia circled the room for the hundredth time, worry deepening with the darkness outside. Rafe had been gone a long time, too long. He should have been back by now.

If he decided to come back.

She twisted the fake diamond ring on her finger, hating the vulnerability of it all. After France, she'd vowed never to care for another man. It was too difficult and dangerous to trust anyone, especially Rafe. Then last night, weakened by her worries and fears, she'd surrendered to him, his caresses and kisses making her forget her troubles.

If only it had lasted past sunrise.

She continued to pace, wishing she could sit still or pause long enough to change her dust-covered travelling clothes, but she couldn't. Last night, with her cheek against his chest and the steady cadence of his heart beating so close to hers, she'd opened herself to the very real chance of being hurt again. The wager scared her more than any other she'd ever made because the only way to know if she would win was to wait.

She hated waiting.

It reminded her too much of her last night with him in Paris.

A knock at the door made her jump. *He's back.*

'Comtesse, a letter arrived for you,' Mrs Linton called through the door.

Cornelia froze, her pulse pounding in her ears

as hope turned to dread. No one but Rafe would send something to her here.

'Comtesse?' Mrs Linton questioned, knocking again.

'I'm coming.' She struggled to cross the room and not collapse beneath the weight of her worry. He might be hurt, in trouble, or worse. He might have decided not to come back.

She opened the door, recoiling at the giddy smile on Mrs Linton's face. The landlady held out an envelope, something of the old crone Cornelia had opened the door to in Paris whispering in the exchange. 'Footman delivered this for Lord Densmore. Said he was the Dowager Countess of Daltmouth's man. Never had the likes of him here before.'

On the envelope, the fine black curves of Rafe's name and title stood out against the white paper. Relief surged through her and she sagged against the edge of the open door. If he or anyone else wanted to send her a parting note, they weren't likely to address it to him. With a shaky hand, she took the envelope from the landlady.

'Are you all right, love?'

'Yes, thank you. Now, if you'll excuse me.' She

closed the door, her nerves stretched too thin for pleasant conversation.

She turned the envelope over and examined Lady Daltmouth's wax seal, tempted to crush it and see what was inside.

No, this was Rafe's business and she needed to trust him enough to wait until he returned.

If he returned.

She laid the letter on the table and resumed her pacing. The floorboards creaked beneath the pressure of her boots, her sturdy carriage dress swishing over her legs as she turned and caught sight of the envelope. It taunted her like the image of Lady Daltmouth drooling over Rafe at the card party. The Dowager Countess had already made Rafe one lucrative offer. The chances of her making another were strong.

She strode away, watching her shadow rise against the wall in front of her.

It didn't matter if the Dowager Countess sent him a thousand notes, trying to lure him to her. He wouldn't accept them, it wasn't his way. At least not now, not yet. There was no guarantee a bad losing streak or an encounter with Mr Smith wouldn't shove Rafe into the Dowager Countess's pocket.

Returning to the table, she smacked the back of

one chair, making it wobble on its uneven legs. If it weren't for Andrew, she wouldn't care if Rafe ran to the Dowager Countess tonight. She shouldn't care. She didn't want to care. They had no more chance of creating a life together than Fanny had of enjoying one with Edgemont. She should have remembered that last night and not fallen for Rafe's enticement to live in the present. He might have cared enough to follow her to Hatton Place, to hold her and make her feel wanted and alive, but he hadn't cared enough to make any promises when she'd pressed him about their future.

Moving to the window, she flicked aside the musty curtain. A watchman ambled across the street below, his square lantern swinging on a stick above him. The flickering lantern reminded her of the ones hanging outside the Red Lion Inn this morning. It seemed like days ago instead of mere hours since they'd been in Sussex, when her faith in Rafe still glowed as brightly as her body beneath his touch.

The watchman wandered away, yelling at a group of passing men who threw taunts at him. Over the rooftops at the far end of the street, the faint glow of the theatre torches silhouetted the buildings. Cornelia had never ventured beyond those questionable streets, but she knew Seven Dials was no place for a gentleman. Rafe might be more rogue than Baron but he was mortal like any other man. Mortal enough to succumb to temptation.

She marched to the table, snatched up the envelope and broke the Dowager Countess's seal. Inside was an invitation to a masquerade ball tomorrow night at the Daltmouths' and nothing else, not even a handwritten note encouraging him to attend. Cornelia laughed, as much from fear of her own weakness as from the silliness of thinking there was anything more nefarious inside. Did she really expect to open it and find a note from Lady Daltmouth inviting Rafe to unmask her in her bedroom?

Yes, she did.

The heavy fall of boots stopping outside the door caught her attention.

He's back.

She tossed the invitation on the table, not bothering to cover the evidence of her curiosity.

The door swung open and Rafe entered. Relief and excitement filled her and she took a step forward, ready to rush to him, but the grim expression sharpening the angles of his face kept her rooted to her spot.

Uncertainty crept in to choke her relief. 'What is it? What's wrong?'

He closed the door, his eyes everywhere in the room but on hers. 'I ran into some difficulty while I was out.'

He approached the table, laying his hands on the back of the chair across from her. Something about him seemed more ragged than before. His sweat-damp hair lay flat against his temples and a fine red dust speckled his coat.

'Are you all right?' She rounded the table and touched his arm, her show of concern hardening the line of his lips.

'As you can see, I've returned.' He moved back, dragging the chair out. 'This time.'

Her fingers curled into a fist, seeking a warmth which was now gone. 'Is there a future time when you intend not to return?'

'I only meant I had some trouble with Mr Smith while I was out.' He smiled, the rogue replacing the taciturn man who'd entered. This look scared her more than his veiled threat to disappear. 'You'll be comforted to know, I've discovered our thief.'

He waved her into the chair.

She settled herself, moving forward as he pushed the chair closer to the table. Despite the nearness of his hands to her shoulders, his strong body steady behind hers, he might as well have stood in the street for all the closeness they enjoyed. 'And?'

He moved across the table and sat rigidly in his seat. 'It seems Lord Daltmouth is more determined to keep his family's secrets than we realised.'

Cornelia's heart dropped. The frail prospect of saving Andrew, of this one last sin of blackmail freeing her from the cards and an uncertain future flickered out. Guilt swept in to replace her lost hope. If she hadn't chosen to blackmail the Earl, he wouldn't have known about the register and she'd still have it and perhaps some other noble's money and Andrew would be safe.

Cornelia clasped her hands together in her lap, rage, regret and fear creeping up her back. There was only one thing left to do. 'We have to get it back.'

'And how exactly do you plan to retrieve it?' Rafe frowned. 'He isn't likely to succumb to your charms.'

Cornelia inwardly cringed. This wasn't the optimistic Rafe who'd left her two hours ago. What had happened in Seven Dials? 'Then we have no choice but to steal it back.'

'Are we to take up housebreaking now?' he mocked her.

'There's no need to sneak in when we can walk through the front door.' She picked up the creased envelope. 'This was delivered while you were out.'

His eyes narrowed on the broken seal. 'Been reading my correspondence, have you?'

'It's no more than you would've done if you were left alone in my rooms.'

'I see your belief in my integrity is as strong as ever.' He plucked the envelope from her fingers, opened it and read it. 'The Dowager Countess must still be ignorant of her son's more suspicious dealings to extend me an invitation.'

Or she's too enamoured with you to be more cautious, she thought, but held her tongue, careful not to taunt him. They were still in this game together and she needed him to keep playing until the end and not change partners. The gilded edge of the card flashed. She didn't want him near the Dowager Countess, and, if the invitation hadn't given them a legitimate reason to enter the Daltmouths' house, she'd have burnt it and thwarted the old sow. 'It's the perfect chance to search for the register. They won't notice us in a crush of masked guests.'

'It's a large house to search.' He flicked the

corner of the card, creasing the fine paper. 'But I'd wager he's hiding the book in his father's old study.'

'Then we'll start our search there,' she encouraged, trying to bolster his determination the way he usually bolstered hers.

'Yes, let's steal through their house and sink to their level. Why not take a trinket or two while we're in there?' He tossed the card and envelope on the table and rose, plucking the wine bottle and one goblet from the peeling sideboard.

'You don't want to get the register back?'

'Even if we get it back, then what? It won't change anything. My title might be safe, but what about your brother?'

'We'll have to choose someone else to blackmail.' The words made her sick. This wasn't who she was or who she wanted to be. It would protect Andrew, but with each step down this path it seemed she became a more despicable person, like her father.

He levelled one finger at her, the cup dangling from his hand. 'No, I won't inflict on any family the kind of uncertainty and suffering inflicted on mine.'

She didn't argue with him, she couldn't because he was right. 'Then it's back to the tables.'

'Yes, the tables.' He poured himself a healthy measure of wine. 'Always the tables.'

He emptied the goblet, then filled it again, almost to the rim.

Desperation drew her to her feet, his fatalism scarring her as much as his sudden thirst. This was how her father used to drink. 'Or we could simply give up and crawl into a bottle, like our fathers.'

He slammed the bottle down on the sideboard so hard she thought it might break, but it didn't. 'Maybe they had it right.'

'No, they were fools.'

'And what are we?'

'Doing the best we can, given our poor circumstances.'

'I see my optimism wasn't completely lost on you.' He raised his goblet in a sarcastic toast. 'You'll excuse me if I don't share it with you tonight.'

'And what will you share with me tonight besides your surly mood? If you think it's the bed, you're mistaken.'

'No, I have no desire to share a bed with you tonight. Or any future night.' He set down the wine, his expression as troubled as the day the British Ambassador fled Paris and war with France became imminent.

Humiliation and betrayal slammed together and nearly undermined her carefully controlled facade. She rose, determined to confront him with what remained of her shredded pride. 'You thought nothing of sharing a bed with me last night.'

'We—I made a mistake encouraging such intimacy when nothing about our lives can support it.'

'How wonderful for you to realise this after you've had your fun.' She dragged in two long breaths to settle her anger and keep herself from snatching up the bottle and breaking it over his head.

He stared into his wine, regret heavy in his dark eyes. 'It was never a jest with you.'

The tender honesty in his words stole her fury. If she meant so much to him, then why was he pushing her away? Why was he leaving her to face the ugliness of the future alone, just like her mother had? The little girl inside her wanted to cry, the crushing abandonment nearly buckling her knees before she locked them straight. The woman who'd survived Château de Vane and a thousand other humiliations silenced the little girl.

'Why realise this now, tonight, when the harm has already been done?' she demanded.

'That's why.' He tossed a pistol on the table and it clattered to a stop over the invitation. 'Compliments of Mr Smith.'

'What happened?' She could guess the gist of it, but she wanted to know, to hear what had turned him so hard against her in the space of two hours. It was a chance to change his mind, to stop him from pushing her away, to make him take back all the hurtful words. The lonely girl grasped at it to the disgust of the wronged woman.

'I have no desire to discuss it.' He drained the cup. 'Nor do I wish to keep leading you down a path you've stated before you have no desire to travel. I'll see to it we get the register back and keep your brother safe. After that, we go our separate ways, just as we originally planned.'

Hope left her as it had the morning her mother died and she'd lost the one person who'd cared about her. Pain churned her gut, roiling up into an anger she'd known all her life. Inhaling slowly, she struggled to keep it from boiling over, to stop herself from flying at Rafe and pounding him with her fists until he experienced even a small portion of the pain squeezing her heart. 'You think too highly of yourself if you believe I want to stay with you when this is all over. I might have been weak last night, but I won't let it lead me into choosing a pauper when there are men like Lord Rollingham to land.'

If the words cut Rafe, he didn't show it, his face as impassive as if he held an excellent hand. She knew from the look he meant to win this game and nothing she said or did could change his mind. Whatever had happened in Seven Dials, it had rent the affection between them as badly as the Comte's treachery.

'You'd better get some sleep. Today was a long one and tomorrow night will be even longer.' He turned to the window and leaned against the frame, the goblet dangling in his hand next to his thigh.

She stared at the expanse of dark wool stretching over his shoulders. He looked so alone, the way he had in the garden at Wealthstone when it seemed as if everything he'd ever wanted and worked for would never be realised. If she could comfort him, lay her head on his back, wrap her arms around his waist and make him realise he wasn't alone, then maybe he'd take back what he'd said.

Instead, she made for the bedroom, desperate to leave before she humiliated herself further by comforting a man who didn't want her. It was finished between them, as much now as the night she'd received the forged letter. Once they had the register, he'd leave her to fend for herself and she would.

She slammed the door behind her. He'd regret this. She'd see to it. She'd marry a man like Lord Rollingham and parade about London in his fine carriage. Then, some day, when the creditors finally seized Wealthstone, she'd buy it. It would happen eventually, she knew it would. He'd been lucky to keep it for this long, but no gambler's luck lasted for ever.

The daydream of revenge was more bitter than sweet and it deepened the pain pooling around her heart.

She locked the bedroom door, then shrugged out of her dusty dress. The cold bit through the thin cotton of her chemise as she tugged loose the strings of her stays and tossed them over the chair with the dress. She plucked the nightshirt, his nightshirt, off the end of the bed and shook it out, her smell mingling with his in the creases and lines of the homespun. Beyond the door, the steady fall of his boots against the floorboards filled the quiet, each thud louder and harder than during the first night she'd slept here.

Instead of sharing his concerns with her, he'd decided to push her away.

She crumpled the nightshirt into a ball and hurled it across the room. To Hades with him. He was beyond her disdain, beyond her concern or ever belonging to her again.

Slipping between the cold sheets, she curled her knees into her chest, fighting the shivers and pain making her teeth chatter. It was better this way, better he tell her to her face than sneak out one night and leave her to wonder and worry.

Settling deeper into the sagging mattress, she willed herself not to cry as she focused on Andrew, Edgemont's threat and the desperate, constant need for money. One by one she considered her possessions, trying to distract herself from the anguish of Rafe's betrayal. She could sell some of her older dresses, maybe even the fake diamonds in Petticoat Lane. The meagre money might fund a few more nights at the tables, give her a few more chances at winning a large purse. It was the only plan she could focus on, the only hope she could muster despite the low odds of achieving it.

The old game was drawing to a close and a new one was beginning with fresh players and stakes.

It was time to forget Rafe and concentrate on the next hand.

If only it didn't hurt so much.

Chapter Twelve

Cornelia and Rafe entered Lady Daltmouth's crowded ballroom. The thud of feet sounded through the room as a long line of dancers turned and parted in a rousing country reel. For a moment, it drowned out the garble of guests' voices bouncing off the high centre ceiling and all the plump nymphs and goddesses painted on it. Greek columns twined with ivy leaves held up the painted Olympus, their footings obscured by Tudor kings and queens, Ottoman princes and medieval princesses. The same parade of history crowded the wide staircase situated in the centre of one wall enclosing the ballroom and helping to support the balcony circling the room.

Any ideas she'd possessed about walking in here and finding the book before the last Henry VIII departed for home vanished. She should have learned by now, nothing in life was ever so easy. She swallowed hard, the strings of her red velvet cape lined with dark blue satin pulling tight against her throat. She hadn't been this nervous since the morning her father had barged into her bedroom demanding she come downstairs and meet her new stepmother.

'Losing heart?' Rafe asked.

'No,' She tugged the cape strings down off her neck, wishing he wasn't so perceptive. 'Not at all.'

'Good.' He studied the room from beneath his father's old domino and the antiquated tricorn pulled down over his brow to touch the top of his mask. There was no humour, no sense of anticipation like the last time they'd entered the Daltmouths', only hard focus. 'I don't think this will be as easy as we first thought.'

She took delight in his uncertainty. 'Then it seems we still have something in common.'

'I'm sure if we tried, we could discover a few more things.'

'We needn't bother. After tonight we won't have anything further to discuss.' *Or any more tortuous interaction,* she thought, but didn't say it, afraid at any moment he might withdraw his help just as he'd withdrawn his affection last night. His promise to stay with her until the end might be thin, but it was all she possessed and she'd cling to it until it was of no more use. Then she'd be done with him and loving any man except Andrew.

A passing group of knights pressed her against Rafe. She didn't want to be so close to him, but she didn't step away once the Lancelots passed. His solid body next to hers was a barrier and a frail comfort against any threat lingering in the crowd. If Lord Daltmouth wished to silence them, it wouldn't be hard for his dubious footman to slither in among the guests and slip a knife in their backs. No one would notice until they collapsed bleeding on the floor. By then the murderer would be gone, protected by the Earl and his ten thousand pounds a year. She and Rafe would be dead and Andrew would be sent to the West Indies to join them soon after.

She couldn't invent a more gruesome tale if she wanted to.

The crowd moved forward, carrying them along with it. She tightened her grip on his arm, wishing she didn't need to cling to him, but he wasn't the only gentleman wearing a domino tonight, or taking advantage of a mask to attend. Judging by the crush, the better quality must have finally deigned to accept one of the Dowager Countess's invitations. The *ton* was never so brave as when hiding behind silk.

Rafe shifted them around a poorly disguised MP and she held tight to his arm, determined not to get separated from Rafe. She didn't want to waste precious time unmasking strange men in order to find him again.

'We'll keep to the sides where it's darker and we won't stand out.' They wound through the crowd, making for one of the columns on the far side of the room. Here, the lower ceiling created by the balcony blocked the light from the gilded chandeliers hanging in the centre of Olympus. Down the length of the chair rail, punctuated by the many floor-to-ceiling windows open to let in the night air, a row of footmen stood at attention. Their eyes were draped with black masks as if they weren't men, but marble statues decorated for the event. Hopefully, their height would help disguise Rafe's and Cornelia's and provide even more anonymity.

'Do you recognise anyone?' Rafe leaned close to her, his breath whispering across her cheek beneath the silk mask, teasing her with the promise of everything she couldn't have.

She snapped off a lose thread on her cape. 'No, do you?'

'The Earl is over by the food.'

She looked to where Rafe nodded, wrinkling her nose at the pudgy man made rounder by his red Tudor doublet. It was difficult to believe he was behind the theft, or anything more taxing than selecting the cakes for tonight's refreshments. 'He seems too busy eating to notice us.'

'No, but the tall man in the blue domino by the obelisk topiary has been eyeing us ever since we entered the room.'

She shifted on her feet, trying to see around the tall feathers of two Marie Antoinettes standing between her and the blue domino. When the two women finally moved, Cornelia caught sight of the man. 'Who is he?'

'Given his height and curiosity, I'd say he's the footman who stole our book.'

Her hand tightened on Rafe's arm, the silk mask covering her eyes more stifling than protective. 'Then the Earl suspects we know.'

How long until she felt cold steel slide between her ribs?

'The Earl is probably just being cautious, which means we'll have to be more careful,' he warned her, his voice less curt and more comforting.

'Then let's get on with it so we can leave.'

'I'll lead the way.'

He escorted her along the edge of the crowd towards the stairs. They'd walked no more than ten paces when Rafe halted and swung around to face her, his back shielding her from the other guests. 'Damn.'

'What is it?'

'Edgemont.'

'Where?'

'Near the window, in the black, lace-edged tricorn speaking to a queen of hearts with a larger bosom than your stepmother's.'

She rose up on her toes to peer over Rafe's shoulder, dropping down behind him the second she spotted the Baron. 'If he sees me, he'll expect the pages.'

'Then you'll have to disappoint him.'

'But Andrew?' She couldn't stop the panic from escaping.

Rafe clasped her hands in his, the tenderness as painful as it was comforting. 'There's little he can do tonight and if he takes any action tomorrow, we'll find a way to undo it.'

She pulled her hands out of his, wary of his assurances. There was nothing binding him to her, nothing to guarantee he would keep his promise or not turn his back on her the moment he got the incriminating pages, just as he'd pushed her away after they'd made love. 'We have to find the register first.'

'And we will.' He lifted the tricorn to wipe his forehead, then settled the hat back over his hair. 'It'll be easier to move once we get upstairs.'

The musicians began the next set, the scraping first note of the violins tightening her fear.

She eyed the wide staircase crammed with revellers, both eager and apprehensive. She might worry about a murderous stranger in the crowd, but at least the other guests offered some protection. Above stairs, there would be no one to help them if they were caught.

Steeling herself against the encroaching anxiety, she held her head up high as she followed Rafe through the throng of laurel-wreathed Caesars and gauzily clad Cleopatras surging onto the dance floor. A small but equally determined crowd made for the stairs and it was easy to fall in with the steady stream of knights and ladies heading for the balcony and a prime view of the ballroom below.

On the landing, Cornelia stopped to look back over the long room. The man in the blue domino was nowhere to be seen, not on the dance floor or at the bottom of the staircase. Not so for Edgemont. He looked up from the Queen of Heart's bosom, his eyes catching hers. Even beneath the silk mask she could see them widening before they narrowed.

She grasped the edges of her cloak and caught up to Rafe. 'Edgemont recognised me. He's sure to come after us.'

'He isn't the only one. Our footman is also following us.'

She looked down the stairs, finally spying the footman struggling to get around two portly chess pieces. There wasn't time to see if he succeeded as Rafe grabbed her hand and pulled her across the balcony and down the wide hallway on the other side.

Most of the candles in the candelabras along the walls had been snuffed out. Smoke rose from a few recently extinguished ones, filling the semi-darkness with a faint grey haze. Costumed couples crammed together in alcoves or pressed against one another on small benches, leaning back into the shadows cast by the columns supporting marble busts of old Daltmouths.

Rafe swept off his hat and dropped it onto one of the bald marble heads. He pulled her down towards the centre of the hall, making for the only unoccupied alcove. He pulled off his domino and blew out the candle in the nearby holder. He untied the strings of her cape, reached over her and turned the garment around. Laying it over her shoulders, he tugged it closed over her body, hiding the deep red velvet with the even darker blue.

He pressed her into the shadow of the alcove, leaning in against her so she could just see over his shoulder. Murmurs and giggles drifted with the smoke down the hallway, the sound as faint as the steady rhythm of Rafe's breath in her ear. The scratchy beginnings of stubble along his jaw grazed her skin and the weight of his hand on her back increased the agony of being this close to him. She gripped the cloak tight against herself, wishing they were just two more couples stealing a few moments in the darkness, their only regrets being not enough time together.

'Do you see him?' he whispered.

She opened her eyes, struggling against the rising heat in her body to focus on the danger. 'Our footman has reached the top.'

'Does he see us?'

She slid one hand out from beneath the cloak and laid it along the side of Rafe's face. Her fingers curled in his hair as she drew his head down a touch more so she could see.

The masked footman moved slowly down the hall, peeking into the alcoves and trying to see the people entangled there. At one particularly deep alcove, he leaned in too close, jerking back as a Marie Antoinette whacked him with her fan. He stumbled back, saved from hitting the floor by the Queen's Sultan who dragged him up by his collar and shoved him towards the stairs. The footman skulked away under a hail of hissed curses before the Sultan and his French Queen returned to their former diplomacy. The dimly lit faces of the other revellers who'd roused to watch the scuffle faded back into the shadows.

'He's gone now,' Cornelia whispered.

'There's one stroke of luck in our favour.' He angled his head, poised above her so achingly close she could see each hair curling over his forehead. Her thumb caressed the back of his neck as he leaned down, his mouth hovering so close to hers. Her toes curled in her shoes as she waited for the sweet taste of him and everything it implied. Then he stopped, his lips drawing tight with regret. 'Let's hope luck stays with us.'

She withdrew her hand, fear crushing desire

and hope. Luck wasn't likely to stay with them. It never did.

He backed out of the alcove, looking down the hall before waving her out. 'We'd better go in case he comes back, or Edgemont finds us.'

She followed him down the hall, ignoring the people pressed together on either side. At the end, they stopped at the foot of a small staircase leading to the next floor.

'Are you sure this is the way?' Studies weren't usually so close to the family rooms, and so far from any guest who might hear her scream if something went wrong.

'I came here once with my father when he needed the old Earl's support for a bill. He kept a small study on the third floor. Judging by what I've seen of the house, they haven't changed much since then. I doubt Lord Daltmouth has moved his father's sanctuary.'

'It's certainly a more private, convenient place to meet with a housebreaking footman than the main floor.'

'And a more secure hiding place for incriminating books.' Rafe looked back one last time, then urged her up the stairs.

At the top, another long hallway greeted them. A

single candle in a sconce in the centre illuminated the gilded frames of landscapes hanging on the papered walls. She paused, almost ready to take her chances with the footman and Edgemont than continue forward. This reminded her too much of the corridors of Château de Vane and the desolation lingering in those old stone walls.

Rafe caught her hand, squeezing it as he drew her forward. She didn't pull out of his grasp, but held on tight, following him through the wavering candlelight.

None of the adventurous couples from below had found their way to this secluded part of the house. If they had, then they were already hidden behind one of the many doors dotting the long expanse.

'Which room is it?' she asked.

'I'm trying to remember.' They crept slowly past one door, then another. 'I think it's at the end, on the garden side.'

Of course. Why shouldn't the one they need be in the darkest corner of the darkest hall in the house?

Rafe stopped in front of the last door at the end. She squinted at the lacquered wood, the light from the candle having given up trying to reach here.

'I hope we don't open it to find King Arthur showing Guinevere his Excalibur,' she whispered, trying to draw from Rafe's courage to brush away her childish fears.

His cheeks rose with his smile. 'I wouldn't bet on it, but there's something to be said for startling Kings and Queens. It makes them more likely to flee.'

He laid one hand on the doorknob. 'Are you ready to find out?'

Once they were behind the door, there were no excuses they could make and nowhere to go if they were caught. 'Yes.'

'Brace yourself for Camelot.' He flung open the door.

Mercifully, no one was inside, but someone must have been here recently.

An oil lamp on a table near the single window illuminated the narrow room. A petite French cabinet of polished burled wood decorated one wall, dwarfed by the sturdier English desk and chair wedged in close to the fireplace.

Rafe ushered her in, then closed the door and locked it.

'What'll we do if the footman finds us?' There was no other way out of the study.

'We'll have to improvise.'

'Then let's not dawdle.' She hurried to the desk,

shoved aside the curved chair and pulled open the top drawer to rifle through a stack of old correspondence.

Rafe didn't move, but stood in the centre of the room, staring at the tall screen standing in the corner. The myth of Daedalus and his son Icarus was beautifully embroidered on each of the three panels. On the first, the son and his father worked to fashioning the wax wings. The second showed them flying away from the labyrinth, mouths wide with hope and exhilaration. It all ended on the third panel as the boy, his wings singed and limp, fell towards the sea. While Icarus flailed, his father flew on, failing to notice his son's last tumultuous moments.

'What is it? Do you think it's behind the screen?' Cornelia asked, sliding the drawer closed and reaching for the next.

'No. I remember this from the last time I was here. I hated the last panel.'

Cornelia tried the bottom drawer and it rattled, but refused to budge. 'This drawer's locked. Something important must be in here.'

Pulled from his memories, Rafe rushed to the desk and kneeled in front of the drawer to examine the lock. 'Let's hope it's the register.'

'Or something we can use against the Earl to get it back.'

Rafe rose, towering over her. 'I need one of your hairpins.'

'Of course.' She reached up and slid one pin free from her hair. A single curl tumbled from her coiffure, falling down her shoulder and curling over the tip of one breast.

Rafe stared at the curl, his look as fiery as if she stood before him naked. He raised his hand and her breast tightened, eager for him to cup it, but his palm lingered flat, waiting in the air between them.

She laid the thin metal across his hand, her fingers grazing his warm skin. In the feathery touch she offered the slightest invitation, the merest hint of forgiveness, the chance for him to apologise and take back everything he'd said last night.

His fingers curled over the pin, catching hers. She waited, noting each solid thump of his pulse against her skin. She shouldn't want him, but she did and she felt sure he did too.

'Cornelia, I—' he began to say, his grip tightening.

The pin pricked her skin. She flinched and pulled

back, the pain sobering. There would be no forgiveness. She didn't want him and he didn't want her.

'I think we should hurry,' she said, rubbing away the sting.

'You're right.' He knelt in front of the drawer and slid the pin inside the lock, jiggling it until the metal clicked.

He looked up at her, anticipation heavy between them, as if they were on the verge of winning a hand like no other they'd ever played before.

He slid open the drawer, smiling in triumph as the black leather cover of the register came into view.

Cornelia reached down and pulled it out, opening it to the page marked with a blue ribbon. Running her finger over the list of names and dates, she smiled at the many times the Daltmouth name appeared. 'France made the late Earl a very rich man.'

'Where's my father's name?' He took the register from her and laid it flat on the desk. 'I want to see it. I want to see for myself where he sold his soul.'

'I don't remember what pages they were on,' Cornelia stammered, surprised by his determination.

'Then let's start from the beginning, shall we?'

He flicked all the pages over and a puff of dust whooshed into the air. 'I haven't had the pleasure of perusing it like you have.'

'You can look at it later. We need to go.'

He ignored her, running his finger down the lines on the first page before turning to the next. Outside, the faint strains of music drifted up from the ballroom below.

'Here he is.' Rafe thumped the yellowed page. 'Five hundred pounds for passing on secret Parliamentary papers to the French.'

He tore the page from the book and held up the ragged sheet, reading the neatly printed words. 'I wonder what hell benefited from that transaction?'

He flipped it into the grate. It sat smoking on the coals before the edges ignited and the whole thing turned in on itself, the flames flaring across the paper before dying down into a black, crumbling pile.

'Rafe, there isn't time for this.'

'Ah, here's another one, with an increase in pay.' He tore the paper from the book. 'Do you know what we could have done with a sum like this? How many debts he could have paid? Instead, he just tossed the money away.'

He crumpled the paper between his hands and threw it in the grate.

'Rafe, we have to go,' Cornelia urged. 'The longer we stay here, the more time the footman has to search for us'

He ignored her, too entranced by the book.

'He betrayed his country and for what?' He ripped another page from the book, crushed it and flung it into the fire. 'Hundreds of pounds to just gamble away.'

Cornelia grabbed his hand as he reached for another page. 'We have to go. Now.'

His eyes whipped to hers, his fury so intense she let go of him and stepped back.

'I'm not walking out of here with this hanging over me.' He slammed his fist against the register. 'I'm not leaving until all evidence of my father's treachery is gone.'

He turned another page and then another, his finger running down each one, searching for the next incriminating line.

She'd never seen him like this, not even after the sharp cheated them during their first day in Paris. His rage scared her, but she understood it. It was the same bitter hate she'd cursed her father with as Lord Waltenham had dragged her into the garden.

'How could he have done this? How could he have done this to us?' He tugged at another page then snatched back his hand, opening it to reveal a small cut in the crease between his fingers. The blood only increased his rage and he tugged out the stubborn page with enough force to rattle the inkwell on the desk.

He threw it in the fire and the page ignited, the Edgemont name above the Densmore name glowing before the flames consumed them both.

He flipped the book shut. 'I want this whole thing gone, all of it.'

'No.' Cornelia slammed her hand down on the cover.

'Let go of it,' Rafe insisted, but the anger in his eyes didn't frighten her this time.

'No.' Her fingers curled over the edge of the leather, ready to fight him for the book. 'You said last night you couldn't ruin anyone's life like your father ruined yours. You destroy the register, you destroy all evidence against Edgemont and any hope I have of using it to save Andrew. I know you don't care about me, but don't consign Andrew to suffering. He doesn't deserve it.'

His grip on the register loosened and she snatched it up, clutching it to her chest. She tried to back away, but the chair behind her blocked the way. Her muscles tightened, waiting for him to lunge for it.

He didn't move, the revenge blazing in his eyes calming like water in a bowl.

'You're mistaken about my not caring.' He brushed the dangling curl back away from her face. 'I care too much.'

'Don't think you'll flatter the book away from me.' Her voice wavered, the feathery sweep of his fingers through her hair, the hint of apology in his words weakening her conviction.

'I'd never do that to you, any more than I could have left you to suffer at Lord Perry's.'

Her grip on the book slackened as she struggled to reconcile the conflict raging inside her. She wanted him, he wanted her, but he'd turned away from her last night. Now, his gentle voice beckoned her back, asking her to trust and follow him once more.

'Rafe, I—' she stammered, not knowing whether to embrace him or thrust him away.

'Shhh.' He settled his palm against her jaw and his thumb swept the arch of her lip, silencing her. 'You've always meant more to me than—'

'This way. They can't have gone far.' Lord Dalt-mouth's voice filled the hallway.

The danger broke the delicate connection and Cornelia's racing heart jerked to a halt. 'They've found us.'

They didn't move, listening for more voices, Rafe's hand tense against her face.

'Do you think they've gone?' Cornelia whispered when they didn't hear anything.

Rafe eased himself around the desk to face the door. 'Not likely.'

Cornelia jumped when the brass knob turned, but the lock below it kept the door in place. A furious, muffled exchange began on the other side before someone shook the knob so hard the entire door rattled against the jamb.

'Step aside,' the familiar voice of a woman commanded, followed by the clank of keys on a ring.

It would only be a second before whoever was on the other side entered.

'This way.' Rafe hustled Cornelia behind the embroidered screen, pulled the pistol from beneath his cloak and pressed it into her palm. 'Don't reveal yourself and don't use this unless you absolutely have to.'

'What about you?'

'You'll see.' He pushed her deeper between the screen and the brown wall behind it, then hurried round to the other side.

Cornelia peered through the small gap between the panels. She drew in a long breath, struggling to calm herself. If she was discovered, she'd need to use her wits, not bolt like some scared rabbit.

Rafe stood before the desk, facing the door, the calm he practised at the tables coming over him as the heavy oak swung open.

'Good evening, Lady Daltmouth,' Rafe greeted, his face not registering even a speck of the surprise making Cornelia's mouth drop open.

Could it be that it wasn't her son who'd stolen the book, but her?

'Good evening, Lord Densmore.' The Dowager, dressed as Queen Elizabeth, strode into the room, followed by her son and the tall footman. A starched ruff rose up at the back of her neck, but remained open at the bosom. Her ample breasts pushed hard against the top of the gold-brocade bodice, a wide diamond necklace covering them and protecting her modesty. She approached Rafe, as relaxed as if she were encountering him in a receiving line, not behind a locked door in her house.

'Have you found something of interest in my late husband's study?'

'The screen. I was curious to see if you still had it.' Rafe pointed to it.

Cornelia clamped her lips closed to keep from gasping or even breathing as she eased back from the gap. *What's he doing? Trying to give me away?*

'You were curious about the screen?' The Dowager Countess snorted, clasping her hands in front of her and facing him like a petite queen ruling her castle.

'I was here once with my father while he and your husband discussed some Parliamentary business. I don't remember much about the visit except this screen and how my father persuaded Lord Daltmouth to vote in favour of the matter.' An odd sense of nostalgia softened the edges of Rafe's cavalier smile, as though he was a boy again, watching his father debate matters of government with another peer and not in danger from the Dowager Countess and her thieving footman. 'He could be so persuasive and likeable when he wanted to be.'

'Yes, your father was quite the clever man. Until the cards ruined him.'

Rafe's cavalier smile sharpened, wiping the fog of nostalgia from his expression. 'And your husband was a brilliant general. Until the French ruined him.'

'You're impertinent, too. Another trait you share with your father, along with his debts.' The Dowager Countess swept around him to the back of the desk, the wide skirt of her costume bouncing about her legs. She peered down at the open bottom drawer, her lips pursing in irritation.

Rafe didn't turn around, but examined the cut on his hand. 'I must say, Lady Daltmouth, I didn't expect to find you involved in this business.'

Neither did Cornelia.

'Of course.' The Dowager Countess lobbed the key ring at her son and the keys clanked wildly together as he fumbled to catch them. 'Do you really think I'd leave such an important errand to my brainless son?'

'Mother?' the Earl protested before a slicing glance from his mother rendered him speechless.

She closed the drawer, then came around the desk to stand in front of him, dwarfed but not cowed by Rafe's superior height. In fact, his looming presence seemed to arouse more than annoy her, the hungry look in her eyes as strong as her rosewater perfume. 'Now, where's the register?'

'The Comtesse de Vane has it,' he stated bluntly.

'And she left you behind to face us.' Lady Daltmouth crossed her arms under her wide bosom and touched one finger to her chin. 'It seems rather selfish of her, wouldn't you say?'

'Not at all. I told her to go. If I don't return safely within an hour, she has instructions to deliver the delightful tome to Lord Twickenham. I wager he'll enjoy some light reading before bed tonight.'

The Dowager Countess dropped her arms, her hands curling into balls as she whirled to face her son. 'Find the Comtesse. She can't have got far.'

'I'm not going to leave you alone with him.' The Earl flapped one pudgy finger at Rafe.

'Mr Green will ensure Lord Densmore behaves.' She motioned to the footman who stood by the door as though waiting to help serve tea, not guard a man. 'And find Lord Edgemont while you're down there. I'm sure he'll want to join this little gathering.'

'Yes, Mother.' The Earl shuffled off to do her bidding.

The Dowager Countess faced Rafe again, raking him with the same lusty gaze she'd mauled him with at her card party. 'Now, my dear Lord Densmore, what are we to do?'

'We wait until Lord Twickenham comes storming in here.' Rafe crossed his arms and leaned back against the edge of the desk. 'You know how much he enjoys making a dramatic show of uncovering treason.'

'I don't think we have to stoop to such levels.' The Dowager Countess moved closer to Rafe, the embroidered hem of her Elizabethan costume swishing over the tops of his boots. She fingered her necklace, straightening it over her smooth skin, the glare from the twinkling stones distracting from the nearly indecent cut of the bodice. 'Not when there are much more pleasurable ways of dealing with the matter.'

Cornelia wasn't sure whose eyes grew wider, hers or Mr Green's.

'You have my full attention.' Rafe eyed the Dowager Countess's assets before returning his attention to her face.

Cornelia's fingers tightened on the register, wondering what he was playing at. He had his knife and she had the pistol. He could shove Lady Daltmouth aside and they could both make for the door. With the two weapons, they could easily escape the footman before Lord Daltmouth returned with Edgemont. Why was he waiting?

'How perceptive of you to guess your attention

is the very thing I want.' The Dowager Countess beamed as bright as her diamonds, tilting her head like a little coquette. 'Among other things.'

'I can well guess what those other things might be.' Rafe answered.

'I'm sure you can.' She rubbed her hands across his waistcoat, smoothing out a wrinkle in the silk before grasping the bottom and tugging it straight. 'But business first.'

Rafe shrugged. 'If you insist.'

'I do, because I think you'll find what I have to say very interesting. Today I visited a gentleman with whom you are well acquainted, a Mr Smith of Fleet Street. It seems you owe him a great deal of money.' She wagged one ruby-clad finger at him, the stone blood red in the low light. 'Very naughty of you, Lord Densmore.'

Cornelia waited for the insult, the snide remark streaking through his eyes, but he said nothing. He uncrossed his arms and rested his hands on the edge of the desk, as if opening himself up to the Dowager Countess and encouraging this disgusting flirting. 'I enjoy being naughty.'

'I don't doubt you do. As do I. You see, I paid your debt.'

Cornelia bit down on her lip to keep from gasping in surprise and giving herself away.

Whatever Rafe's real reaction to the Dowager Countess's revelation, he hid it, his teasing, languid look never changing. 'How very generous of you.'

'You know such generosity comes with a price.'

'Doesn't everything?'

She pressed closer to him, her panniers keeping her pelvis from completely touching his. 'I think you'll enjoy paying this one.'

'It does look promising.'

Cornelia gripped the pistol tighter, afraid it might slip out of her sweaty palm and crash to the floor. It was tempting to let it fall and end this infuriating flirting between Rafe and the Dowager Countess. Whatever game he was playing with the older woman, she had to stay hidden until it reached its conclusion. Assuming it really was a game. Of course it was, it had to be. There was no other reason why Rafe would entertain the old bat's advances.

'If you return the register to me, and forget all about its existence, I'll cancel your debts,' the Dowager Countess offered.

Cornelia's stomach dropped, his reluctance to

escape or push Lady Daltmouth away beginning to make terrible sense.

'All you want is for me to forget the register?'

'And that flighty little Comtesse. The money-grubbing whore doesn't deserve the attentions of a man of your talents.'

Cornelia clamped her mouth shut against an answering insult, burning to grab the lusting shrew by her starched collar and fling her across the room. Who was she to cast aspersions on Cornelia, not when she was practically straddling Rafe's leg in the middle of her traitor of a husband's study? Cornelia leaned closer to the crack, anger and disgust overriding her sense of caution.

The Dowager Countess tilted forward, sliding one finger beneath the end of Rafe's cravat and drawing it out from beneath his waistcoat. 'You see, despite your crooked ways, there's something about you I'm drawn to.'

'My wit?'

'Your skills.' The Dowager Countess's hand tightened on the cravat and she used it to practically scale his chest. 'With the cards, people and, apparently, sneaking through houses. It's the whole reason I invited you here tonight, to discuss my proposal, though I didn't think it would happen quite like this.'

'Surely there are other men better equipped to help you. Your talented footman, perhaps?' He flicked a glance at the man who stood at attendance, pretending not to listen.

'I need a man with a title.'

'Then why not Lord Edgemont?'

Her lip curled in disgust. 'We have an arrangement, but he isn't as talented as you and he thinks too much of himself.'

'When he should be thinking of you.'

'How perceptive, Lord Densmore.' She tapped him on the nose. 'I know you have no desire for lofty government appointments or what you can gain from the bargain beyond reviving the respect of your family name and title.'

'You're right, I don't.' His fingers trilled on the polished mahogany desk before going still. 'Tell me, did you kill Mrs Ross?'

She sank down off the balls of her feet, practically sliding down him in the process. 'No, but her death proved quite the convenient accident, didn't it?'

'Not for her.'

'But certainly for me.' She pushed away from

Rafe, her flattened dress front snapping back into shape. 'It brought your little whore out of the shadows to blackmail my son. I wouldn't have known the register existed if it wasn't for her greed and my son's stupidity in thinking he could raise a thousand pounds without my noticing.'

'What could a woman as charming as you need with such an ugly thing like the register?'

She began to pace, the starched ruff bouncing behind her head with each clipped step. 'I've tried for years to make society forget my husband's betrayal and to secure a place for my son in the government. The *ton* has proven stubborn and I'm tired of waiting. If I can't persuade them to forget, then I'll force them to forget by threatening to take away the very titles and privileges they hold dear. I'll blackmail my way into the best houses and see my son appointed to the most prestigious positions.'

'A clever plan, but if I give you the register, then you hardly need me.'

'Oh, but I do. Not every family has a name in the book, but they all have secrets and weaknesses. I need a rogue like you, a man with a title and no honour who can move through society learning their secrets or trapping them in his debt at the tables. Then we can use it against them to gain entrance into the highest levels of society.'

The Dowager Countess was so caught up in her scheme she failed to see his chest rise once, then again, her insult about his honour hitting the mark. Cornelia noticed it and waited, silently urging him to throw Lady Daltmouth's offer back in her face for daring to insult his pride and integrity. He didn't and the Dowager Countess continued with her tirade.

'If you help me force my way back into the *ton,* I'll pay your debts and be generous with an allowance. Think what you can do with my money, what you can do for your mother. She might even return to London and take her place in society where she belongs.'

The room shifted as if the tide had rushed through, swirling around the Dowager Countess and drawing everything to her. In her lurid promise was everything Rafe sought, everything Cornelia could never give him. The disparaging things the Dowager Countess said about Cornelia meant nothing next to this reality. Cornelia's arms drooped under the weight of the register. She could never be anything more to him than a partner at the tables, a body in his bed and a way to amuse himself until the promise of something better presented itself.

He won't accept the offer. He can't. This isn't who he is, she tried to convince herself, but the strength of her argument paled beneath the Dowager Countess's more persuasive invitation.

Hopelessness flooded through her as if she stood again in the Paris apartment reading the forged letter from Rafe, her world crumbling around her. Only this time, there was no mistaking who sent the message wrenching them apart.

'What about him?' Rafe pointed to the footman. Mr Green's face was stony as he listened to the exchange. 'I don't play second fiddle to a servant.'

The Dowager Countess didn't bother to look at the man, but dismissed him with a toss of her head. 'He can go back to the country. I don't need a peasant when I can have a Baron.'

The footman ground his jaw, breaking the clean line of the bottom of his face beneath the mask. Red spread across his skin, highlighted by the blue domino. Cornelia took faint comfort in his silent reaction. At least she wasn't the only being tossed aside tonight.

'All we need is the register.' The Dowager Countess's voice slithered through the room again.

Cornelia clutched the register tighter against her chest, anger bolstering her courage. She might not have Rafe, but she had Andrew and the pistol and the register. She wasn't about to give up while her brother depended on her. She'd make sure Lady Daltmouth didn't get it, even if it meant shooting one of them. Let them have their lofty plans and each other. She'd use the register to ruin all their grand dreams the way Rafe had ruined hers.

'Think of what I can give you.' The Dowager Countess leaned against him, rested her forearms on Rafe's chest and licked her lips, eager to taste the goods she was buying. 'All you need do is say "yes".'

'Isn't this a cosy scene?' Edgemont's jeer thudded through the room as he strode in.

The Earl followed behind him, gasping at the sight of his mother wrapped around Rafe. 'Mother! What are you doing?'

'Hold your tongue,' the Dowager Countess snapped, peeling herself off Rafe and moving to stand beside him. 'Where's the Comtesse? Have you found her and the register?'

'She never came downstairs,' Edgemont answered, removing his mask and tossing it on a chair. 'And I've been watching the stairs ever since they crept up here.'

'Then she must still be here somewhere.'

'I think she's closer than you realise.'

Cornelia moved back from the screen as Edgemont pulled it to one side. It teetered on its small legs, threatening to topple over before the Earl rushed forward to steady it.

Cornelia levelled the gun at Edgemont and pulled back the hammer. 'Good evening, Lord Edgemont.'

He looked down the barrel, then at the register before grimacing at her. 'Still the little minx, even when you're trapped.'

'I won't be trapped by a dog like you.' She had nothing to lose now except the register and she wasn't about to let it go. They would pay, all of them, even Rafe. 'Now move back.'

She advanced on him and he retreated until he stood next to the Dowager Countess.

'Why are you letting her dominate you?' Lady Daltmouth jeered. 'She has only one bullet.'

Edgemont sneered down his nose at the woman. 'And I'm not about to take it.'

'Coward. She can't be much of a shot.'

'I trained her myself and I assure you, like me, she never misses.' Rafe looked at Cornelia.

She glowered at him, but it didn't break his roguish smile and she debated unloading the weapon into him. However, without the single shot, she was as good as caught.

'Mr Green, see to it,' the Dowager Countess ordered.

'See to it yourself since ya clearly have no more use for peasants.' The man spat at the Dowager Countess's feet and stomped from the room.

'Useless servant,' Lady Daltmouth thundered, then turned to her son. 'Get the register.'

The Earl went pale. 'But, Mother, surely there must be a better way to resolve this.'

'There is,' Cornelia announced. 'I'll walk out of this room with the register and you, my dear Earl, and your darling mother will abide by our original agreement. If you fail to pay, I'll deliver the register to Lord Twickenham and all your precious plans with Rafe, Lord Edgemont and society will come to nothing.'

'How dare you threaten me, you little trollop.' The Dowager Countess balled her hands in front of her, shaking with rage. 'You can't think to get clear of my house with only one shot. And even if you do, I got the book from you once. I guarantee I'll get it from you again.'

'Why, how many of your other footmen are housebreakers, murderers and thieves? It's a wonder you sleep safe in your bed at night with a house full of such men.'

The Dowager Countess opened her mouth with a retort, but Rafe spoke first.

'She's right, Cornelia, you can't escape with only one bullet, or expect to stay safe if you do.' Rafe's tender voice burned through her as if she'd turned the pistol on herself. He'd thrown his lot in with the lecherous old woman, allowing the Dowager Countess to insult and threaten both of them while abandoning Cornelia to her enemies.

All the while Edgemont stood there, gloating over her humiliation the way he used to gloat whenever he brought her father low. Anger, hate and betrayal swirled inside her like smoke choking out the air.

Let them crow at her. She still possessed the pistol and the register. She inched towards the door, careful not to take her eyes off of the lot of them. 'I'll take my chances.'

'She's made it worth my while. Why not let the Dowager Countess make it worth yours?' Rafe encouraged, his manner too calm, too sure for this horrid scene.

The Dowager gaped at Rafe. 'You make quite free with my purse.'

Rafe took the Dowager Countess's hand and raised it to his lips. Cornelia ran one finger down the curve of the trigger, eager to blow the sweet look from his face. Only Andrew's future stopped her from exacting such immediate and messy revenge. She might be a gambler who'd sunk to blackmail, but she was no murderess.

'She's in need of coin as much as I am,' Rafe continued. 'You can buy the register and her silence, and all of us can walk out of here alive.'

'I don't want anything of hers or yours, except to see you all suffer,' Cornelia cried.

'Come now, Cornelia, think what the Dowager Countess can offer you.'

'And what of my interest in the register?' Edgemont demanded.

'Once you don't have a pistol pointed at your gut, I'm sure you and Lady Daltmouth can work out a suitable arrangement,' Rafe replied.

Edgemont scowled at Rafe, then eyed the Dowager Countess, looking for her assurance.

'Yes, yes, we'll keep to our original bargain.' She waved off his concerns with a dismissive hand.

Whatever arrangement they had, Cornelia sensed Edgemont wouldn't fare well in the deal.

Apparently, so did he. 'You'd better uphold your end. Your money can't buy my silence about the register for ever.'

His threat only increased her haughty disdain. 'It's already bought your massive debts and if you don't start cooperating, I'll call them in and ruin you.'

'So, the illustrious Baron of Edgemont is in debt,' Rafe gloated, drawing the Baron's silent ire.

'Heavily,' the Dowager Countess clarified, then wrinkled her nose at Cornelia. 'Just like this little impoverished French noble. How much do you want to keep your mouth closed?'

What Cornelia wouldn't give for a few more bullets. She didn't want to kill the Dowager Countess, but wound her enough to take the superior sneer off her imperious face. 'I want the thousand pounds your son agreed to pay me.'

Disdain deepened the crease between her eyebrow. 'You're hardly worth such a sum.'

'But my silence is.'

'And if you don't stay silent?'

'Who'll believe her?' Rafe added. 'Without proof, what good is her word?'

'What good is yours?' Cornelia shot back, his cut burning like lemon in all the wounds he'd inflicted on her over the past day.

'Fine.' The Countess huffed. 'Give me the register and you'll have your thousand pounds.'

'I'm not turning it over on a promise so one of your housebreaking footmen can kill me in my bed.'

'I think a small token of your intention to keep your end of the bargain might be wise.' Rafe's even voice soothed the Dowager Countess, easing the lines marring her forehead.

'If I must.' She marched to the short, burled-wood cabinet against the far wall, snatching the keys out of the Earl's hands as she passed. She flipped through the collection to find the smallest, then slid the dainty key into the centre drawer lock. She pulled it open and withdrew a stack of pound notes.

Out of habit, Cornelia exchanged a glance with Rafe. She could practically hear him wishing they'd picked the lock on that drawer first.

'Here's two hundred pounds.' The Dowager Countess flapped the notes at Rafe. 'You give it to her and get me the register.'

Rafe held out his large hand. The Dowager

Countess laid the bills in his palm, taking a wicked delight in her command of him. It disgusted Cornelia to see him doing the older woman's bidding and all because of money. She should have known he was this selfish, this desperate. If only she'd realised it sooner.

He closed his fingers around the bills, folding them in half and then half again as he approached. Cornelia gripped the pistol tightly. He could overpower her and snatch it away. She didn't want to shoot him, but if it meant surviving the night, she would.

He stopped in front of her, so close the tangy scent of him made her heart constrict. Why? Why had he chosen to abandon her so completely? Last night, she'd granted him his freedom, making no demands on him except the return of the register, something they both wanted. He didn't need to crush her so completely, or humiliate her in front of her enemies. He was free to chase after the Dowager and her riches, the same way Cornelia had run to the Comte.

Guilt followed her pain and she understood some small portion of his revenge.

'Your money, madam.' He held out the bills between his two fingers.

There'd be no more after this. She caught it in the arrogant triumph making Lady Daltmouth's eyes sparkle. This would be enough to protect Andrew for now, but it wouldn't be long before she was back at the tables, wasting away her life with the cards.

Her heart dropped as she eyed the notes.

'Take the money, Cornelia. After all, with this, two talented people could take the tables by storm.' He cocked his head slightly and arched one eyebrow in serious invitation, the gesture hidden from the others as he faced her.

She breathed once.

Two talented people.

She inhaled again.

His signal to believe any messages from him.

He wasn't leaving her for the Dowager Countess. It was all part of a plan, a way to escape with enough money to save Andrew.

She let out a long breath, centring herself to keep the surprise from lessening the tightness of her face or changing in even the most subtle way the anger in her eyes. With Edgemont and the Dowager Countess watching like two hungry cats, she couldn't give away the bluff.

She lowered the pistol and his lips turned up in

a proud smile. He'd seen her sign, her subtle acceptance. She would follow his lead, just as she had when she'd abandoned the faint safety of Hatton Place to set out with him for London and an uncertain future. Tonight, she would do it again.

He moved closer, sliding the bills down her bodice.

Edgemont leered at Cornelia, enjoying the intimate exchange. His delight helped her maintain the facade of hate, even as Rafe's fingers curled to brush the side of one breast as he tucked the money in the small pocket in the front of her stays, the caress gentle but heavy with meaning.

Then he withdrew his hand and held it out to her. 'The register, if you please.'

'Yes, hurry up. I have guests to attend to,' Lady Daltmouth huffed.

Cornelia laid the book across his palm, her life and faith in him bound up in the simple gesture. He wouldn't disappoint her, she was sure of it now. Whatever he had in mind, it was to both of their benefits. She only needed to watch and follow his lead as she had in all the card rooms of Paris.

'Thank you, my dear.' Rafe thumped the register with one knuckle as he returned to the Dowager Countess.

Lady Daltmouth trilled her fingers against her dress, eager for Rafe and the register.

Edgemont didn't share her sense of triumph. 'I always knew you were a dog, Densmore, but I didn't think you'd sit up and beg so easily.'

'Don't despair, I'm not done surprising you.' He flung the book in the fire and a shrill scream of horror escaped from the Dowager Countess's mouth.

'No!' She lunged for the fireplace and the tongs hanging on the stand next to it. The wide skirt wedged between the wall and the desk and she batted at it, trying to flatten it enough to fit through the narrow gap.

'Damn you, Densmore.' Edgemont lunged at Rafe, slamming against him hard and sending both men backwards to the floor, crushing a small side table beneath them.

The Earl rushed towards his mother, but Cornelia levelled the gun at him.

'Don't move.'

He worried his cravat, torn between not getting shot and helping his mother.

'Don't you dare try to stop him.' The Dowager Countess flew at Cornelia, grabbing her arm and pulling it down. Cornelia held tight to the pistol, trying to pull it away when a finger caught the trigger. The gunpowder exploded with a roar, sending both women staggering back.

The bullet struck the lamp near the window, shattering it and splattering oil all over the curtains, table and floor.

The men continued to struggle, their blows and curses dampened by the ringing in Cornelia's ears.

The Dowager Countess wavered on her feet, shaking off the shock before recovering herself and pouncing on Cornelia. Cornelia swung the empty pistol at the Dowager, trying to drive her back, but the woman grabbed the barrel and twisted hard, trying to pry it from Cornelia's hands.

'If you think I'm going to let some whoring daughter of an impoverished squire ruin my plans, you're wrong,' she hissed over the metal, her knuckles white from gripping it.

'If you think you're going to get Rafe or hurt me, then you're wrong.' Cornelia shoved hard and let go of the gun, sending the Dowager Countess stumbling back in a confusion of flailing arms and gold brocade. She caught the edge of a wingback chair and twisted, landing hard against the floor on her side.

Across the room, Rafe and Edgemont were

locked together, pushing back and forth against each other, knocking over chairs and tables. The shorter man clung to Rafe's waist and Rafe rammed his elbow between Edgemont's shoulder blades. Edgemont grunted, but didn't let go, landing a punch to Rafe's stomach.

Cornelia looked around for a weapon, anything to help Rafe when the ring of metal against brick clanged through the room. At the fireplace, the Earl struggled with the tongs to pull the register from the flames.

'I've got it.' He raised up his charred prize, coming around the desk before the burning book slipped from the tongs and thudded to the floor. In an almost comical dance, the Earl stomped on the flames chewing at the edges of the register, adding the reek of smouldering leather to the eye-watering stench of lamp oil.

'Give it to me.' The Dowager Countess hauled herself to her feet. 'Give me the book.'

'No, you won't have it.' Cornelia grabbed the woman by one arm and swung her away from her son. Lady Daltmouth tripped on a broken table leg, pulling them both to the floor and wrenching Cornelia's arm. Cornelia cried out against the pain, but grabbed tight to the woman's ruffed collar with her other hand, pulling her down as she struggled to rise.

Rafe kicked Edgemont's legs out from under him and the Baron crashed to the floor. Edgemont rose with surprising swiftness, ramming his fist up and catching Rafe along the cheek. Rafe punched Edgemont hard in the gut, knocking the wind from him and forcing him to his knees. Then he hurled himself at the Earl. The round man's mouth fell open and he shuffled backward, stumbling over the rug. As he fell, his foot kicked the register and sent it sliding across the floor. It stopped beneath the dripping curtains, igniting them in a flash.

Cornelia shielded her eyes against the blinding light and wilting heat. The silk dropped in burning tatters as flames licked up the wall, charring the plaster ceiling above, their fury fed by the old books lining the shelves on either side of the window.

The Dowager Countess stared at the fire in disbelief.

Cornelia let go of her and moved back towards the door, coughing as the thick smoke burned her throat and stung her eyes.

Rafe rushed to her and pulled her up. 'Are you all right?'

She rubbed her aching arm. 'I will be.'

'Get the register before it's lost,' the Dowager Countess ordered her son. She staggered to her feet and towards the flames, arms raised against the heat, her dishevelled hair and torn lace collar glowing in the intense light.

Lord Daltmouth backed away, his chins quivering. 'We must go, warn the guests and get everyone out before the whole house burns to the ground.'

'Forget those fools,' Lady Daltmouth snapped. 'Edgemont, get me the register or I'll see to it you're ruined. Do you hear me? Ruined!'

Edgemont hauled himself to his feet and rushed towards the flames. 'I'll get it all right, and then we'll see who's ruined.'

He reached for the discarded metal tongs. They lay at the edge of the carpet, just beyond the reach of the flames, but not their heat, and he dropped them fast.

Lady Daltmouth dived for the tongs, but not before Edgemont ripped a doily from the table and gripped the metal handles. He fought against the heat and the Dowager Countess's grasping hands to try to pinch the book, his high forehead shiny with sweat.

'Leave it.' The Earl tugged at his mother's arm as she struggled to get around Edgemont.

She batted her son's hands away. 'I'm not leaving until I have it.'

'Let's get out of here,' Rafe yelled, pulling Cornelia into the cool of the hallway.

'But the register.' She drew in a mouthful of clean air, her lungs stinging, her eyes tearing from smoke and ash. 'What if they get it?'

'It doesn't matter.' He tried to pull her down the hall, but she dug her heels into the carpet.

'We have to make sure they don't get it.'

'The flames will do that. Come on.'

'But your title, Wealthstone, Andrew's future. It'll all be lost if they get the register.'

He took her by both arms, riveting his eyes to hers. A nasty red bruise marred his cheek and soot stained his forehead and shirt. 'It doesn't matter, none of it matters if we die in there. If they get it, we'll figure something out, together, always together, no matter what. Do you understand?'

His words cut through the roar of the flames and cracking timbers, silencing every desire she'd ever had to possess the register. All that mattered was Rafe and their future. Nothing was settled, nothing safe or secure, but they were together and they would face whatever came as one. 'Then leave them to it.'

'Good girl.'

Chapter Thirteen

'Fire! The house is on fire! Get out!' Rafe shouted as they burst into the hallway below.

From the crevices and shadows people straightened, a murmur of confusion following Cornelia and Rafe as they raced down the hallway to the main stairs.

'Fire!' Rafe roared again from the top of the staircase, pulling Cornelia down through the crush. The musicians screeched the music to a halt and people looked up through their masks, lifting them in shock before the words sank in. In one massive wave, the direction of everyone on the stairs shifted as people started down, scattering at the bottom as they searched for a way to escape.

Rafe gripped Cornelia's hand, his bruised knuckles smarting from the pressure, but he wasn't going to lose her or see her crushed to death in the panic.

The open windows and doors leading to the garden were filled with a steady stream of fleeing guests, but without the dangerous bottleneck at the front of the house. The room was emptying fast, but there were still people on the balcony hurrying down. Many above and on the dance floor stopped to shed their cumbersome costumes, littering the way with obstacles. Rafe kicked a large, horse-head chess piece to one side and pulled Cornelia in the direction of the nearest open French door, staying close to the wall to avoid the mass.

Cornelia kept pace until they were almost to it. Then she stopped, bringing him to a halt

'Rafe, wait,' she shouted over the confusion.

He turned, loath to hesitate until she pointed to the corner of the room. Lady Treadaway slouched in a chair, gasping for breath, ignored by everyone rushing to escape the smoke beginning to drift down from upstairs. Without a second though, Rafe pulled Cornelia towards her.

'Hold on tight to me, both of you,' Rafe commanded as he scooped the old woman into his arms and carried her through the crowd. Cornelia gripped his coat as he made for the door, all of them eager to be through it and in the safety of the open air beyond.

They descended the garden steps, following the flow of people around to the front of the house, across the main pathway and out of the wide front gate. The wrought iron hung ragged on its hinges, torn loose by the surge of fleeing revellers.

Rafe carried the old woman across the wide thoroughfare, joining the long line of guests gathering there to watch the flames rising from the upper rooms or to search through the crowd for lost companions and loved ones.

Rafe lowered the Lady Treadaway to the pavement. 'Are you all right?'

'I will be.' She took Rafe's hand and clasped it to her chest. 'Thank you, Lord Densmore.'

'It was my pleasure.' He rubbed her shaking hands between his, offering what comfort he could in the middle of the street. Cornelia removed her cloak and draped it over the woman's narrow shoulders.

'Thank you, my dear, thank you both.' Lady Treadaway focused on Rafe and patted his cheek, the light from the fire highlighting her fond grin. 'You're so much like your father. You have his tendency for goodness.'

'Most days, I do.' Rafe smiled wryly, trying to rise, but she held on to him.

'I never listened to all those nasty stories about him. I hope you didn't either. He was such a sweet man, helping me secure funds for the orphanage when no one else would.' She pointed a serious finger at him. 'You make sure and remember the good in him and forget the rest.'

Rafe sat back on his heels, clever remarks failing him.

'Mother!' A woman's voice cut through the chaos around them. 'Mother!'

A young Guinevere pushed through the throng, dropping to her knees next to Lady Treadaway and throwing her arms around her.

Rafe rose as Miss Treadaway's male companion knelt to embrace both women. Cornelia slipped her hand in his and gently drew him away. He followed her, the woman's kind words ringing in his ears as loud as the roar of the flames.

He opened and closed his hand, the cut in the crease of his finger from where he'd ripped the register stinging. In the distance, the bells of the fire brigade sounded, steadily drawing closer.

'I'm sorry I was so rough with you over the register. I hated seeing the proof of my father's waste and betrayal.' He rubbed at a drop of dried blood on his skin, ashamed. Losing the control he prided himself on hadn't been his proudest moment tonight.

'You don't need to apologise. I understand.' Curls tumbled around her face, one neat ringlet brushing the torn seam of her dress. Soot dusted her forehead, but her eyes glowed in the roaring light of the fire. The trust she'd shown him in the darkness outside Hatton Place and again tonight when he'd revealed his bluff echoed in their clear blue depths. 'And now?'

'It's gone, all of it.' And it was. All the hate and anger he'd carried for so long. Until tonight, he hadn't realised how much his desire to overcome the past and anger at his father had consumed him. Lady Daltmouth's obsession with the past had destroyed her house just as Rafe's had nearly destroyed him. The register was gone, but so was his father and there was nothing he could do to change any of it.

Despite his father's poor choices, they weren't the only memories Rafe carried of the man. For a short time in the study, when he'd seen the embroidered screen, he'd remembered his father before the cards and how much he'd admired the man. His father might have been weak, but the longer Rafe held on to his father's faults, the more it would eat at him. There had been good in his father at one time, love and happiness. It was time to remember it and let the rest go.

He turned to watch Lady Treadaway being led away by her young companions. 'Her compliment was the first time in a long while I've heard someone, other than my mother, speak fondly of my father.'

'Your mother loved him.'

'Yes, she did.' He gently wiped away a black smudge on Cornelia's temple. 'There's something to be said for such love.'

Across the street, beams cracked and glass shattered, raising gasps of terror from the crowd.

Rafe drew Cornelia back with the rest of the watchers. She clung to him, her shoulder beneath his arm, her body pressed for safety and comfort against his. Relief swept through him as the flames began to consume the second storey. The register was gone, his debt to Mr Smith paid, his title safe and Cornelia by his side. It didn't erase all his troubles, and an inferno wasn't his preferred resolution to the matter, but it was done. Rafe could face tomorrow without the threat of murder and ruin hanging over him.

A large pump wagon drawn by two sturdy horses

stopped in front of the house. The men on board jumped down to unfurl the hoses while the driver stared in slack-jawed awe at the burning house. Flames jutted from the upper windows, licking at the roof tiles and spewing massive black plumes of smoke into the night sky.

'Do you think they got out?' Cornelia asked.

'Not all of them.' He nodded to where Lord Daltmouth stood alone in the centre of the street.

The poor man stared at the fire, his hose torn, his fine velvet doublet singed along his shoulders, which slumped with a loss deeper than his house and one no wealth could replace.

At the broken iron gate, firemen feverishly worked the pumps of their wagon, the water spewing from the hoses doing little to tame the blaze.

'It's our fault. It's my fault.' Cornelia covered her mouth with her hands as a flash of flame drove the firemen back. 'He was more innocent than any of us. He didn't deserve to suffer like this.'

Rafe tucked one finger under her chin and turned her face to his. 'It's not your fault. Lady Daltmouth and Edgemont could have left, but they chose the register and greed over everything else.'

'And what have we chosen?'

'Each other.' He pressed his forehead to hers. 'I love you, Cornelia.'

She fell into the curve of his body and twined her arms around his neck. 'I love you, Rafe.'

He covered her mouth with his, drinking in the salty, smoky taste of her like the finest champagne, losing himself in the supple pressure of her parted lips. All the anguish of losing her in Paris and the fear of letting her go last night faded beneath the press of her body against his.

'Seigneur de Densmore.'

Rafe ignored the far-off, foreign sound of his name. Only Cornelia and the feathery play of her fingers in his hair mattered now. The moist caress of her tongue meeting his drove away the strange nightmare playing out on the street. He'd chosen her over riches and the register, and she'd chosen him and life.

'Seigneur de Densmore.'

He had no plans for what they would do next, but it didn't matter. In her embrace, he knew everything would be all right, somehow, they would make it that way, together.

'Seigneur de Densmore!'

The eager voice finally broke through the intoxication of Cornelia's kiss. Rafe pulled back and squinted over her head at the tall man pushing through the crowd to reach them.

Cornelia twisted in his arms, holding up one hand against the glare of the fire. 'Who's that?'

'An old friend.'

Monsieur Fournier stopped, shoving his crisp white domino up onto his high forehead. 'Seigneur de Densmore. I'm so happy to finally find you.'

'Bonsoir, mon ami.' Rafe laughed, noticing the Frenchman's fine cloak and the new fullness in his face. It was quite a change since the last time he'd seen him. 'It appears lady luck has graced you.'

'She has become my *maîtresse en titre.'* He winked. 'And I have you to thank for it. The money you gave me at the hell, it changed my luck for good. Ten thousand pounds I win. *Merci,* Signeur de Densmore. No more tables for me.'

At least someone he knew was finally winning. 'Congratulations, Monsieur Fournier.'

'Signeur de Densmore, you helped me, gave me money when I had nothing. Now, it is my turn to help you.'

The roar of crashing stone filled the street. They all turned to watch as a section of roof collapsed, sending a shower of sparks and flames leaping into the air. The firemen working the pump yelled for their brethren to get away and abandon the house to the fire.

Rafe shook his head at his friend. 'I'm afraid I'm beyond help, Monsieur Fournier.'

'No such foolishness. Let us come away from this horrible scene. We have much to discuss.' He danced back, waving for them to join him.

'Shall we?' Rafe asked, dropping a small kiss on the tip of her nose.

'Why not? What do we have to lose?'

They followed Monsieur Fournier through the awestruck crowd to the end of the street. A mass of carriages filled the road. Small groups of people wound between the wheels and horses looking for their conveyances while drivers yelled at one another as they struggled to break free of the jam.

The three of them waded into the tangle, making their way to the far side where Monsieur Fournier's black town couch waited.

'Madame.' Monsieur Fournier extended his hand to Cornelia, helping her up into the shiny lacquered carriage.

Rafe followed, settling next to her on the soft leather squabs. The interior was spacious and fine with enough height to keep Rafe from having to curl his spine to fit inside.

The Frenchman climbed in and took the seat across from them, then turned up the flame in the brass lamp.

'How did you acquire such a carriage so fast?' Rafe asked, pulling Cornelia close and curling his arm around her back.

'Lord Edgemont sold it to me. I think he was not as wealthy as he wanted London to believe.'

Rafe exchanged a knowing look with Cornelia before she turned to their host.

'Monsieur Fournier, what did you want to tell Rafe?'

'After my grand night at the hell...' he kissed his fingers and raised them to the ceiling '...I thought of nothing but how I could help you.'

'Nothing?' Rafe laughed in disbelief.

'Well, almost nothing.' The Frenchman shrugged. 'I am only human. But, I knew I must help you. I read through the notes from my survey of your land. I can't believe I was such a fool to have missed it.'

'You found it?' Rafe perched forward on the squab. 'You found Grandfather's lead seam?'

'Alas, no, but there is something equally valuable beneath the soil. I'm so sorry I did not see it before, but I was so focused on finding lead and distracted by all my misfortunes since leaving France. You understand?'

'More than you know.'

'What did you find, Monsieur Fournier?' Cornelia asked, hugged tight against Rafe despite the generous width of the seat.

'Blue limestone.' The man threw out his arms, proud of himself.

The carriage rocked forward on its sturdy springs, creaking as it broke free of the crush.

'Limestone?' Rafe failed to share his friend's enthusiasm.

'A grand vein of it, the best kind, too, much in demand for smelting iron for cannons or making mortar for all the best builders in London.' He perched one elbow on his knee and leaned forward. 'It is worth a fortune.'

Rafe flexed his fingers and slid them between Cornelia's, his excitement flaring and then fading. 'Even if it's there, I don't have the means to extract it.'

'Oh, it is there.' Monsieur Fournier clapped his hands together. 'And you do have the means.'

'No, I don't even have enough to try to win the money.' Rafe ground his teeth, the answer to all his prayers so close and still just out of reach.

'We have Lady Daltmouth's money.' Cornelia patted her bodice.

'No, the two hundred is for Andrew, I won't risk his future by frittering it away at the tables.'

'There's no need for anyone to fritter anything at the tables, Seigneur de Densmore.' Monsieur Fournier chuckled. 'I will provide the money, you will provide the land, and we will share the profits.'

Rafe stared at the Frenchman in disbelief. After so many years, a thousand card games, debts, moneylenders and one ruined house in Mayfair, could it all be this easy?

Monsieur Fournier sat back in triumph. 'No more tables for us, eh, Seigneur de Densmore?'

If the Frenchman was right, if he took this gamble, then everything they'd ever sought and more would be theirs.

He titled his head and cocked an inviting eyebrow at Cornelia. 'No more tables for us?'

She licked her lips, as if on the verge of entering Madame Boucher's to play once more. 'Never again.'

Chapter Fourteen

Wealthstone Manor—one year later

Rafe grabbed Paul by his collar, pulling the running boy back before he knocked into one of the workmen carrying a bucket of plaster. 'Young gentlemen do not run through the house.'

Rafe let go and the boy jerked his jacket straight.

'Sorry, Lord Densmore. Me ma keeps saying the same thing.'

'My mother keeps telling me the same thing,' Rafe corrected.

'Yes, my lord.' Paul bowed like a perfect little prince. He strolled over to the stairs, tossing his wooden ball into the air and catching it as he waited at the bottom for his mother.

Miss Allen came down, wearing a neat dress with a crisp white apron, her dark hair pulled into a twist at the nape of her neck. It highlighted her now full cheeks and the faint pink the country air and good food gave them. Andrew walked next to her, chattering away about the toy soldiers clutched in each hand, a pouch full of them hanging from his waist and nearly pulling down his breeches.

'A strange choice for a governess and a Baronet's schoolroom companion,' Rafe's mother observed, stepping up beside him, the silk of her new gown rustling as she moved.

They watched as Miss Allen led the boys past the workmen climbing the scaffolds to repair the ceiling. Paul moved forward, holding the front door open with all the formality of a footman. He looked to Rafe, who nodded his approval at the boy's refined behaviour.

It didn't last long as Andrew shoved a soldier in Paul's hand and the two boys tore off through the garden, Miss Allen hurrying behind them.

'She kept her son alive and fed during rough times,' Rafe observed, enjoying the childish shouts carrying in through the open windows. 'She knows a thing or two about helping young boys.'

'Indeed, she does. She also tells me the most interesting stories when she helps me dress.' His mother started for the sitting room.

'Really?' He fell into step beside her. 'What kind of stories?'

'The kind not fit for a gentleman's ears.' His mother left him to join Mr Wilson, the draper, at the window and examine the selection of fabrics laid out on the seat.

Near the fireplace, Cornelia sat at the small table with Monsieur Fournier, examining the accounts he'd brought over this morning. She nodded as he spoke, one hand holding the papers while the other rubbed her round belly. The large diamond wedding band adorning her finger sparkled in the firelight. A yellow-silk dress flowed over the curve of her shoulders and across the widening expanse of her breasts. Her dark hair pinned in loose curls on her head shone with an onyx lustre, making her skin as luminous as the strand of pearls around her neck.

At his approach, she looked up, beaming at him with pride. 'Rafe, you must see these figures, they're astounding.'

She moved to rise, but he waved her back into her seat. He leaned over her shoulder to examine the paper, too distracted by her sweet honeysuckle scent to focus on anything but her.

'Impressive. But not as impressive as you.'

He swept her lips with a kiss.

'Bonjour, Seigneur de Densmore. I was explaining to the *belle madame* the increase in mining since we found seam *deux. Excusez-moi.*' He slid another paper out from beneath her elbow and held it up to Rafe. 'The increase in profit is grand, no?'

Rafe took the paper, examining it with the same pride he once used to count his winnings, still amazed by his change in fortune. Here was the money he'd always craved, free of any taint, the wealth managed with the respect worthy of a Baron. Soon, the house would be grand, too, his loved ones safe and secure for good inside the old walls.

He handed the paper back to the Frenchman. *'Très magnifique.'*

'Lord Densmore!' Lord Hartley boomed as he entered the room, his buckskin breeches smudged with plaster along one thigh. 'I had a devil of a time squeezing around all those workmen just to get through the front door.'

'It can't be helped. There are years of neglect to deal with.'

Lord Hartley tugged off his leather riding gloves. 'When are you coming back to London?'

'When our new town house is ready.'

'I can't wait.' He wiggled his fingers in the air. 'My palms itch just thinking of the card games we'll enjoy there.'

'Then your fingers will have to be disappointed.' Cornelia rose and Rafe took her elbow, helping her up. 'You know very well we no longer gamble.'

'And it's a shame, too, letting talent like the both of yours go to waste.' He brushed off the top of his tall riding hat. 'Though it does level the playing field for the rest of us, even if a man can't get a decent game in this part of the country.'

'I'll play you,' Monsieur Fournier offered. 'If you don't mind very low stakes. I did not work so hard to—how do you say it, Seigneur de Densmore?—fritter away my money at the tables.'

'And so you shouldn't.' Lord Hartley shrugged. 'I suppose I shouldn't either, or so my wife keeps telling me.'

'She isn't the only one who's warned you about poor wagers,' Rafe teased.

Lord Hartley slapped his gloves against his palm. 'You're never going to let me forget the boxing match, are you?'

'I haven't decided.'

The crack of breaking glass filled the room, followed by the soft thud of a wooden ball landing on the carpet. Outside, the boy's faces went pale as they looked through the broken pane. Then they took off running across the lawn, Miss Allen chasing after them with a string of curses unfit for a country house.

'And to think, we just had that window repaired.' Rafe plucked the ball from the centre of the shards. 'With those two rascals, we'll have to hire a full-time glazier.'

'You certainly can afford it.' Monsieur Fournier clapped him on the shoulder, then motioned to Lord Hartley. 'Shall we?'

'I can't say no to some friendly play.' Lord Hartley followed the Frenchman from the room, side-stepping a workman carrying a plank of wood.

Cornelia shook her head. 'We'll have to tell the boys to be more careful when they play.'

'Leave them be. It isn't the first broken pane and it won't be the last.' Rafe tossed up the ball, then caught it. 'Mother, how many did I break?'

'Too many to count.' She laughed. 'I'll get one of the footmen to clean it up. Come, Mr Wilson, we must discuss the dining-room curtains.'

She led the draper from the room, their discussion of brocade and silk following them out into the entrance hall before being lost in the steady bang and hum of hammers and saws.

Rafe rolled the pitted ball between his hands, enjoying the sound of the boys shouting across the wide and now well-tended garden. He looked through the broken window and past the statue of the girl at the end, her flowing dress free of roses and vines. Above her shoulder in the distance, smoke rose from behind a hill where the miners worked to extract the precious limestone from the ground.

The first profits from the mine had gone to Fanny, who'd been more than happy to accept a generous settlement in return for Cornelia and Rafe's guardianship of Andrew. The chit was now enjoying the Season in London, trying to trap another man after the end of Edgemont. She'd been more frustrated than upset at the news of his demise.

Andrew would be tutored here at Wealthstone for a few more years until it was time for him to take a place at Eton or another school befitting a Baronet and the brother-in-law of a Baron.

'It won't be long before our child is out there with those two heathens.' Cornelia wrapped her arm around his waist and laid her head against his chest.

'Better out there than inside with a deck in his hands.' He stroked her stomach, feeling the life inside kick against the pressure, eager to meet the little one and to be for him everything their fathers never were for them. 'We'll make a fine gentleman out of him, my love.'

'We will.' She slipped her hand behind his head and drew him down to her. 'As fine a man as his father.'

* * * * *